JACKPOT RIDGE

*Also by Ralph Cotton
in Large Print:*

Powder River
Ralph Compton: Death Along the Cimarron
Vengeance Is a Bullet

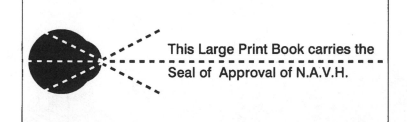

JACKPOT RIDGE

RALPH COTTON

Thorndike Press • Waterville, Maine

Published in 2004 by arrangement with NAL Signet, a member of Penguin Group (USA) Inc.

Thorndike Press® Large Print Western.

The tree indicium is a trademark of Thorndike Press.

The text of this Large Print edition is unabridged. Other aspects of the book may vary from the original edition.

Set in 16 pt. Plantin by Al Chase.

Printed in the United States on permanent paper.

Library of Congress Cataloging-in-Publication Data

Cotton, Ralph W.
    Jackpot ridge / Ralph Cotton.
      p. cm.
    ISBN 0-7862-6441-1 (lg. print : hc : alk. paper)
    1. Poker players — Fiction.   2. Outlaws — Fiction.
    3. Revenge — Fiction.   4. Large type books.   I. Title.
    PS3553.O766J63 2004
    813'.6—dc22   2004047930

For Mary Lynn . . . *of course.*

National Association for Visually Handicapped
—————————————— serving the partially seeing

As the Founder/CEO of NAVH, the only national health agency solely devoted to those who, although not totally blind, have an eye disease which could lead to serious visual impairment, I am pleased to recognize Thorndike Press* as one of the leading publishers in the large print field.

Founded in 1954 in San Francisco to prepare large print textbooks for partially seeing children, NAVH became the pioneer and standard setting agency in the preparation of large type.

Today, those publishers who meet our standards carry the prestigious "Seal of Approval" indicating high quality large print. We are delighted that Thorndike Press is one of the publishers whose titles meet these standards. We are also pleased to recognize the significant contribution Thorndike Press is making in this important and growing field.

Lorraine H. Marchi, L.H.D.
Founder/CEO
NAVH

* Thorndike Press encompasses the following imprints: Thorndike, Wheeler, Walker and Large Print Press.

PART 1

CHAPTER 1

Jack Bell crouched in knee-deep snow against a high-reaching pine on the edge of the jagged ridgeline. The morning sun stood behind him. Above him lay a white canopy of sagging pine limbs, dangerously laden with snow. Bell knew better than to fire his rifle beneath the snow-covered limbs. He'd only moved in beside the tree to get a good look. On the white stretch of flatlands below he watched the four horses struggle as their riders goaded and spurred them on. These men had been dogging his trail for the past five days, ever since he'd left Elk Horn. Yesterday he thought he'd given them the slip.

But no such luck, he thought to himself, watching them look down at his horse's hoofprints in the deep snow while above them he levered a round up into the chamber of his Henry rifle. He'd circled up into the snowy hills a half mile ahead. Then he'd ridden back above his own trail, keeping them on his tracks while giving himself a hawk's view of them. Jack had reined his horse and the pack mule to a scrub cedar a few yards back from the edge to keep from skylighting them. He looked at the big buckskin. The horse stood knee-deep in the snow. Next to the horse, the pack mule, the shorter of the two animals, stood with snow touching its belly.

Jack Bell studied the sky as he moved from beneath the pine canopy, keeping back from the ridgeline and taking a prone position behind a snowcapped rock. There was more snow coming. It would be here by noon — this evening at the latest, he estimated. He didn't want to be caught out on the flatlands in it . . . not with four of Philpot's gunmen on his trail. Now that he'd gotten a good look at them, he knew that's who they were. He recognized the horses as much as the men, having seen the chesty roan and the big dapple gray at the hitch rail outside Philpot's Sporting Life Saloon.

Bell didn't know if Philpot had sicced them on him or if they had gotten a sniff of his winnings and followed on their own like hounds on a scent. Either way, they weren't out to do him anything but harm. He took off his right glove, ran a hand along the barrel of the Henry rifle and placed the butt to his shoulder. He raised the long-distance sight atop the barrel, looked down through it and made a quick adjustment. He didn't

10

want to kill anybody if he could keep from it.

But killing was something he wouldn't rule out just yet, not if they kept coming. The mining camp, Nolan's Gap, lay only a few hours farther north, higher up. His eyes went in that direction for a second, considering the snowy pass and the steep trail. If this didn't do it — didn't shake them off his trail — he'd have no choice but to lay in wait up in the pass. He didn't want a fight, but if there had to be one, he'd take whatever edge he could get. Then he settled himself in and readied himself for the shot.

On the snowy flatlands below, the four riders pushed the tired animals along single file. Steam billowed from the nostrils of both man and beast. Rance Hardaway, the man in the lead, spoke over his shoulder in a long ribbon of steam. "There's times I think a man would do just as well getting himself a job and working it till he drops."

"What the hell brought that on?" said Stoy Manlon, riding right behind Hardaway. As he asked Hardaway, Stoy looked back at the muffler-covered face of Delbert Hanks for some sort of acknowledgment. But Delbert Hanks just stared through him and straight ahead, his eyes as flat and lifeless as those of a corpse. A thin sliver of steam through Delbert Hanks' wool muffler was the only sign of life about him.

"Just speculating is all," said Rance Hardaway without looking back. Beneath him the big dapple gray struggled with the deep, dry snow.

"He's speculating is all," Stoy said to Hanks, turning in his saddle again and speaking to Hanks' blank, dark eyes in a sarcastic whisper. Still there was no response from Hanks. Behind Delbert Hanks rode the kid, Billy Freeman. The kid tried to imitate Delbert Hanks any way he could, right down to the way he'd cocked his hat low to the left, shadowing out most of his face, as if he had something worth hiding from the world.

"What'd he say, Delbert?" Billy Freeman asked Hanks.

"He said Hardaway's just speculating," Delbert Hanks growled over his shoulder.

"Just speculating what?" Billy Freeman asked.

"Shut up, Kid," Delbert hissed through his muffler. "It's too cold to jaw with you." He stared ahead at Stoy Manlon and said, "I would kill a sumbitch for a long drink of whiskey right now."

"You and me both," said Stoy, grateful

for any kind of response from Delbert Hanks. Since Hanks' arrival in Elk Horn a few weeks back, Stoy Manlon and the other local toughs had gone out of their way to get on his good side. Hanks had been gaining a reputation as a crack shot with a pistol. He was just the kind of man someone like Stoy Manlon and Billy Freeman wanted to be associated with.

"Try to keep up, Stoy!" Rance Hardaway barked, looking back and seeing the other three had dropped back a couple of feet farther behind him. "This ain't the kind of weather to go straggling behind in."

"Who's straggling?" asked Stoy Manlon, feeling embarrassed about being singled out and called down in front of Delbert Hanks. "You won't never have to wait up for me, Rance . . . nor come looking for me in a snowbank neither."

"That's good to know, Stoy," Rance Hardaway said wryly. "I'd appreciate it if you and Billy Boy would both get in front of Delbert and stay there."

"Oh? Why's that?" Stoy asked in earnest, goading his horse a little harder in the snow.

"So it'll keep me from having to pull your noses out of his behind if he stops too quick," Rance Hardaway said with no change of expression in his level voice.

Delbert Hanks let go with a snort of laughter, followed by a puzzled silence as Stoy Manlon and Billy Freeman let the words sink in. Finally Stoy Manlon's face turned crimson. He said in a bitter growl, "That's real damn funny, Rance!" Balling his hand into a fist, he batted his heels to his horse's sides, trying to get alongside Rance Hardaway. "Get down off that horse. We'll see who — !"

His words stopped short as a bullet thumped into the snow near the front hooves of Rance Hardaway's big dapple gray. "Mercy sakes!" Rance Hardaway shouted, reining the horse up so sharply it reared up just as the sound of the rifle shot reached down to the flatlands. Before the big dapple had time to settle, another bullet thumped into the snow beneath its raised front hooves. Instead of coming straight down, the dapple veered sideways, the snow causing it to lose its balance. Rance Hardaway flung himself from the saddle as the horse came crashing down in a spray of snow.

The next shot hit near the hooves of Stoy Manlon's horse. But before the horse could spook, Stoy kicked it out from the others, making a slow, awkward getaway. The tired horse lunged step after step through the deep snow until Stoy finally slid down from the saddle and decided to take his chances on foot. Billy Freeman also jumped from his saddle, but instead of trying to run — seeing what an awful task it was for Stoy — he hunkered down into a ball behind his horse.

"Stop running, you chickenshit sumbitch!" Delbert Hanks shouted at Stoy Manlon. He whipped his pistol from his holster and fired two shots dangerously close above Stoy Manlon's head.

"Don't shoot, Delbert! Please don't shoot me!" Stoy Manlon pleaded, coming to an abrupt halt in the snow.

"Then stand still!" Delbert commanded.

Stoy raised his trembling hands in the cold air. Steam swirled in his breath. "He's seen us trailing him. He's going to kill us!"

Rance Hardaway struggled to his feet, snatching up his horse's reins as it also rose, shaking itself off. Hardaway's eyes went along the snow-covered ridgeline, the shine of sunlight off the snow keeping him from seeing anything clearly. "You damned fool! If he meant to kill you, you'd already be dead!" He waved a hand. "Look at us, out here on the open land like some kind of damned idiots!"

"You're the one in charge, Hardaway," said Delbert Hanks. "We're here because you brought us this way."

"I know it," said Hardaway. "I knew better than to come this way when we started out . . . but what was we supposed to do, go around? I never figured on him spotting us back here till we had him in our sights."

"Then by God, you better figure on it now," said Delbert Hanks. He sat tall in his saddle, facing the upper ridgeline boldly. "I hate getting jackpotted like this, damn it to hell! I ought to shoot you for causing it!"

"What — what do we do now?" Stoy Manlon asked, swallowing a tight knot of fear in his throat.

"Now?" said Rance Hardaway. He turned to face the high ridgeline and waved his arms back and forth slowly. "Now we show him we got the message and hope to God he don't kill us where we stand." He stopped waving his arms and stood with his hands high in the air. "See?" he said, talking to the spot where the shots had come from as if he could be heard from that far away. "We understand, mister. We're backing out of here real easylike. . . . No harm done. Let that hammer down and hold your fire."

"What a bunch of cowards," Delbert Hanks said under his breath, looking all around, smoke still curling from the pistol in his hand. Atop the ridgeline, a large blast of ice and snow crashed down from the limbs of a tall pine. Then a swirling white plume rose up beneath the tree as the limbs bounced and swayed. The weight jarred the earth, causing other trees along the ridgeline to shed their weight the same way until the entire hillside rumbled from the impact. "Good," said Delbert Hanks. "I hope the sumbitch was standing underneath one."

Rance Hardaway winced, letting out a low whistle. "Talk about getting your ticket punched one way!" The four men managed to grin at one another, each getting his own image of the rifleman lying broken and buried beneath a ton of snow, ice and tangled tree limbs.

But their grins quickly turned to looks of concern as they realized the earth beneath them continued to rumble. "Aw hell," said Delbert Hanks, staring up at the ridgeline as it seemed to bare itself of snow and rock and small broken trees. "Here she comes!" The entire hillside beneath the ridgeline seemed to have slipped free from the rest of the earth. A wall of white came rolling and tumbling downward. Whole trees rode the crest as the slide tore boulders loose and hurled them toward the flatlands.

"Ride like hell!" shrieked Rance Hardaway, throwing himself up into his saddle and spurring the dapple gray out toward open land. Delbert Hanks spun his horse in the snow and kicked it frantically. Stoy Manlon didn't bother trying to reach his horse. He turned and ran wildly, gaining very little for all his efforts. Billy Freeman ran, pulling his horse along by its reins. But before any of them had gone twenty feet, the hillside was upon them, spilling out onto the flatland beneath what appeared to be a crystal gray fog.

"Good God almighty," said Jack Bell, looking down from atop the ridgeline, feeling the earth jar and sway beneath his feet. As quickly as the slide had started, it ended soundlessly. Within a few seconds, only a roaring echo lingered. In another moment even the echo was gone. Bell watched the crystal gray fog turn into a looming silver mist as trees and rocks became more visible. Within the silver mist, he watched a horse stand up and stagger in place, stunned, its saddle twisted and hanging down its side. Looking closely, Bell saw an arm reach up out of the snow and claw at the air.

"Don't be a fool," Bell said to himself. "These men might have killed you if they'd

18

had half a chance." He hesitated for a moment, giving it some serious thought. But then he shook his head, turned and walked to his horse and mule with his warm rifle cradled in his arms. "Come on, Whiskey," he said to the big buckskin, sliding his rifle into his saddle boot. "Let's see if we can do any good down there."

On the flatlands, Delbert Hanks lay crushed inside a cold, brutal white void. There was no north or south, no up or down. There was no distinguishable sound, only the roaring silence and the lesser sound of his gloved hand scraping inch by inch, trying to widen the narrow space around himself. As his consciousness began to fade, he felt his arm thrust out of the void and flop around aimlessly. Before blacking out altogether, Delbert took control of his arm and began clawing the air as if there were something there to grasp and hold on to.

A half hour had passed by the time Jack Bell arrived. He tied his animals, took a short-handled spade from his supplies atop the mule, and trudged on foot into the lumpy spill of snow and rocks. A thin veil of snow dust loomed in the sunlight above the half-covered body of a dead horse. When he'd made his way to the lone hand reaching up out of the snow, he found it had ceased moving. But that didn't stop him from falling onto his knees and scraping with the shovel until the shape of the man became more clear. First things first, Jack reminded himself. He pried the ice-locked pistol from Delbert Hanks' holster and shoved it down in his belt. An empty holster lay packed with snow up under Delbert Hanks' left arm. Bell looked all around but saw no loose pistol.

"Up you go," Jack said, standing, taking the arm and lifting the man until he could get a better grip on him. Delbert Hanks coughed. Icy slush flew from his lips. He let out a low groan and tried to speak as Jack raised him to his feet long enough to get a shoulder under his middle. "You can talk about it later," Jack said, laying the limp body back over his shoulder as he stood up. He struggled across the fresh spill to the animals.

Jack took down two blankets: one from the supplies atop the mule, the other from behind his saddle. He sat Delbert Hanks on one blanket and wrapped the other around him. He tucked the blanket up under Delbert's chin, stepped back and looked more closely at his face, recognizing him from the Sporting Life Saloon. "Yep, it's you all right — the young gunman . . . or should I say the young target shooter," Jack said, studying the young man with snow-streaked hair who sat shivering before him. "You hang on. We'll get a fire going in a minute . . . soon as I see if anybody else is alive." Jack glanced at the rifle butt sticking up from his saddle boot. "That rifle's not loaded, so don't go trying something stupid, all right?"

Delbert Hanks tried to nod his bowed head, but his violent trembling prevented him from doing so. He did manage to raise his head enough to watch Jack Bell walk back toward the fresh slide, carefully picking his footing among rocks and broken tree limbs.

"Dirty ambushing snake!" Delbert said to himself in a shivering whisper. His cold hand felt for his pistol beneath the blanket but only found an empty holster on his hip and another under his arm. He looked up at the rifle in the saddle boot. But then he hung his head and trembled more violently, hugging the blanket tightly up under his chin. Never in his life had Delbert Hanks been so humiliated, so beaten, so dazed and helpless. "This is killing me," he whispered hoarsely to the snow-covered ground, his eyes filling with tears of rage.

★ ★ ★

It was nearing midmorning by the time Jack Bell led his horse and mule and Rance Hardaway's dapple gray back into the shelter of a deep overhang. Atop the dapple gray, Delbert Hanks and Rance Hardaway sat slumped against one another, wrapped in blankets. Jack had found Hardaway near the far end of the spill, only partially covered with snow. But there was a purple knot the size of a land turtle on the side of Hardaway's head, where a flying rock had knocked him cold. Jack had spent a full hour looking for the other two men, but he had found no trace of them.

When the animals were grained and sheltered farther back beneath the overhang and a crackling fire licked upward from the circle of stones left by some earlier occupants, Jack melted snow in a small pot and boiled coffee. Rance Hardaway and Delbert Hanks sat in stunned silence, neither knowing what to say to a man they'd been out to rob, possibly to kill. Now that same man had not only saved their lives, he was actually fixing coffee for them. They avoided Jack's eyes altogether and only glanced at one another with expressions of shame.

Finally Jack Bell broke the tense silence as

he poured two steaming cups of coffee and sat them on a flat rock beside the fire. "Boys, I'm afraid there's only two tin cups here. Hope you don't mind sharing one."

"Obliged," Rance Hardaway murmured under his breath. Without looking Jack in the face, he stood up, stepped over, picked up the cup of coffee and stepped back over beside Delbert Hanks. "Here, Delbert, you drink first. I don't mind waiting," he said in a humble tone.

Delbert seethed and gritted his teeth, drawing his hands into tight fists beneath the blanket. But then he took a deep, calming breath, getting control of himself, and said, "No, by all means, Rance, you go first."

In the same humble, polite voice, Rance droned on, holding the cup out to Delbert Hanks. "No, I insist, Delbert, you go first. I know you're cold and tired, and I don't mind waiting until you've warmed yourself and gotten —"

"Hold it, boys," said Jack Bell, cutting them off. "Let's not get carried away here. I know what you were doing out here. If I'm not embarrassed by it, why should you be?"

Delbert took the cup from Rance Hardaway's hand and sipped from it. Hardaway looked at Bell, face-to-face for the first time, and said, "How do you know we were out to do you dirt? We could have just been on the same trail by coincidence, couldn't we?"

"Sure, you could have," said Jack, picking up his own cup of coffee and sipping it through the rising steam. He sat it down and leveled his gaze on Rance Hardaway. "But we both know better." He looked back and forth between the two shivering men. "Don't worry. I'm not going to shoot you. If I wanted blood, I'd have left you both back there in the snow to die. Far as I'm concerned, soon as you're both able to ride, you can clear on out of here. No guns though. I'll keep the firearms."

"No guns?" said Delbert Hanks. "You're going to send us out of here on one horse, with no way to defend ourselves or shoot game for something to eat? Then you might just as well go ahead and shoot us."

"Damn it, speak for yourself, Delbert," said Rance Hardaway, seeing a dark look come to Jack Bell's face. "Mister, you've been more than fair. I thank you for it, and I'm damned ashamed for what I came out here to do. You're right. We came here to take back the money you won at the Sporting Life. As far as killing for it, I can't say. Nobody can say for certain about a

24

thing like that until it's happened, can they?"

"I reckon not," said Jack. "Tell me one thing. Was it Early Philpot sent you after me, or was it your own idea?"

"What difference does it make?" Delbert Hanks asked, his voice taking on a surly quality now that the coffee was warming him and he knew he'd soon be free to go.

Jack shrugged. "Just curious. Just wanting to know for my own satisfaction. If you don't want to tell me, I'm not pushing you for it."

"Good," said Delbert Hanks, "because I'm not telling you a damn thing." He returned his lips to the hot coffee.

"I'll tell you," said Rance Hardaway. "You've been more square with us than I would have been with you in the same situation. Early Philpot sent us sure enough. Said you cheated him in that poker game. Said get his money back however we felt like doing it."

"The more you talk, the bigger your mouth gets, Hardaway," said Delbert Hanks, a warning edge to his voice.

"So what? I don't owe Early Philpot nothing. I wish to hell we'd never come out here."

"But we did come out here," said

Delbert. "Early never forced us to. We came on our own. So bite it off and chew it." He took another sip of coffee, then sat the cup down on the ground at Rance's feet. "There, drink up. Let's get the hell started back to Elk Horn." His eyes turned to stone as he raised them to Jack Bell and said in a sarcastic tone, "Anything you want to ask me before I go?"

"No," said Jack. "I can see you're a real hardcase. No point in asking you anything."

"That's right, there ain't," Delbert sneered. "You don't know me, mister . . . and you don't want to."

"You're right both ways," said Jack. "I heard about all the whiskey-bottle necks you shot off out behind the Sporting Life. Heard how many spokes you shot out of a buggy wheel." Jack spread a flat, mirthless grin. "Tell me something though. Have you ever shot a man? Ever looked a living human being dead in the eyes, drawn your smoker and nailed a hole in his heart? Left him stone dead staring up at the sky?"

Now it was Delbert Hanks' turn to spread a mirthless grin. "Ha," he said, giving Jack a cold stare. "More times than you've got fingers and —"

"Careful," Jack warned him, cutting him off. "Your whole life might depend on how you answer that question. The claims a man makes today are the ones he has to live up to tomorrow. Until you know you've got it in you to kill, all the threats in the world ain't worth a cotton-mouthed spit."

"I don't need no sermon," said Delbert. He noted that Jack Bell's hand was no closer to his pistol butt than it had been. Jack's expression was the same; so was his demeanor. Yet there was a difference now. It was as if a steel wire had been jerked tight in the air between them. It was unseen, but Delbert felt the vibration of it deep in his bones. "You said we're free to leave," Delbert said cautiously. "Does that offer still stand?"

"Get out of my sight," said Jack Bell, singling Delbert Hanks out, no longer seeming to notice Rance Hardaway one way or the other. "Don't ever step back in it."

CHAPTER 2

No sooner had Delbert Hanks and Rance Hardaway started leading the dapple gray down a narrow, snow-filled path away from the ledge overhang than Delbert began looking back over his shoulder and acting anxious to get farther away from Jack Bell. "Quit acting like that horse is made of gold," Delbert Hanks growled, trying to get Hardaway to hurry his pace. "Far as I'm concerned, we could start riding him right now."

"Yeah," said Rance Hardaway, nodding at the deep snow lining the steep path ahead of them. "Then we're sure to have two things to worry about: one horse with a broken leg and the two of us with broken necks."

Delbert grabbed Rance's arm, bringing both man and horse to a halt. "Maybe somebody should have told you earlier, Hardaway, but I don't take no sass or smart-mouthed attitude. I didn't like the way you crawfished all over the place back there, answering questions for that saddle tramp. Early Philpot ain't going to like it neither, once I tell him about it."

"Keep your hands to yourself, Delbert," Rance Hardaway cautioned, "if you don't want to go rolling all over this mountainside." He jerked his arm away from Delbert's grasp and started trudging on, leading the horse along the deep path. "The man had us dead to rights and a cocked gun on us to boot. That's not the best time I can think of to start giving a man any guff. There's times when the best thing you can do with a crow pie is eat it till it's all gone and act like you loved it."

"The hell is that supposed to mean? A crow pie? I never heard of such craziness as that," said Delbert Hanks.

Rance Hardaway shook his head. "You're even younger than I thought, Delbert. You never heard of crow pie?"

"Didn't I say I never?" Delbert snapped.

"How about humble pie?" asked Hardaway, trudging along ahead of him. "I expect everybody's heard of eating humble pie."

"I never," said Delbert, sounding put out by the subject, "and I've been around as much as the next fellow."

"I bet you have," said Rance in a sarcastic tone. "Being around doesn't mean much. A man can circle the world and come back as stupid as he started out, I expect."

Delbert Hanks bristled. "Are you calling me stupid?"

Rance Hardaway chuckled, staring straight ahead down the path. Instead of answering Delbert, he said, "Here's another saying you might not be real familiar with: 'If the shoe fits, wear it.' " Rance grinned. "Ever heard that one?"

"Smart sumbitch," Delbert growled under his breath. He gritted his teeth and clenched his fists, enraged. He looked all around for a rock large enough to cave in the back of Hardaway's head. But none were visible on the snow-covered ground. Before making a move on Rance Hardaway from behind, he looked back over his shoulder and saw Jack Bell standing in the same spot, still watching them leave. He grumbled and turned his gaze forward.

"What's that? What did you say?" Rance Hardaway asked without looking around at him.

"I said when I think of a saying, I'll let you know," Delbert lied.

"You do that, Delbert," said Rance. "If I was you, I wouldn't be feeling so cross and cocky. The man showed you where you stand, telling him what a killer you are. Turns out you ain't killed nothing much bigger than an empty rye bottle."

"Never mind what I can or can't kill," Delbert hissed. "I reckon my guts won't fail me when the time comes."

They struggled onward in silence for the next half mile. At the bottom of the path where the land flattened, they took turns sitting atop the dapple gray a few minutes at a time as they followed their earlier footprints back to the spot where they'd gotten hit by the snow slide. "Think you can find that belly gun?" asked Rance Hardaway, seeing Delbert drop down from the saddle as the horse labored on in the snow. He grabbed the loose reins as Delbert made his way over to the upturned snow where Jack Bell had dug him out of his icy tomb.

"I hope so," said Delbert Hanks. "I've packed it around for a long time. It meant a lot to me."

Rance looked back and forth across the piles of snow and broken brush and timber. "My rifle would be a big help. I better get to looking for it too."

"You damned sure better," said Delbert. "Once I get my hands on my pistol, I've got a saying or two for you."

Hearing the warning tone of Delbert's voice, a worried look came to Rance Hardaway's face. "Hey, Delbert, come on! We've got no reason to start fighting. Hell, we need to stick together out here if we're going to make it back alive!"

"I'm *going* to make it back alive," Delbert Hanks said confidently. "But I ain't real sure about you." He dropped down onto his knees and began probing the large hole in the snow with his gloved hands.

"This is crazy," shouted Rance Hardaway. But even as he protested, he reached down and tied the horse's reins around a long broken tree bough and hurried over to where Jack Bell had found him in the snow. He kicked snow away from pine limbs and searched back and forth in the rocks and rubble. "I never saw a man who can't take a little kidding, Delbert!" he said, his voice almost turning to a plea. He hurried all around, stumbling amid small boulders and the hard, frozen lumps of overturned snow.

"All right!" said Delbert Hanks with a wide, evil grin, jerking his belly gun up from the snow. "Here we are!" He began slapping the pistol against his palm to free it of ice. "How are you coming along with that rifle, Rance?" he called out. "Seems like you'd have found it by now. You know what they say: 'A green duck on a pond ain't worth a red fox in a henhouse.' You ever heard that one?"

"Delbert, damn it! Don't do this to me!

I've never mistreated you! You want the horse? Then take it, go ahead, but don't shoot me!" As he spoke, he trudged toward the horse, realizing he never should have left it. Instead of searching for the rifle, he should have climbed into his saddle and ridden away. But now he was afraid it was too late. The harder he tried to hurry through the snow, the slower he seemed to move, like a man trying to run in a nightmare.

"Well, much obliged, Rance," said Delbert. "I believe I will just take the horse off your hands, since you've offered it." His grin widened. "Reminds me of the saying: 'No need in two men sharing what one of them can do without.' Ever heard that one, Rance, wise man that you are?" He stalked forward through the snow, raising the pistol toward Rance Hardaway at a distance of twenty feet and closing. "Here's another saying for you, Rance: 'Never refuse your coat to a cold man carrying a loaded gun.' Ever heard that one, have you?" He cocked the hammer back on the Colt Thunderer belly gun. Flakes of ice fell from the gun butt.

"Here, Delbert, take the coat too!" said Rance Hardaway, his voice growing shallow and tight. He stripped out of his fleece-lined winter coat as he tried to struggle along sideways toward the horse, already seeing that it was no use. Delbert and his ice-coated pistol were too close upon him. "I'll give you what all I've got, Delbert — only please don't kill me!"

"Naw, it's too late to beg and carry on, Rance," said Delbert, shaking his head. "I've got to kill you now, just on general principle." His words stopped short as his eyes made a sweep across the snow. "Now I wish you'd just looky there, Rance! Ain't that your rifle butt sticking up?"

Rance Hardaway slumped, letting out a defeated breath. Sticking up from the snow only inches from his zigzagging footprints stood the butt of his rifle, its barrel buried in the snow all the way to the chamber. "Damn it to hell," Rance Hardaway whispered.

Delbert laughed aloud, the pistol leveled and ready. "Talk about piss-poor luck. You come mighty near tripping over it. A man with no more luck than that *ought* to be shot, don't you think?"

Rance Hardaway seemed to resolve himself to his fate. The sight of his rifle butt sticking up from the snow so close to where he'd been looking for it seemed to have put life and death into perspective for him. "Go to hell, Delbert. Do whatever you've got to do. You won't last much longer yourself, the way you're going."

"Yeah, but I'll do it in style though." He jerked his head sidelong toward the dapple gray. "And I'll ride a good horse while I get there."

"Take care of that horse," said Rance Hardaway. "That's all I ask of you. Surely to God you'll do that, won't you?"

"We'll see." Delbert shrugged, his gloved hand tightening on the pistol butt. "Who knows? I get hungry; I might skin him down and eat him."

"Rotten bastard."

The Colt Thunderer bucked in Delbert Hanks' hand; slivers of ice flew from it. Then a gray ribbon of smoke curled upward from the barrel. "There now," he said to the body of Rance Hardaway lying slumped in the snow, a long streak of blood stretching from his back. "All the serious brownnosing you did with that saddle tramp never kept you alive very long, did it?"

Delbert stuck the smoking pistol into the empty holster under his arm, stepped over and pushed Rance Hardaway's body down into the snow with his boot until it was partially buried. Then he stooped down and shoveled snow over the body with both hands until it was hidden from sight. "That's a good place for a turd like you, Rance Hardaway," he said. "Just deep enough to start stinking once the weather breaks." He picked up Rance's fleece-lined coat, shook it off and threw it on over his own flimsier winter coat. Then he took up the reins to the dapple gray and stepped up into the saddle. "Let's head back to Elk Horn," he said to the horse. "See what kind of trouble we can stir this into."

It was late evening when Jack Bell wound his way the last mile upward into Nolan's Gap. He'd heard the sound of music and laughter rising up from the rocks and snow before the town came into sight. At length, as he rode the horse at a walk up the steep, tilted mud street, corrugated tin roofs of stilted mining shacks appeared up out of the side of the mountain as if the town had lain hidden in wait for him. He felt the tug of the pack mule on his lead rope and slowed enough to make things easier for the shorter animal. A pistol shot resounded from inside the saloon up ahead. Then a man came sailing airborne out into the snow and mud, his pistol sailing out right behind him.

"Don't let me catch you out here bumming from my customers," a loud voice boomed from the open door.

"Well, Whiskey," Jack said quietly to the buckskin. "Looks like this might be home for a while." He heeled the horse toward the sound of banjo music and laughter as the drunk struggled up to his feet only to slip and fall back down. This time he landed face first in a puddle of muddy, icy water. Jack stepped the buckskin wide of the man and had started to rein up to the hitch rail. But when he saw that the man was making no attempt to rise up on his own, Jack quickly stepped down from his saddle in the middle of the street and grabbed the man by both shoulders.

Yanking the man from the puddle, Jack dragged him back a couple of feet and dropped him onto his side. The man spluttered and coughed and raised a muddy hand to a bloody welt rising on his forehead. "Who — ? Who hit me?" the man asked.

Jack could smell the sour whiskey on his breath. "Nobody hit you that I saw," Jack Bell replied, picking up the man's pistol. He checked and saw it wasn't loaded, then shoved it into the man's holster. "It looked like you knocked yourself cold." He poked his toe along the edge of the icy mud puddle and turned up a rock the size of a large apple. "There's your culprit." Jack grinned.

The man looked at him in confusion as his mind tried to catch up to itself. "You . . . pulled me up from the mud?" He coughed again and spit mud from his lips.

"Yes, something like that," Jack said. He started to stand up and walk back to his horse, but the man grasped his forearm.

"I'm obliged, mister," the drunkard said. "I might have died right here."

"But you didn't," said Jack, casting a glance at the man's muddy hand on his coat sleeve. "Now go sleep it off somewhere." He stepped back and offered the man a hand getting up.

"I'm Ben Finley," the man said through another cough. He eyed Jack Bell as his expression turned wary. "Say now . . . I hope you ain't one of the strong-arm boys Arnold Waddel's got working for him."

"No," said Jack. "I'm nobody's strong-arm boy. My name's Jack Bell. Would it have made any difference if I was one of the men you're talking about?"

"If you was one of Arnold Waddel's flunkies, damn right it would make a difference," said Ben Finley with commitment. But seeing Jack Bell's level gaze and thinking about it for a second, his tone of voice relented a bit. He said, "Well, no. I reckon when a man pulls you from the mud,

38

you're beholden to him, whoever he is."

"That's more like it," said Jack, turning Ben Finley's hand loose as Finley stood a little more steadily on his feet. "Life's too short to go around mad at everybody. Have you got a place to go to get yourself out of the weather? It'll be turning cold tonight."

"Don't worry about me, Mr. Bell," Ben Finley said. "I got me a shack up there that's as good as any man needs and a daughter who looks after me like an old mama cat." He nodded toward one of the shacks on stilts standing up on the mountainside. The glow of an oil lamp shone through a small front window. "I bet my Rosalee is waiting right now with a hot bowl of stew simmering on the stove."

"Good," said Jack Bell. "Then you get on home to your daughter. If you don't think you can make it there on foot, we'll give you a ride up there." He nodded at the buckskin.

"Thank you, sir, but no," said Ben Finley, brushing a hand down the front of his ragged wool coat and freeing it of stiff flecks of mud and ice. "You've done more than enough already." His eyes went across the buckskin but stopped at the pack mule. "Are you a prospector, Mr. Bell?"

"No," said Jack. "Not yet anyway. I won

the mule and prospecting gear in a poker game down in Elk Horn the other night."

"I see. Then you're a gambler?" Finley asked.

"No, not by profession," said Jack. "I just hit a lucky streak at the Sporting Life Saloon and won everything that got in front of me . . . mule and all."

"Anybody wins at the Sporting Life and lives to tell about it really *has* been on a lucky streak," Finley said. He eyed the pack mule a little closer, then said, "I'd need to be more sober to say for sure, but that looks like the mule that left here with an ole boy named Henry Muir. The most profane-speaking man I ever saw."

"That's not the man's name I won it from," said Bell, "but once a mule starts making his way around a poker table, there's no telling who'll end up owning him. If you need a good mule and a mining stake, he is for sale . . . once I get my belongings down off his back."

"Not for me; I'm afraid my prospecting days are over," said Ben Finley. "I found my fortune and lost it before it left the ground. But if I hear of somebody looking for a mule, I'll point him to you."

Bell wanted to ask the old man what he meant about finding his fortune and losing it before it left the ground, but no sooner had Finley finished his words than both he and Bell turned toward the sound of the saloon doors swinging open. On the boardwalk stood a big man wearing a white bartender's apron and garters on his shirt sleeves. At the sight of the big bartender, Ben Finley took a step back, farther away from the front of the saloon.

"Finley, I warned you to get away from here," the big bartender said, rolling up his shirt sleeves as he spoke. His eyes went to Jack Bell. "Is he bothering you, mister?"

"No bother," said Jack Bell.

Ben Finley sounded nervous as he said to the bartender, "See, Stanley? I weren't causing no trouble out here. This man was just helping me collect myself and get on home."

"You had your chance to leave here, Ben. You should have taken it," said the bartender, stepping down from the boardwalk into the mud and slush along the edge of the muddy street. "I think I'm going to have to crack your head . . . teach you to listen when I tell you something."

"Easy now," said Jack Bell in a firm, level tone, taking a half step in between Ben Finley and the big bartender. "He told you he's on his way home."

"Easy?" said the bartender. "I'll show you *easy*. This old bummer put a bullet hole in a brand new oil painting a while ago. I could have shot him down for it, but I didn't. He's got a beating coming. Get out of my way, or you'll get a lesson too."

But Jack Bell stood firm. "I'm afraid I can't do that," he said.

As Bell spoke to the bartender, a man wearing a broad-brimmed dress hat stepped out onto the boardwalk into the waning evening light. A match flared as he struck it and raised it to the tip of a cigar. Seeing Stanley the bartender start to take a step toward Jack Bell, the man said through a fresh plume of gray cigar smoke, "That's enough, Stanley." The bartender caught himself midstep and eased back. The man continued, "You could beat on this knothead all night, and he'd never learn a thing."

Jack Bell's eyes went to the glow of the match just as the man shook it out and flipped it away. In the shadowy light, Jack saw a brace of belly guns partially hidden by pinstriped lapels beneath the open front of a long bearskin coat. "Max Brumfield?" Jack inquired.

"You better hope it's me, Bell," said the voice. "I once saw Stanley Barger here hit a man so hard, the poor fellow's boots fit him

42

backward for the next month." Max Brumfield raised his face enough for Jack Bell to recognize his easy Southern gambler's smile. "How are you, Jack?" A thin mustache mantled Brumfield's lip.

"I'll do," said Jack, stepping away from between Stanley Barger and Ben Finley. "How about yourself?" He and Brumfield shook hands at the edge of the boardwalk.

"Never better, Jack," said Max Brumfield. He passed a glance to Stanley Barger, dismissing him, then gave Ben Finley a cold stare. "You owe me for the oil painting, Ben. Now get on home and sober up before I have Stanley tie a tin can to your tail."

Ben Finley thanked Jack Bell again and bid him good evening. Jack and Max Brumfield watched the old man trudge across the narrow street to a pathway lined with planks leading upward onto the mountainside. Then Max Brumfield gestured a sweeping hand toward the large plank building and said with a short laugh, "Welcome to the Western Palace Saloon. Not the biggest or the best right now, but growing bigger *and* better every day."

"I've sure seen worse," said Bell, looking the big rough plank building over. "Finally got a place of your own, huh?"

43

"Indeed I have," said Brumfield. He turned to the big bartender. "Stanley, take my friend's horse and mule to the livery barn. See to it they're attended while I go pour him a drink."

But before Stanley Barger could make a move to the horse, Jack Bell said, "Much obliged, Max, but that won't be necessary." He stepped over to the buckskin and the mule and gathered the reins and lead rope. "You know me, Max. I tend my own."

Max Brumfield looked him up and down: the battered Stetson, the three days' growth of beard stubble, a wide bandanna draped high around his throat. "Oh yes, I nearly forgot," said Max. "You always were quite the individualist, weren't you?"

Jack Bell smiled. "I never liked being beholden, if that's the same thing."

"Of course it is," said Max Brumfield, stepping forward into the muddy street with him. "I'll just accompany you then. And since you don't want to be *beholden* to anyone, you can buy us both dinner afterward."

"Sounds good to me," said Jack Bell.

"Oh, does it now?" Max Brumfield cocked an eye at him. "My, but that was certainly easy! I take it you have arrived here flush with cash?"

"I got lucky in Elk Horn at the Sporting Life Saloon," said Jack, walking along, leading the animals, Max Brumfield right beside him.

"Did you indeed?" said Brumfield, looking surprised. "Early Philpot does not part with his money easily. Some poor dealer's head must have rolled over that."

"Wasn't a dealer I won it from," said Jack. "I played stud poker with Philpot himself."

"Then I am truly impressed, Jack!" said Max Brumfield, looking even more surprised. "But now that you've told me that, I hope you realize I'm going to have to win all that money away from you."

Jack smiled, staring ahead toward the livery barn. "I realize you're going to *try*."

CHAPTER 3

Delbert Hanks spent three days and nights trudging through deep snow on his way back to Elk Horn. In the dapple gray's saddlebags he'd found a few coffee beans and some jerked elk shank. He'd eaten sparingly, and when he'd crushed the beans and boiled himself some weak coffee, he saved the used grounds and reboiled them. One thing he did not skimp on was his fire. Every evening Delbert grabbed whatever deadfall he could find sticking up out of the snow and whatever limbs and bark he could strip from standing timber. He built a large, licking fire that steamed and crackled with green wood throughout the night.

On the fourth morning, Delbert stoked up the dying fire and piled it high with green pine limbs and long clumps of winter wild grass he had dug up from beneath the snow. He reboiled the coffee grounds until he had a weak-looking cup of coffee steaming beneath his nose. With a piece of elk jerky he'd held over the fire on his knife blade, he sat atop his saddle on the ground with a wool blanket wrapped around himself. He took his time eating with one hand outside the blanket, watching a large cloud of steam and smoke fill the sky.

From fifty yards away a lone rider eased his horse upward atop a low rise of snowy hillside and sat for a moment staring at Delbert's back through a bandanna he'd cut slits into and pulled up over his eyes as relief against the blinding glare of sun and snow. A dead rabbit hung from a length of rawhide looped around his saddle horn. He patted his horse's withers to keep it quiet, then heeled it forward silently until he called out above the loudly crackling fire from no more than ten feet away, "Hello the camp!"

Delbert snapped his head around in surprise. His free hand didn't even have time to reach out for Hardaway's rifle he'd pulled from the snow and brought with him. The sight of the large rifle bore trained at his face caused him to freeze momentarily.

"You can thank your lucky star I'm a white man, eh, pilgrim?" The lone rider laughed under his breath, his words trailing a wake of steam. Then, as if in afterthought, he added, "You can thank God *you're* a white man too! I'm cold enough I'd kill for a cup of coffee."

Without waiting to be asked and without taking the rifle or his eyes off of Delbert

Hanks, the rider stepped down slowly from his saddle and dropped his horse's reins to the snow. The horse seemed to take the gesture as a command and stood as still as stone. The man stepped wide of his horse and eased forward, his thumb across his rifle hammer.

Delbert's voice sounded worried as he spoke. "There's coffee for you here . . . just wish it was stronger though." He cocked an eye at the man and said, "I've seen you before. You're one of those detectives who works for Arnold Waddel. I saw you in Elk Horn a while back."

"Yeah, I'm Fleetus Gibbs. I saw you there too, at the Sporting Life Saloon. You were working for the owner," the man said, eying the rifle lying near Delbert.

"Yep, I worked for Philpot. My name's Delbert Hanks." Delbert rose enough to lean forward, take off his hat and use it as a hot pad as he picked up the small coffeepot and shook it a bit, judging its contents. "Hope you've got a cup with you."

"Sure do," said Gibbs, seeing no reason to fear this young man. Still, he kept his eyes on Delbert's back as he stepped over to his horse, took a tin cup from his saddlebags and came back rounding a finger in it. "As I recollect, you're the one with a reputation for being a shootist."

"I reckon so," Delbert said, playing it modest, "but it's not something I tried for. It just came about, working for Philpot, taking a stand with some of the gunmen drifting through. Of course, I never was nothing to compare with you boys riding for Arnold Waddel. I hear he only hires the toughest of the tough."

"Well . . ." Fleetus Gibbs let his words trail. Then he said with regret, "I don't work for Waddel anymore. We run off all the claim jumpers around on the other side of the mountain. I reckon we worked ourselves out of a job."

"Too bad," said Delbert. "The truth is, I don't work for Philpot anymore either. Not after what's happened out here. Me and some other boys got hit by a small avalanche. Killed them all; damn near killed me too. That's why I'm run out of everything — hardly any food, coffee, ammunition. Luckily I found that rifle. Maybe I can shoot something."

"There's little out here to shoot at with this snow," said Gibbs. "I shot that big rabbit and gutted him last night about dark. I was going to save him for later, but we can skin him and spick him."

"Much obliged," said Delbert Hanks,

"but I'm all right on this jerked elk for now. It's only a couple days' ride back to town."

Gibbs poured himself a cup of weak coffee and squatted down beside the fire with it. He wrapped both hands around the cup, liking the warmth of it. "Two days can be a long time, out like this — only one animal, low on food. Suppose your horse legs out? Suppose you have to hold up an extra day or two? How are you fixed for ammunition for that rifle?"

"Something will turn up for me," said Delbert. "Something always does."

"Stupid pilgrim," Gibbs growled to himself. He studied Delbert's youthful face, his cheeks pinched red by the cold. "What did Early Philpot have you doing out here anyways? Nothing that couldn't wait till the weather changed, I bet."

Delbert offered a thin smile, fixing his eyes on the fire as he spoke. "Early Philpot sent us out to ambush a man who won too much money from him. I believe he meant for us to kill him. Leastwise, that's what we decided to do."

"Whoa now." Gibbs gave him a strange, surprised look. "That's not the kind of thing you ought to be telling somebody."

"Why not?" Delbert asked without taking his staring eyes from the fire.

"Why not?" Gibbs was beginning to think the young man wasn't right in the head. "Because it's illegal, you damn fool! Suppose I was to go tell the law. You'd be in more trouble than you'd ever get out of!"

Delbert turned his eyes to him slowly. "Really? Then I guess I better kill you, huh?" His slight smile widened.

His words stung Gibbs for a second. But seeing the dumb smile on his face, Gibbs took it as a joke and eased back and sipped his coffee. "You shouldn't kid around like that. Somebody might take you serious."

"I am," said Delbert. A pistol shot exploded beneath the blanket wrapped around him.

Fleetus Gibbs saw the streak of blue fire blow through the blanket. He felt the bullet strike the tin cup in his hands and bore through his chest. He fell back with the impact of the shot, the coffee spilling onto his wounded chest in a billowing of steam. He caught a glimpse of tiny flames eating at the edge of the bullet hole in Delbert's blanket, smoke curling out of it. All of these things happened at once, in a dizzying flash, as he realized he'd been shot. "You . . . son . . . of a —"

Before he could finish his words, another shot exploded, this one silencing him as he seemed to melt into the blood-streaked snow. Delbert flipped his blanket aside and patted out the tiny fire his shot had caused on it. "I told you something always turns up for me," he said quietly, cocking his head to one side with curiosity, examining his hand-iwork. He stood up and stretched and took in a deep breath of cold air. "Thank you, Jack Bell. Thank you, Rance Hardaway," he said aloud to himself, gazing up along the distant mountain line. If he'd known it was this easy killing people, he might have started doing it a long time ago.

He scraped snow over the body of Fleetus Gibbs, kicked out the fire and rummaged through Gibbs' saddlebags to see what he had gained for his efforts. Some .45 caliber pistol bullets, a stiff shaving brush, a large chunk of beef jerky, a bag of strong-smelling pemmican. Not much, but that was all right, Delbert thought. It hadn't cost him anything; a couple of bullets was all. He'd gained a horse. That meant a lot, he thought, scraping snow over Gibbs' body until it became only one more white mound on an endless white blanket. When he'd finished preparing for the trail, he left the camp riding the dapple gray, leading Gibbs' dun behind him. For the next two days, he pushed hard toward Elk Horn.

Early Philpot knew a good thing when he saw it, and he saw it the day he rode into Elk Horn. That had been two years ago, shortly before the railroad made the little trading-post town its regular fuel stop and cattle railhead. Philpot had bought the Sporting Life Saloon when it was a nameless, sour-smelling, used army surgery tent. The bar had been a rough plank resting on two rain barrels. But overnight, Elk Horn had swollen to four times its former size, and the Sporting Life was nameless no more.

The army tent was long gone. In its place stood a handsome two-story clapboard building with a broad five-foot-high facade running the width of its high front edge. On either end of the facade stood two giant-sized painted beer mugs tipped slightly toward one another with foam on the verge of dripping over their rims. In the middle of the facade, two painted bare-knuckle prize-fighters stood toe-to-toe, squared off and ready to fight. Above them, fancy gold-trimmed painted letters spelled out THE SPORTING LIFE SALOON. Underneath, in slightly smaller letters, it read: *Earl Leland Philpot, Prop.*

Early Philpot's enterprise had grown into the largest, most prosperous business in town. And he deserved every dime of it, he thought, standing on the boardwalk out front of his saloon, watching the busy street. It might still be too soon for Rance Hardaway and the others to be back yet, but the man he'd sent them after had seven hundred dollars of his money, and that was enough to keep Philpot edgy and anxious.

Not that Early Philpot couldn't afford the loss. There wasn't a week went by that some player didn't get lucky and win a pile of cash at one of the Sporting Life's gaming tables. Of course, they usually lost it back no sooner they'd won it. But this thing with Jack Bell had been a matter of personal pride. It hadn't been one of Philpot's dealers who'd lost the money. Philpot himself had lost the seven hundred . . . and to a nobody! A drifter! And at his own game, the holy game of poker. Early Philpot couldn't stand it.

It didn't even make sense to him *why* he couldn't stand it. All he knew was that it was eating at him. He puffed on a long black cigar and watched Sheriff Taylor Brady walk toward him from the direction of Elk Horn's barbershop and dentistry emporium. Sheriff Brady held a bandanna to his jaw and approached with an expression of pain etched on his brow.

"Good morning, Sheriff," Early Philpot said, already knowing the kind of response to expect.

"Morning hell," Sheriff Brady grumbled weakly. "I'm losing all my blasted teeth one at a damn time. There's no good morning for me."

"My condolences, Sheriff," said Philpot absently as he gazed off into the distance past the edge of town where a lone rider appeared to rise upward into the sunlight. "If there's anything I can do, feel free to let me know." He gestured a soft, clean hand toward the doors of the Sporting Life Saloon. "Drinks are on the house for you, of course."

"Much obliged. I'll take you up on the drinks," said Sheriff Brady. "The way my jaw's aching, I won't make it through the day without something to get rid of this damn pain." He looked back and forth as if to make sure no one else could hear him. Then he said, "The cost of having these teeth pulled is starting to drain me too. Maybe it's time you and me talked some more about what we can do . . . for the benefit of the town and its future." As he spoke, Sheriff Brady took the bandanna from his jaw long enough to rub the tip of his finger and thumb together in the universal sign of greed. "I hope you understand what I'm getting at, Mr. Philpot."

Early Philpot smiled. "Indeed I do, Sheriff. I've been wanting us to get together and talk about this town's future for a long time. Nothing would please me more than for the two of us to become colleagues."

For Early Philpot, this had just turned into an exceptional day. He knew how the game was played between a saloon owner and a local lawman. In the two years it had taken him to build up the Sporting Life into a moneymaker, he'd been at the mercy of the town sheriff. He'd had to abide by the local ordinances, keep the noise down, keep the ground in front and behind his business clean. He'd had to pay a saloon tax just to make sure the sheriff came running when he needed help.

"Colleagues, huh?" said Sheriff Brady, having to take a second to familiarize himself with the word. Finally he nodded. "Then I reckon it's time we get it done."

"At your convenience, Sheriff," said Philpot, not wanting to sound too excited about the proposition. "Now go get some whiskey — ease that pain some." He reached out and patted a broad hand on the sheriff's back, giving him a gentle nudge toward the saloon doors.

No longer would it cost Philpot money every time a drunk fired a pistol or relieved himself in the street out front of the saloon. With the sheriff in his pocket, all that was about to change. The Sporting Life had grown and reached that crucial point where his business had become bigger than the local law or the town council either one. The sheriff had just told Early Philpot that he was ready to deal with him. Ready to get directly onto the Sporting Life's payroll. From now on, Philpot owned the streets of Elk Horn. The sheriff would be eating from the palm of his hand. Smiling in satisfaction, Early Philpot gazed back out at the lone rider drawing closer to the edge of town.

As Sheriff Brady slipped through the bat wing doors of the Sporting Life Saloon, Early Philpot raised his hand and gave the bartender a signal. It was Philpot's give-the-man-anything-he-wants signal. Seeing it, Curly Jones, the bartender, gave a slight nod of acknowledgment and hurried to wait on the sheriff as Brady stepped up to the bar. "So much for that," Early Philpot whispered to himself. He turned and stepped down from the boardwalk over a short pile of snow and onto the walk-planks stretched across the muddy street.

Delbert Hanks saw Early Philpot coming toward the livery barn to meet him. Philpot hurried along in front of him and swung open the barn door just as Delbert rode up, leading the spare horse behind him. "Well? What happened out there?" Early Philpot demanded, closing the door and standing beside Delbert Hanks as he slipped down from his saddle. "Where the hell are Rance Hardaway and the others?"

"Where are they?" said Delbert Hanks, spinning his reins around a stall rail. "I'll tell you where they are: They're all dead!"

Early Philpot stared at him, stunned.

"That's right — dead," said Delbert Hanks. Then he began lying with every breath. "It turns out this Jack Bell is a stone-cold killer. One of the fastest, straight-shootingest sumbitches you ever seen."

"That's why you were along, Delbert," said Philpot. "You're supposed to be the best around!"

"I am the best around, Mr. Philpot," said Hanks. "But we all got separated from one another in a snow slide. By the time I got around it and found the others, Bell had killed them deader than hell."

"Jesus," Philpot whispered, rubbing his chin, thinking about it. He was ready to put the whole matter aside. It had been foolish on his part to begin with. After a moment, he let out a breath of resignation and said, "Well, thank God you made it back . . . and it's all over."

"All over?" Now Delbert Hanks looked stunned. "There ain't nothing over, Mr. Philpot. I hate telling you this, but soon as the weather breaks, Jack Bell is going to come riding down the middle of the street strapped for bear . . . looking for you. He knows you were behind us coming to ambush him! He's going to kill you, unless you're a hell of a lot better with a gun than I think you are!"

Early Philpot turned chalk white. "How does he know I sent yas after him?"

"That damn Rance told him," said Hanks. "Rance was still alive when I found him. He said Bell made him tell him everything. Said Bell vowed he'd be coming for you soon as the weather lifts." Delbert shook his bowed head and added, "Looks like you'd been better off forgetting that money he won. I'm telling you, Mr. Philpot, this man ain't no light piece of work. The best thing you can do for yourself is skin out of town, lay low for a while, I reckon."

"Don't be a fool, Delbert! I can't leave Elk Horn with my tail tucked between my legs!" He tapped a thumb on his chest.

"This is my town. I have a business to run!"

"Then you better hope Sheriff Brady can gather some good deputies and back you up when the time comes." He couldn't help but spread a devilish grin. "Better hope his teeth don't start falling out about the time the shooting starts." He turned and loosened the cinch on the dapple gray and stripped its saddle from its back. He swung the saddle up onto a stall rail. "Soon as you pay me what I've got coming, I plan on heading a few miles down country, lay up until the winter passes."

"Pay you for what?" Philpot growled. "You haven't done what I told you to do! I sent four of you to bring back my seven hundred dollars! Now three of yas are dead, and I've got a gunman coming to kill me! How dare you talk to me about paying you! You're not leaving here. You're not leaving me in this kind of mess. You're staying right here. You're going to guard my back until this thing is settled with Jack Bell!"

With his back still turned to Early Philpot, Delbert Hanks smiled. But then he put the smile away and turned to Philpot. "Like hell I am. The deal was fifty dollars each for going after your money for you. You won't even pay me that, and now you expect me to stick around to face a killer like

Bell? You must be out of your mind!"

"Wait a minute," said Philpot, seeing Delbert Hanks as his best defense. "I'm a little upset." He reached in his trouser pocket and pulled out a roll of bills.

"Naw, forget the fifty dollars," said Delbert Hanks. "I'm clearing out of here. I know when I'm not wanted."

"Damn it, Delbert, take the money!" said Philpot. He reached out and stuffed the bills down into Delbert's shirt pocket. "And don't worry. If you stay and back me on this thing, there's plenty more where this came from." Philpot held the roll of bills up enough to be noticeable.

Delbert Hanks considered things for a moment, looking at the thick roll of bills in Philpot's hand. Finally he said, "All right. I'll stay and help you. But we need to tell the sheriff a little different story about how things happened out there. We can't tell him you had us trailing this Bell, now can we?"

"No, we certainly can't," said Philpot. "Get these horses taken care of. We'll have to think of something."

"While we're thinking of something, here's something else I better mention to you," said Delbert, turning to the late Fleetus Gibbs' dun and loosening its cinch.

He pulled the saddle from its back and pitched it up on the stall beside the other. "I found this horse wandering around not far from the body of another man Bell killed. It was one of those detectives from the mine company. He was dead when I got to him."

Early Philpot gave him a dubious look. "How do you know Bell killed him?"

"Use your head, Mr. Philpot," said Delbert, sounding a bit put out with his employer. "Who else was out there? Nobody, that's who. Jack Bell killed him. Plain and simple. The fact is, even if Bell didn't kill him, it's to our advantage to make it look like he did. Those mine detectives ain't going to take kindly to somebody killing one of their own, now are they?"

"You're right, Delbert." Early Philpot let it sink in for a second, then said, "But you know what? Maybe you ought to say the detective was still alive when you found him, the same way Rance Hardaway was —"

"Hold it," said Delbert. "Do you think I made that up about Hardaway?"

"No, of course not," said Philpot. "But can't you say the same thing about this detective?"

"That would be lying," said Delbert, sounding reluctant.

"Damn it! It's like you said: These detectives aren't going to like Bell killing one of their own. Do you want them on our side or not?"

"All right. I follow what you're saying, Mr. Philpot. This Jack Bell is on some kind of killing spree. He killed poor Billy Freeman, Stoy Manlon and Rance Hardaway." He studied Philpot's eyes as he spoke. "Then he shot this poor detective and left him to die out there."

"There you have it," said Philpot. "I sent the four of yas up to Nolan's Gap to collect a gambling debt from one of the miners. Bell ambushed you on the way."

"Who's the miner?" Delbert asked.

"Hell, I don't know. It doesn't matter," said Philpot. "He probably wasn't even who he said he was." He spread a thin, sly grin. "The lying sumbitch probably didn't even work there. Probably wasn't even headed there when he left here. But you remember him, don't you? A big German named Schmidt? Stood about this tall?" He raised a hand. "Shaggy brown hair?"

"Yeah, now I remember." Delbert returned the sly grin. "That no-good sonsabitch caused every bit of this! We ought to hang him if he ever shows his face again."

"You're a bright boy, Delbert Hanks,"

63

said Philpot. "You know when to speak . . . but you also know when to keep your mouth shut and listen."

"Not only that," said Delbert on his own behalf, still grinning over their private little joke. "When I hear good advice, I take it and act on it." He thought about Jack Bell telling him that he'd better make sure he had killing in him before he went around making threats about it. Yep, that had been good advice — and he'd followed it. Now look how well everything was starting to go for him.

"Then you're going to go far in this world, my boy." Early Philpot slapped Delbert on his back as he directed him toward the door. "Come on now. Let's go talk to that snaggletoothed sheriff."

CHAPTER 4

As he told Sheriff Brady his story, Delbert Hanks reached out every few minutes, poured himself a shot from a bottle of rye whiskey, tossed it back and went on talking. Early Philpot noticed that the more Delbert drank and talked, the more he began elaborating on his tale. By the time Delbert had gotten to the part where he'd gathered the dead detective's horse and brought it back to Elk Horn, the story had taken on an unreal quality. Early Philpot didn't like the skeptical look Sheriff Brady had begun giving Delbert. Bad teeth or not, Brady was a lawman. Early Philpot realized the man had spent the broadest part of his life listening to saddle trash like Hanks lie on any number of subjects.

"Let me make sure I've got this straight," said the sheriff. As Delbert Hanks stopped long enough to refill his shot glass, Sheriff Brady touched his wadded-up bandanna to the corner of his mouth, careful of his swollen jaw. "This Bell fellow, for no apparent reason, shot Rance Hardaway, caused a snow slide that killed those poor idiots Billy Freeman and Stoy Manlon . . . then killed one of the detectives because he thought the man just *might* be trailing him?" He moved the bandanna away from his face, looked at it as though it might possess the secret to some arcane puzzle, then pressed it carefully back against his jaw.

Delbert straightened in his chair as if offended by the sheriff's words. "I wouldn't go so far as to call poor Billy Freeman and Stoy Manlon *idiots*, Sheriff. Those boys were some damn good friends of mine."

"Sure they were," Sheriff Brady said absently. "Now, back to the story. You're telling me that all this happened while you were on your way back from —"

"Sheriff, if you please?" said Early Philpot, cutting the sheriff off. "This man is half-frozen, half-starved and worn to a frazzle. He's obviously told you all he knows. Don't you think any questions you have can wait a few hours, until he's rested enough to make sense of all this?"

Sheriff Brady gave Early Philpot a cold stare. "I find it best to question a man as soon as possible after something like this happens. Keeps their memory fresh, you could say." He looked at Delbert Hanks as he added, "I know Delbert here better than he thinks I know him. It ain't above him to come up with some trickery if he thought it might suit his purpose . . . whatever that purpose might be."

Delbert Hanks rose slightly from his chair. "I won't be talked to in this manner!" he warned. "Not while the law allows a killer like Jack Bell to go running loose, free to do as he damn well pleases!"

"Sit down, boy!" Sheriff Brady growled, his voice distorted by the swelling and pain in his jaw. "I'm the law. I'll deal with this the way that best suits me. You better hope to God you ain't lying to me!"

As Sheriff Brady and Delbert Hanks growled back and forth at one another, neither they nor Early Philpot noticed the two detectives who stepped through the doors and walked over to their table.

"What's Fleetus Gibbs' horse doing in the livery barn, Sheriff?" one detective asked, cutting in on Sheriff Brady, his palm resting on the bone-handled butt of a big Walker Colt holstered across his stomach, easy-reach style. The most noticeable feature of the man speaking was a cloudy blind eye with a fierce jagged scar running through it and down his left cheek. "He was supposed to meet us two days ago."

Both detectives shifted a dark gaze back and forth between Sheriff Brady and

Delbert Hanks as if sensing that the conversation they'd interrupted had something to do with their missing colleague. Sheriff Brady looked the two men up and down indignantly. "Well by God, gentlemen!" Brady said, his face growing red in anger. "Don't let my talking interrupt anything you might want to say. Feel free to just jump right in."

"Much obliged, Sheriff," said the one-eyed detective, who stood nearest him. The man didn't seem to catch the sarcasm in Sheriff Brady's voice or demeanor. "I'm Floyd Finch." He jerked his head toward the other man. "This is Nate Reardon. You've seen us pass through here before. We're formerly with West Track Mining Company. Fleetus Gibbs is one of us." They gave Delbert Hanks an accusing look. "The boy at the barn said some sniveling-looking piece of punk brought Fleetus' horse in a while ago." His good eye stayed fixed on Delbert Hanks.

Delbert rose up from his chair slowly, feeling the unprovoked insult sting him like a slap in the face. "Who the hell are you calling a sniveling piece of punk?" His hand poised near the pistol on his hip.

"Anybody who *is* one," Floyd Finch said almost in a whisper, not the least bit threatened by Delbert Hanks. Floyd's gun hand still rested on his Walker Colt. "I've seen you around here, bottle-shooter," he said. "Now sit down before I hurt you *really* bad all over."

"Gentlemen, gentlemen! Please!" said Early Philpot, standing up quickly and spreading his hands in a show of peace. "We're all of the same accord here! Delbert found your friend's horse out on the range! He also found your friend's body! Right, Delbert?" Early Philpot turned it over to Delbert, then motioned for the bartender to bring over two more glasses for the detectives.

"Ole Fleetus dead?" said Floyd Finch.

"That can't be," said Nate Reardon. He stepped forward, glaring at the others. "Fleetus wasn't dead the last time I talked to him."

"Jesus," Sheriff Brady whispered in disbelief. All four of them just stared at Nate Reardon for a speechless moment.

Finally Floyd Finch said, "Nate, pour us both a drink." He looked at Sheriff Brady, Delbert Hanks and Early Philpot. "Nate don't always say things the way he means them."

"Ain't that the damned truth," Delbert chuckled, sinking back down into the chair, seeing that neither of these two detectives were real bright.

As Nate snatched the bottle of rye and grumbled to himself under his breath, Floyd Finch said on his behalf, "But don't worry about him though; he's tough as they come. Nate can fight his way through a thicket full of wildcats when he has to."

"I bet he can," said Sheriff Brady, taking a long upward look at Nate Reardon. The big detective stood a foot taller than anybody in the saloon. His shoulder width was broad enough to darken a small room. "Now, let's see if both of you together can manage to keep your mouths shut while I question this man about your friend Fleetus Gibbs. He's buried under the snow out there. Delbert here says he knows who killed him."

Both detectives stared at Delbert Hanks. "That's right," Delbert said. "It was a claim jumper named Jack Bell. He killed your friend Gibbs and some friends of mine as well. Then he hightailed it up toward Nolan's Gap as fast as he could. I expect he's there right now."

"A claim jumper?" said Sheriff Brady. "This is the first I've heard you say anything about him being a claim jumper."

Early Philpot gave a slight smile of satisfaction, thinking the claim jumper idea had been a good one on Delbert Hanks' part.

"Well, put two and two together, Sheriff," said Delbert. "The man was leading a mule loaded with mining equipment. He just happened to show up about the time these detectives thought they'd cleaned out all the claim jumpers." He looked at the two detectives and added, "Makes sense, wouldn't you say? Your friend Gibbs stopped him, maybe wondering what he was doing. *Bang,* this Bell fellow shoots him dead before he knows what hit him. Let's use our heads here. We're dealing with a dangerous man."

"That murdering sonsabitch!" Floyd Finch hissed through clenched teeth. "Nate and me'll go up there and get him, Sheriff. You won't even have to dirty your hands with him. We'll bring him back to you on the end of a pole."

"Hold on, fellows," said Sheriff Brady. "You boys ain't going after him, and that's final. I ain't having no half-assed vigilantes out there trying to do my job for me. If this man Bell is in Nolan's Gap, he won't be going nowhere for a while. I'll go there myself. If there's anything to charge him with, I'll bring him back myself."

"Anything to *charge* him with?" Delbert Hanks' voice sounded incensed. "Jesus,

Sheriff! I told you what he did! I'm a bona fide witness that he killed those men!"

"You're also a liar and a snake, Delbert, so don't go counting yourself more than you are." Sheriff Brady stared down at him as the pain throbbed in his jaw. "I don't feel like riding out of here until I get the rest of my teeth attended to. So everybody can just settle down and wait out the weather. The law might work slow sometimes, but it always works steady." He reached out for the bottle of rye on the table, but Early Philpot snatched the bottle away and stuffed it up under his arm.

"Is that so?" said Philpot, an angry expression on his reddening face. "Well, maybe it'll work a little quicker without my whiskey in its belly! You've got no right telling these two men they can't go looking for the man who killed their friend. Are you forgetting what we was just talking about before all this came up — about us working together for the good of this town?"

"I ain't forgot," said Sheriff Brady. He hesitated for a moment, touching the bandanna back to his swollen cheek once again. He seemed to consider everything. Then he said, "All right. I'll go after this Jack Bell soon as my jaw comes down to size." He cut his gaze to the detectives. "Meanwhile, if you two head for Nolan's Gap . . . I've got no right stopping you." He looked down at Delbert Hanks and added, "You neither, for that matter."

"That's more like it," said Early Philpot to the sheriff. "Now why don't you go back to your office and lay down, let that jaw heal up." He stepped back from the table with the bottle snugly under his arm, letting Brady know there were no more free drinks for him.

"Maybe that would be the best thing to do for now," said the sheriff. "All this aggravation is splitting my head open."

Early Philpot and the others watched in silence as Sheriff Brady left the saloon. Once Brady was safely out of sight, Philpot said to the detectives, "There you are, gentlemen. You're free to pursue this killer any time you're ready. The more men on his trail the better, is the way I look at it."

"Yep, us too," said Floyd Finch. He grabbed Delbert Hanks by his shoulder and started to lift him from his chair. "We're even taking bottle-shooter with us."

"Get your stinking, grubbing hands off me!" With his shoulder raised out of position, Delbert made a swipe at his pistol but missed it. "I'm not riding with you lunatics!"

"Oh yes you are," said Floyd Finch. "You're going to have to show us the way to Gibbs' body. We've got no idea where to look for him."

"For God sakes, you're detectives!" shouted Delbert, wrenching himself free from Floyd Finch's grasp. "You can't follow hoofprints in the snow?"

"We like your company, bottle-shooter," said big Nate Reardon, stepping in to grab Delbert's other arm.

Before Delbert could act on his own behalf, Early Philpot interceded by setting the rye bottle down on the table with a loud thump. "Damn it, everybody knock it off!" He glared at the detectives. "This man works for me. He does what I tell him to do!"

"Good. Then *tell* him to come along with us," said Floyd Finch.

"Curly," said Early Philpot in a level tone, raising a hand toward the bar. From behind the bar came the click of metal on metal as the bartender cocked the sawed-off double barrel he'd jerked from under the bar. The detectives' eyes followed the sound, then stopped and fixed on the open-bored ten gauge pointed at them from twelve feet away.

"You two get out of here," Philpot said.

"I'm sick of looking at you. Go find the man who killed your friend, Gibbs . . . if you're smart enough to find your way back to the livery barn and get your horses."

"We've got more friends coming," said Finch, a warning tone coming to his voice. "We're supposed to meet some other detectives here."

"That's fine," Philpot replied. "You can wait for them at that back corner table if you can behave yourselves. If you come back over here starting trouble, you'll need all the friends you can find."

On their way to the corner table, Nate Reardon whispered to Floyd Finch, "You should have told him Black Moe Bainbridge and Dewey Sadlo are the other detectives we're meeting here. He'd sing a softer tune, I bet."

"To hell with him," Finch growled in reply. "Let him find out on his own."

Early Philpot and Delbert Hanks watched the two detectives walk to the corner table, both of them grumbling under their breath. Once they were settled in their chairs, Floyd Finch called out to Curly Jones, who still stood aiming the shotgun at them, "Hey, bartender, think you can quit looking down that barrel at us long enough to bring us a bottle?"

"That's all of those two for a while," Early Philpot said in a lowered tone as Delbert Hanks sat back down at the table. "My guess is they'll both pass out drunk till their friends come scrape them off the table."

"Why don't you take a chair yourself, Mr. Philpot," Delbert said. "We got something we need to talk about."

"All right." Philpot sat down.

"I'm going to need some money," said Delbert.

Philpot stood up. "The hell you are! What for?"

"I need money for ammunition, whiskey and living expenses. I also need a good single-action Colt and a good drawing holster. If I'm going to be your personal bodyguard, you don't want me going around only half-armed." He nodded at the Colt Thunderer double action in the holster under his arm.

"Bodyguard? This is the first I've heard that you're my *bodyguard!*" said Philpot.

Delbert shrugged. "What else can you call it? This Bell comes here to kill you, I'm the man he has to go through to get to you. That spells bodyguard in my book."

"I see," said Philpot. "Then it's a good thing I didn't let those two detectives tear you apart. Who the hell would have looked out for me then?"

Delbert let the snide remark slide past him. "The thing is, I saw this man Bell shoot. There's no question I can take him. But I got to admit he's the best I've seen in a while. For your sake and mine both, I need to get some ammunition and whiskey and get to practicing day in, day out. I want to be ready for him when he gets here."

Philpot just stared at him for a moment. "You're dead serious, ain't you?"

"You're damn right I am," said Delbert. "I saw this man shoot. This ain't no joking matter."

Early Philpot called out to the bartender. "Curly, bring us that big Colt shooting rig from under the bar and gather us some empty bottles."

"Don't forget a full bottle too," said Delbert. "I always shoot better after a little bracer."

Behind the Sporting Life Saloon, Delbert Hanks and Early Philpot looked at the row of six empty whiskey bottles Delbert had set in a row along a rail fence surrounding an empty corral twenty yards away. "This looks awfully far away to me," said Early Philpot. "Especially with you shooting a gun you're not familiar with." He eyed the bottles skeptically. "There's no point in wasting good whiskey and bullets."

"Don't worry about the pistol being familiar," said Delbert. He gauged the distance. "This is how far I always practice." He turned up a long swig of whiskey, then corked the bottle as he let out a whiskey hiss. "The idea is to practice at a certain distance every time until you're deadly at it. Always try to strike that same distance when you face off in a shoot-out." He stuck the bottle down into the snow at his feet, adjusted the holster belt on his hip, loosened the pistol in its holster and stared straight ahead at the row of bottles, saying to Early Philpot, "Holler *go* anytime you're ready."

Early Philpot looked all around. The two detectives had followed them out of the Sporting Life and were watching from a few yards away. "All right," Philpot said to Delbert Hanks. "I'll do this today . . . but don't expect me to stand out here in the cold hollering *go* for you and setting up empty bottles." He looked embarrassed. "This is a job for a flunky."

"I understand, Mr. Philpot," said Delbert, his gun hand poised near his holster, ready to draw. "I just figured you wanted to see where we stand."

"I do, this time," said Philpot. He moved

a step away and got set. But before he could say *go,* Floyd Finch gigged his elbow into Nate Reardon's ribs.

"Go!" shouted Reardon, both he and Finch grinning, each thinking their unexpected interference would throw Delbert Hanks off.

They were wrong. Delbert's pistol streaked up from his holster as his body snapped down into a crouch. His right thumb worked fast and steady, drawing the hammer back and letting it fall. Firing from left to right, with each shot a bottle exploded into the air. When the last shot resounded from the big Colt, out of six empty bottles, only the fifth one remained.

Finch and Reardon offered one another a smug grin, but they were both impressed. Early Philpot stared at the one remaining bottle as Delbert lowered the Colt into his holster and drew the Thunderer from under his arm. He fired one quick shot, and the fifth bottle disappeared in a spray of finely shattered glass. "See?" said Delbert. "That's fine shooting. But if I'm out there protecting your life . . . I still need to practice. Wouldn't you agree?" Delbert looked away with a half smile, already knowing what Philpot's answer would be.

The fast shooting had also impressed

Early Philpot, yet he saw what Delbert meant. He swallowed the peppery taste and the smell of burnt gunpowder and said, "Yes, absolutely! You go ahead and practice all you want. If you run out of bullets, get some more at the mercantile and tell them to put it on my account. If that claim-jumping dog shows his face in Elk Horn, I want to see nothing but the soles of his boots sticking up in the street."

While Early Philpot spoke, Delbert Hanks raised the big Colt from his holster, punched out the spent cartridges and replaced them. Floyd Finch and Nate Reardon, having seen enough, turned and started around the side of the building. But they stopped when they saw the three horsemen step their mounts forward single file along the narrow alleyway toward them. "It's about damn time they showed up," Reardon said to Finch in a guarded tone. "Who's that with them?"

The rider in front wore a thick fur coat with its bulky collar turned up beneath his wide, flat hat brim. He carried a rifle pointed straight up from his gloved fist, holding the butt of it propped against his thigh. Stopping his big brown-and-white paint horse, he said down to Finch as he stared ahead at Delbert and Philpot,

"What's all the shooting about, Floyd? I hate riding into a noisy town."

"I know you do, Black Moe," said Floyd Finch. "So do I." He thumbed back over his shoulder at Nate Reardon. "Me and Nate got here a while ago. I'm afraid we've got bad news for yas. Fleetus Gibbs is dead out there on the trail somewhere. That boy back there doing the shooting is the one who found him. He brought his horse to town."

"His horse, huh?" said Black Moe Bainbridge, staring back through the alley at Delbert Hanks. "Now, that was big of him. What about Fleetus himself?"

Floyd Finch said, "He left ole Fleetus buried in the snow."

"I'm intrigued," said Black Moe, swinging his leg over his saddle and stepping down, still staring at Delbert Hanks as Early Philpot hurried forward and set up six new bottles. Neither Philpot nor Delbert Hanks had noticed the three riders yet. Black Moe said over his shoulder to the other two, "Sadlo, you and the Swede step down here and say if you're as intrigued as I am."

"Hell, you already know I am," said Dewey Sadlo, stepping down from his saddle. Floyd Finch and Nate Reardon stared at the man with long blond hair as he stepped down with Sadlo.

"Who's the new man?" Floyd Finch asked, looking the big man up and down.

"That's Erie Olaffson," said Black Moe. "You can call him the Swede. Don't ever tangle with him toe-to-toe. He can bend a knife blade between his teeth. I saw him do it." Black Moe smiled flatly.

"No fooling? How'd you do that, Mr. Swede?" Floyd Finch wanted all the details. But the Swede gave him a silent, glassy stare and stepped past him, following Black Moe, who had slid his rifle from its boot and started walking forward.

Levering a round up into the rifle chamber, Black Moe stared first at Delbert Hanks, then past Delbert to where Early Philpot stood placing the last of the six empty rye bottles up along the fence rail. "Look at these two daisies," he murmured to himself. "You can tell they think they're up to something real mysterious." His gloved thumb slid up across his rifle hammer. "I bet it'll take every bit of twenty minutes to find out what the hell it is."

At the fence rail, Early Philpot gave Delbert Hanks a nervous glance. He was having a hard time getting the sixth bottle to stand on its own. "Damn it, Delbert, if you're my bodyguard, make sure I'm out of the way before you go shootin' —" His words cut short as a loud shot resounded, and the bottle exploded into a spray of glass. "God almighty, Delbert!" Philpot shrieked, slinging his fingers back and forth, trying to make sure they were all still attached to his hand. But looking at Delbert, Early Philpot saw the bewildered expression on his face.

"What the hell?" said Delbert, trancelike, his pistol hanging loose and unfired in his hand. He turned and looked at the grim smile on Black Moe Bainbridge's face as the big man lowered the rifle from his shoulder and walked forward.

"Surprised, huh?" said Black Moe. "I saw those bottles had you outnumbered — thought I better give you a hand."

Delbert scowled. "Is that supposed to be funny, mister?"

"It is if you laugh about it," said Black Moe. "If not, I reckon it's whatever you turn it into." He levered a fresh round into his rifle chamber. The smile melted from his face, seeing Delbert's grip tighten on the big Colt.

"Ha . . . ha . . . ha," said Delbert without a trace of mirth in his voice.

Black Moe lowered his rifle barrel to dead center on Delbert's chest. "You best quit choking that pistol and slip it into some leather." He gestured toward the Sporting Life Saloon. "You and me has got some talking to do, about what happened to my pal Fleetus."

Seeing the other detectives approach, Delbert eased the Colt down into his holster, turned and walked silently along the narrow alley. "You men might not know this," said Early Philpot, "but I happen to be the owner of this saloon!"

"Congratulations," said Black Moe. "Now shut up and move it. I want to talk to you too."

"To me? About what?" Early Philpot tried to stall in place, but Black Moe gave the Swede a look, and the big man shoved Philpot forward.

"It's going to be hard for you to tell me anything if you're the one asking all the questions," said Black Moe.

CHAPTER 5

The men walked through the narrow alley and into the Sporting Life Saloon in silence. In the lead walked Delbert Hanks, rigid with anger but biding his time. Behind him came Early Philpot, followed by Black Moe. The rest of the men followed Black Moe. As soon as they drew closer to the bar, the men spread out to Black Moe's right along the bar rail. Delbert and Early Philpot kept to Black Moe's left. As soon as Philpot stopped a few feet back from between Delbert and the detectives and Black Moe raised his rifle and laid it along the bar top, Delbert's hand streaked down and came up with the big Colt cocked and pointed at arm's length. He backed six feet away along the bar. Black Moe Bainbridge looked at the pointed pistol and said in a calm voice, "Now, that's a hell of a way to begin a civilized conversation."

"I don't see where you and I have a damn thing to talk about, mister," Delbert hissed. Early Philpot stood frozen in place in the middle of the floor, a frightened look on his face. "I told Mr. Philpot here what happened to your friend out there. If you don't like the outcome, you can just go straight to hell, far as I care."

"Oh, we've got things to talk about indeed," said Black Moe, ignoring Delbert's remark. "For one thing, let's talk about what's going to happen to you once you pull that trigger. You're not really stupid enough to think you can kill all five of us, are you?" Unbeknownst to Delbert, as they had walked into the Sporting Life Saloon, Black Moe had reached inside his open coat, cocked the pistol in his belly holster and adjusted the tip of the holster to his left in what was now Delbert's direction.

"I can't say about all five, but I'll damn sure leave you lying dead on the floor."

"I see," said Black Moe, keeping his gloved hands spread along the bar rail, making no attempt to inch them closer to his rifle but at the same time keeping them within short reach of the inside front of his coat. "But that's provided you can actually pull that trigger."

"What?" Delbert spread a nasty grin. "If you think I can't pull this trigger, you're *dead* wrong about me. I can kill a man without batting an eye." He kept the pistol out at arm's length, the weight of it already feeling heavier to him.

"I have no doubt you're an ardent killer

through and through, young man," said Black Moe. "But it's been my experience that a man faced with impossible odds has a hard time being the one to make the first move . . . knowing it will be his *last,* of course." Black Moe gave him a short smile, then turned to face the bartender and nodded at the bottles of whiskey on the wall. "Jerk the top off one, bartender, and set us up some glasses. Looks like we might be here awhile."

"I ain't kidding around, mister!" shouted Delbert, growing enraged.

"Neither am I," said Black Moe, his voice calm, watching the bartender reach in cautiously and go about his work, setting down glasses and pulling the cork from a bottle of rye, "but what exactly is it you want? You never really said. I'm certain these men are eager to know. Or are you just wanting to point a gun at us, make sure we know how tough you are?"

A murmur of agreement and muffled laughter rose from the men as they showed little regard to Delbert and his cocked pistol. "Stop prodding me!" shouted Delbert. "I can't stand being prodded into a corner! I can't stand answering lots of questions!"

Black Moe shrugged. "I haven't even

asked you one yet." He looked Delbert up and down as he slowly took off his gloves one finger at a time. He reached out and with one finger slid a glass of whiskey slowly down the bar in front of Delbert. "Consider this a lesson in life, young man: The longer a man holds a pointed gun, the heavier it gets."

"I'm warning you, mister!" said Delbert, his gun hand beginning to tremble with the weight of the big Colt.

"Here, drink this and lower that shooting iron," said Black Moe, nodding at the whiskey. "The longer you stand there doing nothing, the worse picture I get of what happened to ole Fleetus Gibbs out there." Black Moe stepped back to his spot and raised his glass of rye, his right hand on the bar near the open front of his coat.

Delbert trembled and cursed under his breath, looking to Early Philpot for direction. "Let it down, Delbert," Philpot said in disgust. "Can't you see it ain't scaring them?"

Still Delbert couldn't let it go. The weight of the pistol caused the tendons to stand out in his neck; his face turned twisted and red. "Can't lower it on your own, kid?" said Black Moe. "Don't worry, I'll have the Swede here bust you across the jaw, make it look like you held out as long as you could." He grinned, then called down the bar to his right, "Hey Swede — come over here and help this boy out."

Without a word, the big blond-haired detective stepped back from the bar and pushed his shirt sleeves up over his thick forearms. He started to take a step toward Delbert. But Delbert let out a long, tight breath and let the pistol slump to the bar top, then seemed to sneak it down into his holster and out of sight.

"Now drink your whiskey like a good boy," said Black Moe with a dark chuckle. The rest of the detectives took little notice of Delbert or appeared to care that some sort of dangerous situation had just ended.

"Damn it to hell!" Delbert raged. He backhanded the shot glass of whiskey off the bar, turned and stomped out the door. Early Philpot stared after him nervously.

"Well, there went your personal protection," Black Moe said to Philpot. "What on earth will you do now?"

"You had no reason to treat him that way," said Philpot. "Delbert wasn't lying about what happened to your detective!"

"How do you know?" Black Moe said bluntly. "You weren't there, were you?"

"I trust his word," said Philpot.

"I bet you do," said Black Moe. "Either you trust him or else you've both got something to hide." He watched Early Philpot's face for a reaction.

"I've got nothing to hide," said Philpot.

Black Moe judged him to be lying by the shallow tone of his voice. "Well, then that's good for you but bad for us," said Black Moe.

"What do you mean by that?" said Philpot.

Black Moe relaxed, reached inside his coat and straightened his holster. "Because if you did have a problem, say with this killer, Bell, for instance . . . me and these men would be just the ones to take care of it."

Early Philpot considered things for a moment, then looked at the bartender and said, "Curly, take a break. Go out back and make sure dogs ain't got into the garbage."

Curly looked back and forth at the staring eyes on him, then said, "Sure thing, boss." He dropped his bar rag, turned and walked to the rear door.

Once Curly was outside and the door had closed behind him, Early Philpot stepped over to the bar and slumped onto his elbows. He lowered his forehead into a sweaty palm and shook his head slowly as he spoke. "This has turned into the damndest mess I've ever seen."

Black Moe eased over close beside him, hooking the bottle of rye and a glass on his way. "Tell me everything. I promise you'll feel better." As he poured a drink for Early Philpot, Black Moe pulled his watch from his vest pocket and checked it. Yep, he thought to himself, it had taken just about twenty minutes.

For the next few minutes, Black Moe and the detectives listened to Early Philpot reveal what had happened, how Jack Bell had won seven hundred dollars from him, and how he had wanted it back. He insisted that Bell had killed Gibbs. He even made an attempt at convincing the men that Bell had cheated at poker, but the detectives only gave him a flat, impartial gaze. When he'd finished talking, he picked up the fresh whiskey Black Moe had poured for him and tossed it back.

"All right," said Black Moe. "I think we can clear this whole mess up for say . . . five hundred dollars."

"Five hundred dollars!" Early Philpot's eyes widened in disbelief. "My God! That's only two hundred less than what I lost to begin with!"

"I know five hundred sounds big to you,"

said Black Moe, "but to us it only sounds like a hundred dollars apiece. It'll be even less when some other detectives show up and throw in with us. Pretty cheap to get rid of this cold-blooded killer, I'd say. And don't forget: We're professionals. We won't do like Delbert. We won't cause you more trouble every move we make."

"Other detectives are going to be coming to town?" Philpot asked warily. "Not Gannerd Woodsworth, I hope."

Black Moe grinned. "He could be coming. We all lost our jobs. We're all looking for our next stake." His grin widened. "You and ole Gan ain't had problems before, have you?"

"Every saloon west of the Mississippi has had trouble with Gan Woodsworth," said Early Philpot. "He gets to drinking, he's got no more sense than a wounded wildcat. I'd just as soon he not be coming to town."

"Yeah, but he's coming to town one way or the other," said Black Moe. "Wouldn't it be better, him working for me, me working for you? Beats him being on his own, all whiskey-drunk and with no constraint, don't it? Who knows, the way Gan Woodsworth gets, he might end up shooting your bodyguard. Then you'd be up a stump for sure."

Early Philpot thought it over again and said in resignation, "All right, I'll pay you the five hundred. But speaking of Delbert, he still *is* my personal bodyguard. I don't want nothing happening to him before this Bell is dealt with."

"Don't worry about Delbert," said Black Moe. "We won't hurt him. Won't let ole Gan hurt him either. I might pick at the lad a little. But to tell you the truth, I kinda like Delbert. I'll take him under my wing, see if I can learn him something." He slid a guarded glance at the other detectives, then looked back at Philpot. "Far as Fleetus Gibbs goes, I wouldn't care much if Delbert did kill him. I've come very near killing him myself a time or two."

Early Philpot looked relieved and sipped his rye. "When will you go after Bell?"

"Just as soon as we rest up and shake the cold off us," said Black Moe. He looked all around the Sporting Life Saloon. "Right now we all need a bath, a room and some good, hot grub." His eyes went back to Philpot and fixed on him. "Now that we're working for you, I see no need in us staying in that cold, crowded hotel." He tossed back his whiskey, licked his lips and ran a thumb across each side of his long, thin mustache. "You own a nice, big house someplace around here, don't you?"

By late afternoon, Black Moe and the rest of the detectives had left the Sporting Life Saloon long enough to stow their saddle-bags at Early Philpot's ornately trimmed two-story house standing at the far end of town. When they'd returned to the saloon, they began drinking in earnest. By evening, all the other customers had left the saloon as the detectives turned more and more wild-eyed drunk and belligerent.

From the dusty window of his office, Sheriff Taylor Brady had kept a close eye on the comings and goings to and from the saloon in spite of the terrible pain in his jaw. When the sheriff recognized Gannerd Woodsworth and two other riders come into town, he murmured to himself, "Now here comes this troublemaking sonsabitch. I've seen all of this I'm going to take." He walked to a battered gun rack, took down a double-barreled shotgun and loaded it. "I know you're up to something, Early Philpot," he growled as if Philpot were standing there beside him. "*Colleagues* or not, I aim to know what it is."

As the other two riders followed Gannerd Woodsworth to the hitch rail out front of the Sporting Life Saloon, Black Moe Bainbridge stepped through the saloon doors onto the boardwalk to meet them, tipping his hat slightly. "Evening, Red Tony . . . Ellis Dill," he said, acknowledging the two men with Woodsworth. Black Moe's right hand stayed partly hidden behind his back. Gannerd Woodsworth took note of it, watching Red Tony Harpe and Ellis Dill exchange greetings with Black Moe. Gannerd could tell by Black Moe's smug, drunken expression that something was in the works. As he stepped down from his saddle, he said, "Bainbridge, don't even try talking to me until I get half a belly full of warm rye in me."

"I'm ready for you," Black Moe grinned. His hand came from behind his back with a full bottle of rye in it. He pitched the bottle to Gannerd and watched the big man pull the cork with his teeth and blow it away from his lips.

"Won't be needing that," said Gannerd, watching the cork stick into the pile of snow along the boardwalk. He looked at Harpe and Dill as they stepped up onto the board-walk with him. Seeing them stare at the bottle in his hand, he said, "Get your eyes off my whiskey," as he raised the bottle toward his lips. "You boys want a drink, get on inside and get your own." Gannerd turned up a long swallow and released a hiss. The two men grumbled but hurried inside as if drawn to the bar by unseen hands, leaving Black Moe and Gannerd Woodsworth standing in the evening cold.

"I don't suppose you've found any work yet, eh?" Black Moe asked, looking Woodsworth up and down with a grin.

"No, not a lick," said Woodsworth. He gave Black Moe a curious gaze. "I can see you're busting to tell me something, so come on, spit it out."

Black Moe laughed, then said, "You ain't going to believe what I've found for us to do. We're going to make five hundred dollars off of Early Philpot just for riding up to Nolan's Gap and shooting some poor sonsabitch for him."

"Five hundred split how many ways?" Gannerd Woodsworth asked.

"It don't matter how many ways," said Black Moe. "Five hundred dollars is just for starters. Philpot's scared to death of this man we're going after. We'll call our own shots on this thing. Hell, me and the boys are already living in Philpot's big ole house. We'll be sleeping in warm, clean beds tonight, taking hot baths, eating and drinking like kings." He nudged his elbow into Woodsworth. "Not bad for some ole boys who just lost their jobs with the mining company, don't you think?"

Woodsworth spread a slight grin, considering all the possibilities. "Not bad at all." He raised the bottle to his lips. "We ain't breaking any laws doing this shooting for Philpot, are we?"

"Hell no," said Black Moe. "That's the sweetest part of it. Besides, what if we was? You think we wasn't breaking laws, chasing miners off the side of the mountain?"

"They were claim jumpers," said Woodsworth, correcting him.

"Bull," said Black Moe. "They had every right to be there mining their claims. They weren't on the mining company's land, and we both know it. If there had been a court of law for those miners to go to, we would all have been thrown into jail for what we did."

Gannerd Woodsworth widened his grin. "That's what I like about the law of the gun. It always favors the person quick enough to hold it in their hand first. Only thing wrong with the job we done for the company is that we done it too good. There ain't an independent miner left up here. We should have chased them away slower, made this job last till next summer at least."

"So, are you with me on this?" asked Black Moe. "We'll take our time, spend a couple days here enjoying Early Philpot's hospitality. With Philpot in the palm of our hand, we can ride roughshod over this whole damn town if we take a notion."

"Well, hell yes!" said Gannerd Woodsworth. "You knew I was going to be with you when you saw me riding in."

They both laughed. But then their laughter stopped short as they looked up and saw the open bore of the sheriff's shotgun staring at them. "Don't mind me, boys," said Sheriff Brady. "Just go right on talking. I want to hear more about how you can ride roughshod over this town." He jiggled the double-barreled shotgun in his hands. "Speak slow and clearly, so's Little Bertha here can hear you."

"Easy there, Sheriff," said Black Moe Bainbridge, keeping his voice calm and even, his hand relaxed but slightly poised near his pistol butt. "We were having ourselves a private conversation here. Ever heard of a man's right to privacy?"

"Nope, that's a new one on me. Have you ever heard of a man's right to a burial at public expense?" Sheriff Brady barely opened his lips as he spoke, carefully avoiding cold air against his sore teeth. "Because that's about the only *rights* you're going to get out of me this evening. Now lift them pistols with your thumb and finger. Drop them . . . then get your sorry asses onto some saddle leather and clear out of here."

"Jesus, Sheriff! What's going on out here?" said Early Philpot, stepping out onto the boardwalk just as Sheriff Brady cocked both hammers on the shotgun. "Bainbridge works for me! He's a lawman! They all are, the same as you!"

"No they're not," said Sheriff Brady over his shoulder, not turning around toward Early Philpot. "They're hired thugs, that's all. You should have heard what this one just said, how he's got you in the palm of his hand . . . how they can ride roughshod over this town —"

"Sheriff, for God sakes!" said Philpot, cutting him off. "That's just loose talk, I'm sure. I've hired these men. They look after my interests now."

"What do you need with gunmen and saddle trash like this?" Brady asked, his hand still clenched around the shotgun stock. "What the hell have you gotten yourself into, Philpot? It's all got something to do with that man up in Nolan's Gap, doesn't it?"

"Damn it, Sheriff! This ain't the time for me to explain everything to you! I've got problems. These men are going to help me settle them!"

Sheriff Brady eased down a bit. "You're saying you don't want my help? You want to let these men do as they damn please?"

"Give me some room here, Sheriff, is all I'm asking," said Philpot. "I know what I'm doing."

Sheriff Brady lowered his shotgun slowly, keeping his gaze on Black Moe and Gannerd Woodsworth. "You better know what you're doing, Philpot," he said. "You've turned down my help. From now on, you better be able to keep these men in line. I'm washing my hands of it."

Behind Early Philpot, the rest of the detectives had crowded into the doorway, staring through drunken, bloodshot eyes. They started to lunge forward, but a look from Black Moe stopped them. "Go on back inside, men," Black Moe said. "The sheriff was just leaving."

Black Moe, Gannerd Woodsworth and Early Philpot watched as Sheriff Brady lowered the hammers on the double-barreled shotgun and backed away. "You better keep this side of the street quiet, Philpot. I'm warning you."

When Brady had turned and walked away into the grainy evening light, Philpot turned to Black Moe and Woodsworth. "I know it was only loose talk, but damn it, let's have no more of it. I need to know you men are on my side. Is that too much to ask?"

"No, sir, Mr. Philpot," said Black Moe in a slightly mocking tone.

"And you," said Philpot, turning to Gannerd Woodsworth. "I know how you are when you're drinking. I don't want any trouble at all out of you. Is that clear?"

"Clear as rain," said Woodsworth, trying to keep from spreading a smug grin.

"All right then," said Philpot, tugging down on his vest. He turned haughtily and walked back inside the Sporting Life, the men in the doorway parting way for him.

"See what I mean?" Black Moe said to Woodsworth, gigging him again with his elbow.

"I sure do," Woodsworth replied. "This whole thing could get to be more fun than a hog killing."

CHAPTER 6

Good fortune seemed to smile upon Jack Bell from the minute he arrived in Nolan's Gap. By the end of his first week in town, his bankroll had grown by over three hundred dollars. Max Brumfield had played it cautious and observed his friend's luck before going heads up with him across the poker table. Like any shrewd saloonkeeper, Max had held back from playing the game with any great commitment. Instead, he would only sit in for a few hands each evening, just long enough to be sociable. Then he'd gather his money, shake his head and excuse himself.

"There's no winning against dumb luck, gentlemen," Max said jokingly one windblown night after the drinking crowd had left and all that remained were the serious poker players. "If you men are smart, you'll get out of here before Jack ends up owning your shirts."

"He can have my stinking shirt," grumbled an old miner through a faceful of wild whiskers. "It's my gold poke I hate seeing him dip into."

Jack Bell took the ribbing in stride, offering a slight smile as he dealt a card from the deck and turned it faceup in front of the miner. "Well, Wilfred," Jack said, "there's a four of diamonds to go with your seven of spades and your nine of clubs. See what happens when you complain? It just gets worse."

"Ah, hell with it — I fold," said the miner in disgust. He threw his hole card down and shoved the hand away from him. "Stud poker never was my game."

"But you're the one called the game," said Ed Munley, the town blacksmith. A chuckle arose from the other players around the table.

"I don't care if I did," said Wilfred Sayre. "It still never was my game." He raised a shot glass to his lips and emptied it, setting it down loudly on the tabletop.

Jack Bell turned his attention to Ed Munley, sitting at Wilfred's left. "It's your bet, Ed."

Munley studied his hole card shrewdly, then tried to read Jack Bell's eyes the same way. Finally he sucked air through his teeth, pitched his cards into the center of the table and said, "No. I fold too. I've misjudged you two hands in a row. I'm not about to try for a third."

"Thank you, gentlemen," said Jack Bell,

reaching out and raking the winnings to his side of the table. As he adjusted the poker chips into stacks and pushed the paper money to one side, Rosalee Finley stepped through the door and walked over to the table.

"Mr. Bell, may I have a word with you, please?" she asked in a polite but apprehensive voice.

"Yes, ma'am," said Jack Bell, looking up at her from his stack of chips.

"I mean privately," Rosalee Finley said. Then she added, leaning slightly toward him, "Please? It's about my father. I'm afraid he's gotten himself in trouble."

"If you gentlemen will excuse us for a spell." Jack Bell gave the other players a glance, then stood up and gestured a hand toward the far end of the bar. "Let's step over here where we can talk." As he followed at her side, Jack asked in a lowered tone, just between the two of them, "What kind of trouble has Ben gotten himself into now?"

Rosalee stopped at the end of the deserted bar and turned, looking Jack squarely in the eyes. "He has stolen your mule and mining gear, Mr. Bell." The grim tone of her voice relayed the gravity of the situation.

"I see." Jack Bell just stared at her for a

moment before offering any further comment. He wasn't about to downplay what this young woman obviously believed to be something of major importance. "Well . . . I can't say that I'm too upset over that mule. I've been trying to get rid of it ever since I got to town. As far as I'm concerned, let's just say Ben is borrowing it. Does that help any?"

He'd met Rosalee Finley his first day in town, when she'd walked into the Western Palace to thank him for helping her father the night before. She had been courteous yet reserved. Bell remembered wondering how a beautiful young woman like Rosalee Finley had managed to remain unattached in the midst of a mining town filled with single men. But it hadn't taken him long to see that there was a seriousness about Rosalee that discouraged even the offer of friendship, let alone romance.

"Yes, Mr. Bell, thank you," said Rosalee. "That helps greatly."

But Bell noticed that her demeanor didn't change. She still looked worried. There was more on her mind. "All right, Miss Rosalee," Bell said, "what else is bothering you?"

"Nothing, Mr. Bell," she said. "At least, nothing that should concern you." She turned her eyes away from him.

But Jack Bell wouldn't let her off that easily. "Try me," he said, following her eyes until she felt compelled to face him. "I happen to like your father, Miss Rosalee. He's a harmless old man with lots of old stories. Let's not fault him for that."

Rosalee nodded, considering Bell's words. "Yes, you're right. My father means no harm to anyone . . . but sometimes I'm afraid he gets too wrapped up in those old stories. He's wandered off toward the high passes, looking for the gold he claims he found last year."

"You mean he's up there somewhere with nothing but that little mule of mine?" Bell said.

"Yes. That is, he's on his way there unless I can catch up to him and talk some sense into him. I'm afraid he has really outdone himself this time, Mr. Bell."

"What kind of a start does he have?" asked Bell.

"I can't say exactly," said Rosalee, "but I think he must've left shortly after noon today. He didn't show up for supper. I saw that his two blankets were missing from his bed. I went to the livery barn and found out that your pack mule was gone. I'd say he's been gone ten hours or more."

"A man can cover lots of ground in that length of time," said Bell, considering it.

"Yes, and my father doesn't stop once he gets his mind set on something," said Rosalee. She lifted a nod toward the distant mountain range. "In this weather, he could die up there before I can get to him."

"Before *you* get to him?" Bell gave her an apprehensive look, noting that she wore heavy miner's boots and a pair of men's wool trousers. "You don't mean you're going up there after him!"

"Of course I'm going after him, Mr. Bell. What choice do I have? He's my father."

"But surely you don't intend to go alone, do you?" asked Bell. He gave a quick glance around the nearly empty saloon. "We'll wake up the town . . . get together a search party."

"No, we mustn't do that," Rosalee said quickly. "If my father sees a group of men following him, he'll only try to get away, or else he'll hide. In his frame of mind, he'll think they're trying to follow him to his gold." She shook her head. "I have to find him and hope I can talk sense into him, if he hasn't completely lost his reasoning. It's the only thing that will work."

"Then at least let *me* go with you, Rosalee," Bell offered. "Your father trusts me, I know he does."

She looked at him as if considering his offer.

"Think about this," said Bell, still trying to persuade her. "What if he has completely lost his mind? What if you find him and he refuses to come back here with you? What can you do all by yourself?"

"Perhaps you're right," she relented. "Once he gets it in his head that he can find that gold, he'll be awfully hard to deal with. Used to be I could talk to him. But lately he's gotten more and more difficult to deal with. He's convinced that the longer he waits, the less he'll be able to remember where he found the gold."

"Was there ever any gold, or is this whole thing his imagination?" Bell asked.

"I don't know," said Rosalee. "Last year a party of miners found Father lying near death up in one of the high passes. Everything had been taken from him. His belongings, his supplies. Even his coat and shirt were gone. All he had on was his trousers and boots. He had an old leather satchel clutched to his chest. Someone had wrapped him in an Indian blanket and left him there. He'd been shot in his side with an arrow. Someone — or perhaps he himself — had broken the arrow off."

"Indians?" Bell asked curiously. "I thought all the tribes from this part of the country had been moved to reservations years ago."

"They have, except for a lone wolf now and then who can't stand reservation life. I know how strange this sounds," said Rosalee. "But when Father was better and able to talk, even though his memory was vague, he recalled the image of an Indian hovering over him. It was as if he were haunted by it. He has never been able to piece together what happened to him up there. The doctor said he might never. I suppose that's why it haunts him so badly."

"Yes, I can see why it would," said Bell, working on it in his mind as he spoke. "Did anyone happen to look at the arrowhead, try to see what tribe it might have came from?"

"Yes, Mr. Bell," Rosalee said. "There was a man named Bratcher living here at the time who used to scout for the army. He looked at the arrowhead. He said he'd seen only a few like it before. It was probably Ute, he told us. But he couldn't be sure."

"Do you still have it?" Bell asked.

"No. I haven't seen it since Bratcher gave it back to my father. Father might still have it, but if he does, it's with him right now. Why do you ask, Mr. Bell?"

Jack Bell shrugged slightly. "Never mind. I don't suppose it matters." He looked back at the card game, then let out a breath and said, "Let's go gather some supplies. It looks like we've got a long, cold night ahead of us."

As Rosalee Finley left the saloon ahead of Jack Bell and walked to the livery barn, Bell picked up his money from the poker table and excused himself from the game. Max Brumfield walked up beside him and asked, "Is everything all right, Jack? I don't like losing a player, especially one I'm getting ready to pluck like a Christmas goose." The players looked up at Bell with detached interest, bid him good evening, then turned their attention back to their cards.

Bell offered Max Brumfield a thin smile. "Looks like you'll have to save your plucking till the next time, Max." With a glance, he gestured Max away from the game table. When they stepped over to the door, Bell told him about Ben Finley.

"Well, this really rips it," said Brumfield. "Surely you're not going out after that old fool!"

"Yep, I sure am," said Bell, "so save your breath about it. I've already made up my mind."

"Then my suspicions about you are

right," said Brumfield. "You really are a hopeless do-gooder."

"Afraid so, Max." Bell smiled.

"My God." Brumfield shook his head. "I could see you doing this if maybe you thought it would give you some sort of advantage over Rosalee. But that can't be it. As lovely as she is, she's still about as warm and cuddly as a porcupine."

"That never entered my mind, Max," said Bell. "She needs my help. I can't let her go up there by herself . . . and she's the type who'd try it."

"Maybe craziness runs in their family," said Brumfield. "Old Ben is as crazy as a june bug." He shook his head. "I think you better get up a search party."

"Nope, that's out of the question," said Bell. "Rosalee says it'll only spook the old man."

"Then I'm going with you," said Brumfield. "I can be ready in two minutes."

"No, Max, but thanks," said Bell. "Seeing you along would spook ole Ben worst of all."

Brumfield thought about it. "Yes, you have a point. It would spook him all right. But damn it, I hate to see you and Rosalee traipsing out after him in this kind of weather. If you think it's bad now, wait until

111

you get up in those passes and get a blizzard dumped on you. Are you sure you want to do this?"

"*Want* to do it?" said Bell. "I'd be a fool to *want* to do it. There are some things you do even if you don't want to, Max. Remember those?"

"Oh yes," said Brumfield jokingly. "I do seem to recall those sorts of things. *Virtuous,* I believe you Good Samaritans call them."

"That's right," said Bell. "*Virtuous* — the sorts of things you wouldn't mind your folks hearing about. You ought to try it sometime . . . just to see if it makes you sleep any better."

"Heaven forbid," Brumfield said. "I sleep good enough as it is. I always say, if a man sleeps too soundly, it's a sign that he's missed a chance at making a profit somewhere."

"Don't act tough to me, Max. It's too late. You offered to go along; I turned you down. Your heart was in the right place, don't try denying it."

"Shhh, watch your language," Brumfield joked. "Someone might hear you. I can't have these buzzards know that there might be a shred of decency running through me."

"Don't worry," said Bell. "I won't tell if you won't."

"Good," said Brumfield with resolve. He placed his black cigar in his teeth and clamped down on it. Then his expression turned somber. "Don't let these two get you killed out there, Jack. I mean it . . . or I'll be awfully upset with both of them."

"I'll try not," said Bell. "But whatever happens, don't blame Rosalee. She didn't twist my arm any. Neither did old Ben. Who knows," he said as an afterthought, "maybe we'll get lucky, find that gold old Ben claims is up there somewhere."

"Ha! Don't count on it," said Brumfield. "If there was any more gold left up there, West Track Mining Company wouldn't have pulled out of here. You can rest assured of that."

"I know," said Bell. "I'm just trying to make myself feel better about going out in this weather." Outside, the wind began to moan as if on cue. "See," Bell said, jerking his head toward the low, foreboding sound, "it's calling for me right now."

"Good luck," said Brumfield. He touched the tip of a finger to his hat brim.

When Jack Bell walked out of the Western Palace and closed the door behind him, a saloon girl named Dolly Lisko, who'd been watching the poker game from a small table in the corner, got up and walked over to where Max Brumfield stood at the bar. "What was that all about?" she asked, stifling a yawn with the back of her hand.

Brumfield shrugged as he poured himself a double shot of rye whiskey. "Old Ben Finley took off again . . . took Jack's mule with him."

"Looking for his lost gold?" said Dolly, sounding bored with the idea of it.

"Sure, what else?" Brumfield chuckled. He slid a clean glass over in front of Dolly and filled it for her.

"And your friend Bell is going to look for him." She shook her head. "Are you sure Bell isn't simpleminded?" She touched a fingertip to the rim of the shot glass, then touched it to her tongue.

"Don't worry about Jack Bell," said Brumfield. "He's just one of those kind of men who always wants to do the right thing. I can't say nothing against a person for being that way." He picked up his whiskey glass, looked at it and said, "Here's to dogooders — may they do enough good to make up for the rest of us."

Raising her glass, Dolly said with a wry smile, "I'll drink to that any time. It keeps *the rest of us* from having to worry about it."

They tossed back a drink. When they lowered their glasses, Dolly let out a whiskey sigh and said, "Maybe this time the old man won't make it back."

"Always the pessimist, eh, Dolly?" Brumfield chuckled in a dark tone.

"Why not?" Dolly sipped her whiskey and raised a thin black ladyfinger cigar to her lips. "I figure if the old man's out of the way, I can talk sense to Rosalee . . . get her to give up washing clothes and sewing for the miners. Put her to work with me, providing a service these men *really* appreciate."

Brumfield looked at her for a second, then said, "That's not going to happen, Dolly. Rosalee's not the type."

"Oh? Don't be so sure," Dolly replied. "Let that old man walk off a cliff and freeze to death, we'll see what type she is. Give me a chance to comfort her . . . take her under my wing, be the mama she's never had after all these years of her having to take care of that old fool, Ben. You'd be surprised what I can turn her into."

"Lord, Dolly," said Brumfield, "you are one cold, bitter, heartless shrew!" He raised his glass as if in salute and spread a wicked smile. "I've always admired that in a woman."

CHAPTER 7

"At least we'll have plenty of moonlight starting out," Jack Bell said, noting the soft gray light through the open door of the livery barn as he raised the globe of an oil lantern and lit the wick. "But if this wind keeps up, it'll bring in some heavy cloud cover." He trimmed the wick and lowered the globe. A small circle of golden light ringed him and Rosalee as they walked to where Whiskey stood looking out at them above the stall door. Whiskey nickered and tossed his head restlessly. Steam billowed from the big buckskin's nostrils in the cold air.

"Always ready to go, aren't you, big fellow?" Bell ran a hand down Whiskey's muzzle, then lifted a harness from a peg as he opened the stall door. At the far end of the barn, Bell saw a little roan barb standing saddled and ready. Bulging saddlebags hung behind the roan's saddle.

"I hope you've packed plenty of supplies," said Bell, watching Rosalee walk to the roan, unhitch its reins and come leading it back toward him. A gunbelt lay looped around the roan's saddle horn. An old

LeMat pistol stood in a well-worn holster.

"I hoped I wouldn't need too much, but to be safe I put on a week's worth of grub. I have coffee, flour, some beans, some dried beef and a slab of salt pork. We can stop by the house and get more, now that you're going with me."

"I'll be all right," said Bell, "long as there's plenty of coffee." Leading Whiskey from the stall, he stood the horse in the center bay, smoothed a saddle blanket onto his back, then lifted his saddle from a rack and laid it up. "My saddlebags are at Max Brumfield's, where I've been staying. I always keep a few pounds of pemmican and a few airtights on hand in case I have to leave town in a hurry."

"Leave town in a hurry?" Rosalee looked a bit surprised. "That sounds like the sort of thing an outlaw might be required to do, Mr. Bell."

Bell saw the apprehension in her eyes as he snuggled up the cinch beneath Whiskey's belly. "No, ma'am, that's not the way I meant it at all. A traveling man should always keep himself prepared against the elements, in case of an emergency — like tonight, for instance."

"Oh, I see . . ." Rosalee quietly weighed his words as she watched him prepare the big buckskin for the trail. After a moment, she said bluntly, "Mr. Bell, am I going to be safe traveling with you?"

Bell stopped and just looked at her for a second. Finally he said with a trace of a smile, "Only if you'll stop calling me *Mr. Bell*."

"Well, I —" Rosalee stopped and rethought her words. Then she offered an embarrassed smile and loosened up some. "All right then, Mr. Bell, what should I call you?"

"Call me Jack or Bell, either one," he said. "Just drop the mister; it sounds like I've come to collect your mortgage."

"Of course then, *Jack*," Rosalee said with resolve. She folded her gloved hands in front of her and stood a bit rigid. "I simply wouldn't want you to get the wrong impression about us traveling together."

Bell understood. Finishing with the buckskin, Bell pushed his hat brim up and turned to Rosalee. "Ma'am, I'm glad you brought it up. Believe me, I realize the seriousness of this situation. My intentions toward you are honorable."

Rosalee blushed in the glow of the lantern. "Pardon me for speaking so boldly."

"Not at all," said Bell. "It's the sort of thing a person should establish, I suppose."

He looked away, a bit bashful himself. "The fact is, you are a beautiful young woman, Miss Rosalee. I would be lying if I said I hadn't noticed. But this is a search for your father. I'm not a man to take advantage. I try to talk straight, and I try to live straight. I leave the game on the gaming table. You and your father have been good to me since I arrived here. My only intentions are to help you find him."

"Thank you, Mr. — I mean, *Jack*," said Rosalee. "I apologize for bringing it up. Sometimes I can speak a little too bluntly for some folks."

"No, ma'am, don't apologize for speaking your mind," Bell said. "The nature of the world we live in requires us to do so, ma'am. I take no offense at it. It's the only way we know where we stand with one another. It's the folks who don't make themselves clear that I have trouble with."

"Please call me Rosalee," she said, almost cutting him off. She neither saw nor sensed any guile in this man. Indeed, she realized that if she had, she would never have gone this far. She would not have accepted his offer of help in the first place. Rosalee Finley was not a trusting woman. There were no stars in her eyes, she reminded herself, looking Jack Bell up and down as he turned back to readying his gear. Experience had taught her to be wary of men and their underlying intent. Yet when she *allowed* it, this man had a way of disarming her. Perhaps she should *allow* it more, she told herself.

"I do trust you, Jack," she said. His eyes were clear and sharp but not hardened. His body exhibited strength, but it was a strength that he appeared to have mastered with patience and confidence. She watched how his hands moved deftly, quick and gentle, about the big buckskin.

Bell gave a passing glance, dropping the stirrup down Whiskey's side. "Thank you, Rosalee." Then he turned, with no more to say on the matter. "Do you want to wait here for me while I go get my saddlebags?"

"Yes. I'll be out back looking for Father's tracks," said Rosalee.

Jack Bell left the livery barn and walked to Max Brumfield's small cabin behind the Western Palace Saloon. When he returned to the livery barn, he filled a small flask with oil for the lantern and put money for it and his livery bill in the cigar box near the front door. Then he joined Rosalee out back. He held the lantern low to the ground as the two of them led their horses back and forth, searching the rutted mud and snow for any sign of tracks left by Ben Finley and the pack mule. Throughout the day, the path had turned to slush in the sunlight owing to the amount of traffic to and from the barn. But as soon as the sun had gone down and the temperature dropped, the gray slush had hardened into ice. It crunched beneath their boots.

In moments Rosalee found a pair of boot prints followed by the sharp hoof prints of the little pack mule. "Here they are!" said Rosalee, sounding hopeful. As Bell led the buckskin over beside her and looked down, holding the lantern out for better light, Rosalee said quickly, "I know those are Father's boots!"

"Oh? What makes you so sure?" Bell asked.

"See right here?" Rosalee stooped down and touched a finger to the right boot print where a corner of the heel was missing. "I clipped off this piece from his right boot heel . . . just in case something like this ever happened again." She stood up, gathered her wool coat at her throat and raised her wool muffler over her nose against the cold bite of the wind.

"That was good thinking on your part," said Jack Bell, extending the lantern. Inside the shelter of the soot-streaked globe, the lantern flame rose and fell to the draw of the wind.

"My poor father. I've had to treat him almost like an unruly child at times," said Rosalee.

There was hurt in her voice that Bell didn't feel needed his acknowledgment. He only nodded and stepped forward with her, the two of them seeing the tracks head out past the circle of lantern light and reach out wide of town before being swallowed by the darkness.

"Let's use this moonlight as long as we've got it," Bell said, trimming the wick down until the lantern turned dark. "The way this wind is kicking up, we could have cloud cover moving in any time now." They both turned and stepped up into their saddles, Bell holding the hot lantern out away from the buckskin's side.

Morning still lay black beyond the horizon when the last two players stood up, stretched, pocketed their money and left the Western Palace Saloon. At the edge of the boardwalk, the two men stopped long enough to look up at the gray swirl of clouds boiling above the wind. They commented quietly on the weather as they adjusted their hats and heavy coats and lifted their collars before stepping out onto the street and hurrying away in the grainy darkness.

As the last two players disappeared, Max Brumfield stepped back, closed the door against the wind and took a fresh cigar from his pocket. "Another night, another dollar," he said tiredly. He walked back to the bar, where Dolly Lisko stood pushing her hair up into place and pouring them both a shot of rye. "Well, how did we do?" she asked.

"*We* did good, as usual," said Brumfield, putting some mock emphasis on the word *we*.

Dolly smiled and let it pass, seeing Brumfield take out a thick, flat stack of dollar bills from inside his lapel and count off a sizable amount of them into his left hand. Arriving beside her at the bar, Brumfield put the large stack of money away, folded the amount he still held in his left hand and held it out to Dolly. "For you, dear lady," he said.

"My oh my!" Dolly squealed quietly, snatching the money from him and fanning it out in front of her eyes. "I don't know if I've ever made this much money with all my clothes on!"

"Get used to it. Business is growing bigger and better every day. All we need to do is continue giving the players a fair shake for their money. Word soon gets out, doesn't it?" Brumfield struck a match and held it to his cigar, turning the cigar back and forth, watching Dolly's eyes light up as she counted the money again, folded it three ways and shoved it down inside her soft pink cleavage.

"Oh yes! It most certainly does," Dolly replied, smiling as she patted her large breasts. "Now, if you'll excuse me, it's been a long night. I'm going to crawl under the sheets until noon." She gave Brumfield a look. "Care to join me?"

"Much obliged, Dolly, but not right now. I'm done in. As soon as Stanley gets here to clean up and take over, I'm going to grab some sleep myself." He raised his glass, sipped his drink, then both he and Dolly turned toward the door at the sound of voices and boots on the boardwalk.

"What's this?" Dolly murmured. The front doors swung open wide, and four soldiers hurried inside. The first two soldiers supported a thin, shivering young man between them, their arms around his waist, his own limp arms looped across their shoulders. Behind the four troopers a young officer stepped to one side and began unbuttoning his heavy wool coat. He nodded toward the large gaming table and said, "Sit him there, and get some warm whiskey poured into him."

Max Brumfield recognized the officer as Captain Luchen Stovall. Stovall led a monthly payroll detail to a small frontier garrison eighty miles south of Elk Horn. Seeing the battered condition of the man as the troopers hurriedly sat him down into a wooden chair, Brumfield gestured for Dolly to get a new bottle of rye from behind the bar. "From the looks of him, Captain, we'd better pour quickly. Who is he?"

"We don't know yet, Mr. Brumfield," said the captain. "We found him half-frozen night before last as we crossed the flatlands. No horse, no gear, no gun. Just a holster full of ice, if you can picture that."

Max Brumfield only nodded. He *could* picture it, based on what Jack Bell had told him about the incident.

"It looked like he'd dragged himself a long ways through the snow and found shelter inside a stand of rocks. It's a miracle he's alive. He's been in and out of consciousness until only an hour ago. When he came to, he began shaking uncontrollably. We haven't even learned his name. All we've managed to learn from him thus far is that someone tried to kill him."

"Oh?" Brumfield gave the young man a

dubious look. "He seems to be coming around quickly enough now." He narrowed his gaze at the young man. "You wouldn't happen to be one of the men from Elk Horn, would you?"

The young man responded with a trembling nod.

"I see." As Brumfield spoke, he reached out across the bar and took the fresh bottle of rye from Dolly. He picked up a clean shot glass and stepped over to the game table. He uncorked the bottle, poured a shot into the glass and held it down to the trembling young man. "Here, can you hold this for yourself?"

"I — I — I'll do my — my best," came the shivering reply. The young man wrapped both hands around the shot glass to control them and concentrated on raising the glass to his lips. Half the rye sloshed over the edge of the glass, but he managed to swallow the rest. Brumfield took the glass, refilled it and placed it back into his hands. This time when the young man downed the whiskey, his trembling subsided. He said in a stronger voice, "I was riding with some men from Elk Horn . . . but it was all on the up-and-up. We weren't causing nobody any trouble."

"I bet you weren't," said Brumfield.

Turning to Captain Stovall, Brumfield saw the captain's inquisitive look.

"What do you know about this, Mr. Brumfield?" Captain Stovall asked.

"I heard about some trouble that happened out there the other day. A prospector who passed through here said he had a run-in with some of Early Philpot's men who'd followed him out from Elk Horn. Had to take a couple of warning shots at them to shake them off his trail."

Brumfield looked back and forth between the captain and the young man at the table, seeing if his story was going to be challenged. The young man bowed his head over the whiskey glass as if in submission. The captain had no reason to doubt what Brumfield had to say. "Turns out it was all some sort of misunderstanding," Brumfield lied.

The captain looked down at the young man, seeing that the rye had begun to settle his shivering. "Is that correct? Was this all some sort of misunderstanding?"

"It — it could have been," said the strained voice. "Everything happened so fast . . . I ain't sure."

"You're not sure," Captain Stovall said. He and Max Brumfield exchanged a glance. Then the captain asked, "What's your name, young man? You're reasonably sure of that, aren't you? Now that you have an adequate amount of whiskey glowing inside you?" Stovall's voice sounded a bit cynical.

The swollen face turned up to the captain, taking on a defiant air. "Yeah, I can remember my name. I'm Billy Freeman . . . and I ain't done *nothing* wrong."

"There, you see, Captain?" Brumfield spread his hands and offered a trace of a crafty smile. "That only confirms what I heard . . . that it was all just a terrible misunderstanding. I won't bore you with the particulars of it, unless you really want to hear them."

"I can live without them," Captain Stovall said in a clipped tone. He studied Billy Freeman for a moment, looking at the young man in a whole different light now that he'd caught a glimpse of this new, sullen attitude. "Now that we've brought him here, I don't care what any of this was all about. I just wish someone else had found him. I've wasted all this time on him . . . now that he's coming around, all I get is he 'ain't done nothing wrong.' "

"Well, it's true. I *ain't* done nothing wrong!" Billy Freeman protested, his voice stronger now but still shivering a bit. "I appreciate you bringing me here, Captain, saving my life and all. But I ain't got no more to say about what happened out there till I talk to my boss, Mr. Philpot."

"Nothing like gratitude, eh, Captain?" said Brumfield.

"I'm used to it," said Captain Stovall. He looked away from Billy Freeman and at the four troopers who stood shivering, their faces pinched red by the cold. "All right, men, three drinks each. But no more. We're going to warm up and leave in half an hour. Every man *will* be sober." He turned back to Brumfield, the sound of the troopers' boots shuffling quickly across the floor as Dolly stepped behind the bar and grabbed some clean shot glasses and another bottle of rye.

Stovall said to Brumfield, "I trust you'll tell the proper authorities whatever they need to know about this? Since it isn't an army matter, I want nothing more to do with it."

"Don't worry, Captain," said Brumfield, looking back down at Billy Freeman as he spoke. "You've done your part. I'll take it from here."

"Suits me," said Captain Stovall. He looked down at Billy Freeman and said, "I want you to realize that since there's no sheriff here in Nolan's Gap, I'm taking it upon myself to act on the army's behalf and give Mr. Brumfield here the authority to do as he sees fit. If you give him any trouble, for all I care he can throw you in chains and hold you for a federal marshal or else ride you out of town on a rail. Are we clear on that?"

Billy Freeman only nodded his lowered head.

"Don't worry, Captain," said Brumfield. "I won't have any trouble with him." He looked down at Billy Freeman with a dark glint in his eyes.

CHAPTER 8

Ben Finley awoke before dawn in the shelter of a deep cliff overhang where he'd built a small fire and spent the night. Long icicles hung along the edge of the cliff opening like the fierce teeth of some earth-locked beast. Within the mouth of that beast, Finley listened to the howling night wind subside as he stoked up the fire with dry wood he'd found scattered about on the rock floor. When the fire grew stronger, he melted snow in a small coffeepot and boiled coffee.

The mule watched placidly from its spot against the back wall, its ears only perking up when Ben Finley scooped a double handful of oats from a feed sack. "There now, you haven't been forgotten," said Finley, walking over and pouring the oats into a mound in front of the animal. The mule twirled its tail and ate heartily. Finley rubbed its coarse mane, saying as if the mule could understand, "We'll have to keep your strength up. You've got a big job ahead of you, carrying all that gold down the side of this mountain."

The mule crunched grain in its hungry

jaws, showing interest in neither man nor gold. But Finley didn't let the mule's lack of interest discourage him. "They all think I'm a crazy man right now." He stooped and patted the mule's lowered head. "But you watch how quick all that changes when we come back with the gold."

Firelight flickered on Ben Finley's weathered face. The excitement in his faded eyes bordered on madness. His aging body ached with an exhaustion that a restless night of broken sleep had not been able to repair. But he could not afford to sleep right now, no matter what the loss of it cost his tired body. In his struggle to resurrect, reassemble and discern the events of the past, sleep had become his enemy. For three days now, a picture had been forming more and more clearly in his mind, a picture of the very spot where he'd found the gold. He dared not sleep or allow himself to concentrate on anything else lest this elusive image slip away from him.

The picture had first come to him grainy and vague like the misty remnants of a dream. But this was no dream, he reminded himself. This had happened; and the harder he concentrated on it, the clearer the picture grew. This was the spot; he was certain of it. So certain that his hands trembled in anxious anticipation. He tried through sheer mental force to draw in more details out of the thick gray surrounding his memory, but the picture only came to him at its own pace. He could only wait for it and hope to capture it in its entirety before something robbed him of it again.

He sipped strong coffee and stared into the dancing flames, letting the image come to him. He dared not let himself think about Rosalee, that she would be worried sick about him. He dared not think of anything that diverted his thoughts from the gold and its secreted whereabouts. As if through a thin, watery veil, he caught a glimpse of himself stepping down off of a narrow trail and into the mouth of a cave, a cocked rifle in his hands. He had followed something to that cave, but what was it? He reached down deep inside himself for it, but the image would not surface.

"For God sakes, what is it?" he murmured to himself in the stillness of the crackling fire and low whir of dissipating wind.

In his recollection, he saw himself standing outside a cave whose entrance was almost completely covered by a tangle of deadfall and dried brush. He seemed to have followed a blood trail there, for a large splotch of it glistened on the ground. As his recollection grew stronger, he looked back over his shoulder at where his horse and mule stood tied to the bleached skeleton of a cottonwood tree. Beyond the animals there was something in the background he was supposed to see, something clinging to the side of the mountain. "What is it, please!" he pleaded with himself.

It was something important, he knew. Yet that image still lay just beyond his mental grasp as if it had hit a snag in the road and stuck there. He tried hard to focus more intently on it, but nothing came to him. In a moment he felt the image slip further back into the gray haze. "Blast it all!" he said to the fire, rubbing the back of his trembling hand against his forehead. His skin felt clammy. He breathed deep and sipped his coffee until his cup was near empty. Then he stood up and looked east at the silver wreath on the distant horizon.

Ben Finley put out the fire, poured out the few remaining drops in his coffee cup and walked back over to the mule. He went over his supplies quickly and in doing so chastised himself once again for not bringing along his old LeMat pistol. His only protection was a single-barreled ten-gauge shotgun with a weak hammer. Often it would take a half-dozen tries before the hammer would strike hard enough to fire. Not a good form of defense in country where matters of life or death had to be determined in the blink of an eye. But there was no turning back now, Ben Finley reminded himself, running a hand across the shotgun stock as he prepared the mule for the trail. He picked up the leather satchel from the ground and slipped it up over his shoulder.

In moments, man and animal had slipped out their ancient shelter and trudged upward off the familiar trail and onto a snow-covered path winding up toward the high passes, the image lying just beyond his mind's eye, taunting him, drawing him onward. He did not know if he was traveling by memory or by sheer hunch, but within a mile something drew him off of one path and onto another. He struck out on a steeper path for no more reason than the fact that it felt right to him. It felt like a place he'd been before. He hoped to God he was right.

Jack Bell and Rosalee Finley traveled side by side steadily throughout the night, not pushing their horses through the deep snow but rather letting the animals set their own pace. By dawn they'd followed Finley and the mule's trail up off of the flatlands and stopped to rest in the shelter of a cedar thicket out of the cold wind. "We've kept his tracks in sight across the flatlands," said Bell. "There's a good chance we'll find him before nightfall, tomorrow at the latest, unless we get snowed in."

"What makes you so sure we can find him that soon?" Rosalee asked.

"Because he's not trying to outrun anybody. He's just searching for something," said Bell. He swung down from his saddle and took the reins to Rosalee's horse while she dismounted, stepping carefully into the calf-deep snow. "The harder he searches, the slower he'll have to travel until he finds it."

Rosalee considered it. "Yes, you're right. And if I know Father, he's thinking of nothing now except the spot where he thinks he found the gold. I doubt if he's even thought that someone might be on his trail. This thing has been eating at him so badly ever since you arrived in Nolan's Gap."

"I'm sorry if I brought you problems," said Bell. "It sure wasn't my intention." He took Rosalee by the elbow and escorted her and the horses to a downed pine lying lengthwise across a short stand of snow-covered rock. He slapped snow from the pine log, and Rosalee sat down. "I suppose your father and I did spend too much time the other night talking about gold strikes. But to be honest, I didn't do much more than listen. Ben did most of the talking."

"No, Jack, I know this isn't your fault," said Rosalee. "And I appreciate your taking time to let my father get all of his gold fever talked out. I had hoped he would talk it all out of his system. But I'm afraid that seeing you and that pack mule with its prospecting gear only brought things fresh to his mind again." She patted the log beside her with her gloved hand. As Bell sat down, she continued, saying, "I can't say that I blame him. Father never made that *big find* that he and men like him always dream of. Some men come to realize that their dreams are never going to come true, and they learn to accept it. I'm afraid my father only grew more and more desperate . . . until it finally pushed him over the edge. I only hope we can keep harm from coming to him."

As Rosalee spoke, Bell caught a glimpse of something moving among the snow-covered rocks a few yards below them. "Don't worry," said Bell, "we're going to do just that." It had been just a quick flash;

then it was gone. He made no mention of it to Rosalee, but he kept a close watch out of the corner of his eye. He saw nothing. Standing up, dusting snow from the seat of his trousers, Bell deliberately moved closer to the horses until he laid a hand on his rifle boot and unsnapped the safety strap.

"I think these horses are rested enough, don't you?" Bell said.

Rosalee gave him a curious look, noting something in his voice and knowing they'd only been there for a few moments. Steam billowed from the tired horses' nostrils. But seeing the changed expression on Bell's face, she stood up, glancing around, and walked over beside him.

"Yes, I'm sure they're rested," Rosalee said. She saw Jack Bell draw the rifle from the saddle boot and run a gloved hand along the barrel as if inspecting it. But then she noted his thumb cocking the hammer and holding the rifle poised as his eyes moved back and forth across the tops of rocks and snowcapped brush.

"What is it, Jack," she whispered close to his ear without looking conspicuous.

"Nothing, I hope," Bell whispered in reply, not taking his eyes off the snowy terrain. "But I could have sworn I saw someone or something dart across the trail." He let the rifle droop slightly in his right hand but kept his finger close to the trigger. Taking a step, Bell felt Rosalee's hand tighten on his forearm.

"Don't go down there," she whispered urgently.

"I'm not," Bell replied, placing his gloved hand over hers in reassurance. "If we're being followed, we'll find out soon enough. But let's ride a little farther up before we rest these horses. We're in the open a little too much to suit me."

As they mounted their horses, Bell thought he heard a sound from behind a stand of snowcapped brush. Yet when he darted his eyes toward it, he saw nothing. Bell drew his horse back enough for Rosalee to put her horse in front of him on the narrow trail. They moved upward cautiously, Rosalee resisting the overpowering urge to keep looking back over her shoulder. Bell kept his rifle across his lap, his gloved hand around the small of the stock, his thumb across the hammer, his finger ready on the trigger.

They climbed slowly and steadily. Nearly an hour passed before they once again stopped the horses midtrail and turned in their saddles to look back. There was no sound below them but the low whisper of cold wind; nothing moved but the lazy sway of tall pines and the restless drift of gray-streaked clouds. "Perhaps it was nothing after all," Rosalee said in a guarded voice. "Maybe it was just something on the wind, something playing tricks on your eyes."

"It was *something* all right," Bell replied. "But we may never know what. Whatever it was, I doubt it was a person. If it was, we'd have known it by now. It wouldn't make sense to trail us this far without making a move." He stepped down from his saddle and watched Rosalee do the same.

"So what do you think?" Rosalee asked.

"Some sort of critter, I suspect," said Bell. "Weather like this sends critters searching wide for their feed. It could've been a big cat, a wolf, who knows?" As he spoke, his eyes made another, more cautious search across the cold, rough terrain.

Rosalee shivered a bit from the cold and drew up inside her wool coat, offering a critical smile. "I don't like thinking we might have been looked at as some creature's *feed*."

"Neither do I," said Bell, "but it's something worth remembering at all times. Out here, being something's dinner is a simple fact of life."

"I hope Father is all right," Rosalee said

absently, looking upward along the meandering trail.

"I didn't mean to scare you," said Bell,
seeing the look of apprehension come upon
her face. "When the ground's this deep
under snow, an animal will range twenty or
thirty miles in a day if it has to, to feed
itself." He pulled gently on his horse's reins,
saying, "Come on, Whiskey," and walked
off the trail toward the shelter of some tall-
standing rocks. Rosalee quickly looked back
once more, then hurried along, leading her
horse behind him.

Pushing the horses the extra hour on the
uphill trail had taken a toll on the animals.
Seeing how tired they were, Bell took out a
small coffeepot, a tin plate, some coffee
beans and jerked beef from his saddlebags.
He said to Rosalee, "We're going to have to
give these animals a little longer rest. Why
don't I fix us some hot coffee and warm beef
while we wait? We'll have time to eat and
still make another eight to ten miles by
dark."

"Good idea," Rosalee said. "I'll get us a
fire going. I don't know about you, but I'm
cold to my bones."

Rosalee gathered dried brush, shook
snow from it and heaped it beside a standing
rock where she'd cleared snow from a wide

141

patch of rocky ground by scraping her boot back and forth. While she did this, Bell stooped down, brushed snow from the flat surface of a rock, then took a bandanna from his pocket and poured some coffee beans into it. He wrapped the beans into a tight ball and crushed them with his pistol butt until they were suitable for boiling. He scooped clean snow into the pot.

The moment Rosalee had a small fire rising up from the center of a small pile of deadfall kindling, Bell sat the pot atop the flames and the two drew closer to the heat and watched in quiet anticipation. As the coffee began to boil, Bell took his long knife from its sheath, ran the blade back and forth through the fire, then stuck some jerked beef on the tip of it and held it over the licking flames. When the coffee reached its strength, Rosalee poured two cups and set the pot to one side of the crackling fire. They ate the warm beef and drank hot coffee until only a small portion of each was left.

Bell offered the last of the beef to her, but out of politeness Rosalee turned it down. She thought he would eat it himself, but surprisingly, Bell flipped the beef off the tin plate into the snow a few feet from the fire. Seeing Rosalee's questioning gaze, he said,

"If something is sizing us up for dinner, I'd like to get a look at it, get it in my gunsights before it decides to attack."

"You're baiting it, doing this to draw it in closer?" Rosalee asked.

"I either want to draw it in and kill it or else spook it away from us. I don't want us at its mercy this whole trip."

"What do we do now?" Rosalee asked.

"Now we go on about our business," said Bell. Holding the tin plate over the flames for a second, he stuck the plate into the snow, then rubbed a handful of snow around it to clean it. He scooped snow into the coffeepot and rubbed it around, cleaning the pot as well. Then, standing up, he slung the coffeepot back and forth to dry it some. As he did so, he gestured toward a protruding ledge sticking out above the trail a hundred yards ahead of them. "We'll get up there and take a few minutes, see if anything shows up down here." He scraped in snow with the side of his boot and put out the fire.

"Here, give me those things," said Rosalee. She offered a faint smile, taking the tin plate and coffeepot from him. "If we have something watching us, I'd rather see your hands free to carry the rifle."

Even as the two of them prepared their

horses for the trail, less than twenty yards away a pair of eyes watched as steam curled upward from flaring nostrils and drifted away into the sheltering tangle of brush. Breath thrust in and out of the big cougar's chest like a powerful bellows. The smell of live, warm flesh, both human and beast, permeated the air, the muskiness of it taunting the cat's senses, causing its long claws to instinctively press down into the snow, find a length of downed pine and sink themselves into it. The smells lured the cat forward, low and snakelike across the ground.

Jack Bell swung his leg over his horse and had just settled into his saddle when, beside him, Rosalee's horse grew nervous and tried to bolt sideways from beneath her, nickering in fear.

"Whoa!" Rosalee coaxed, the horse having caught her by surprise and nearly thrown her from her saddle. Luckily Rosalee was no newcomer to checking down a spooked horse. She caught her balance quickly, sat back hard and low on the reins, keeping the horse's head down and tucked back. The horse could neither rear nor bolt away without considerable effort. It gave a short bucking kick in protest but settled, stepping sidelong against Jack Bell's horse.

"Easy, Whiskey," Bell said, seeing that his horse too had been on the verge of spooking. He reached over, took a firm grip on the bridle of Rosalee's horse and drew it close to him, he and Rosalee working together to keep both horses under control. With the rifle in his free hand, Bell took a quick glance around the area. Then, realizing what an awkward position they were both in, he said, "Let's get out of here."

Bell let Whiskey go forward. Holding on to Rosalee's horse's bridle until the animal saw that they were on their way and stopped trying to bolt, Bell turned loose and let Rosalee have the lead of the animal. Still the horse tried to rush forward, but Rosalee kept control. She let it hurry but not bolt. Rosalee and Bell both looked back now, keeping a wary eye on their trail as the nervous horses climbed higher.

"Something's moved in awfully close to us," Bell said as they moved farther away from their camp spot. "Whatever it is, it's getting more and more daring. Looks like we're going to have to deal with it sooner than I thought."

At the sound of the horses whinnying and the voices of the people ringing out, the big cat had crouched flat to the snow and remained deathlike still until the horses had gone a good thirty yards or more. Watching the horses and their riders move out of sight around a bend in the upward-reaching trail, the cat slinked forward soundlessly, its nose close to the ground. It clamped the piece of beef jerky in its jaws as if the meat might try to suddenly get away, then darted out of sight and swung wide of the trail. The cat stopped only long enough to down the beef and lick its paws. Then it climbed high off the narrow trail, keeping the scent of live flesh close and beneath it where it could see them clearly yet remain hidden from their view.

CHAPTER 9

From atop the rock ledge, Jack Bell and Rosalee Finley looked back on the twisting trail below. But they saw nothing out of the ordinary. "After what just happened down there, I suppose coming up here is a waste of time," said Jack. "I've got a feeling we were about to be hit by a big mountain panther. If these horses hadn't caught scent of it, we would have been in big trouble."

"Is that what you think it is?" Rosalee asked. "A cougar?"

"Cougar, panther, mountain lion; I've heard it called all three." Bell shrugged. "But yep, I think that's what it is. In fact, I'd bet on it now. The way it's taken its time, following us so closely without making its move. A big cat likes to get its prey into rocky terrain — the rockier the better. Once a cat takes the high ground above you . . . it's got the advantage. You're no longer calling the shots. All you can do is wait and see what it has in mind for you."

As Bell spoke, he surveyed the land ahead of them, then looked back on the campsite, still hoping the predator might show itself.

But Bell knew the cat had already taken the beef and gotten out of sight. Looking upward along the snow-laden ridges above them on the left, Bell had a pretty good idea the cat was already up there, flanking them.

"You sound like you've had quite a bit of experience with big cats," said Rosalee, hoping his answer would be *yes*.

"Sorry, Rosalee," Bell replied quietly, his eyes still searching the rough, frozen land. "Right now I'm wishing I did, but the truth is, I don't. I've fired warning shots at a couple over the years, just to keep them away from camp and livestock. Other than that, all I've got to go on is what I've heard from others." He gripped his rifle in his gloved hand and looked squarely at Rosalee standing beside him. "Usually a panther is nothing to worry about. They shy away from people, keep to the high country and live on small game, unless they're lucky enough to find some elk or mountain goat. But if other game is scarce, any big animal will attack whatever it thinks it can take down. Weather like this, a big cat gets on your trail hunting food, he'll stay on it until he gets what he's looking for."

"And there's no chance we can out-travel him?" Rosalee asked, already knowing the answer as she looked out across the rugged land.

"Not on this terrain," said Bell. "This cat won't turn loose until it takes one of us or one of the horses. This is a serious hunt."

"And no hunter wants to go home empty-handed," Rosalee commented in a grim tone.

"You've got the picture," said Bell, turning and stepping up into his saddle, his rifle ready and resting across his lap. "This panther knows the rules of the hunt. We've either got to kill it, or it's going to end up killing one of us." He patted Whiskey's withers. "This horse has been with me too long to end up fed to a mountain cat." They turned their horses back toward the narrow trail, where the prints of the mule and Ben Finley wound upward into a wide world of whitecapped mountains.

They traveled on until the shadows of afternoon lay long and broken across the terraced slopes to their right. Upward on their left lay the higher rock ledges and sparse pine and spruce that appeared to cling to the mountainside by thin, gnarled fingers. Along the rock ledges hung icicles the length of a grown man. With a sound like the crack of a small rifle shot, the icicles would break free and tumble down from two hundred feet up, crushing themselves into tiny wet fragments by the time they came spewing across the trail.

Jack Bell and Rosalee rode along, saying very little since they'd stopped on the rock ledge and looked back down on their abandoned campsite. They remained alert, their eyes keeping a vigil on the rocky ground above them. Only now and then did they glance at the tracks they were following. Ben Finley and the little mule were closer now, the steady walking gait of the horses gaining on them with every passing mile. Jack Bell predicted they would overtake the man and the mule by noon the following day and with any luck soon be on their way home.

But even as Bell thought about finding Rosalee's father and heading home, his eyes moved warily, searching along the ledges for the big cat that he was convinced was stalking them. Once he thought he'd caught a glimpse of it streaking out from behind one rock and disappearing behind another; yet, upon watching that spot closely as the horses pushed on, he saw nothing else. So engrossed was he in watching the upper ledges that when Rosalee called out his name from twenty feet ahead of him, the suddenness of her voice startled him.

"Jack! Look here!" Rosalee called out as

Bell let out a breath and relaxed his grip on his rifle stock. "Father camped here, beneath this overhang! There's his boot marks."

Bell heeled his horse forward and swung down from his saddle beside Rosalee, who had just done the same. He saw the boot prints and hoofprints inside the overhang; he also saw the big paw prints and the dark stain where the cat had left its mark in the dirt and on the rock wall.

"Your father's been here all right. So has the cat," said Bell, stooping slightly for a closer look at the paw prints. "A big one from the size of its paw print." Cautiously looking back deeper into the darkened space beneath the overhang, seeing the blackened spot where Ben Finley had made his campfire, Bell said to Rosalee before venturing in, "Wait here and hold the horses until I get a good look around under there." He handed her his horse's reins, then stepped under the overhang with his thumb ready across his rifle hammer.

Ten feet back beneath the ledge, Bell could see the space was empty. He felt relieved and called back to Rosalee, "All right, bring the horses in."

Seeing the big paw prints herself as she led the horses in beneath the overhang,

Rosalee asked in an anxious tone, "Do you suppose this thing is also tracking my father?"

"It's hard to say what this cat is up to," said Bell, still looking the place over. But not wanting to compound her fear, he added, "It probably just came by after Ben had camped here and left." He pointed at the marked boot heel prints in the dust and at the mule's hoofprints leading to the narrowing back wall. The cat's prints circled along the rear wall to another dark streak on the wall, then led out the far end of the overhang and disappeared upward into the rocky slope. "This looks like as good a place as any for us to spend the night, with that cat out there prowling."

"We could get another hour of traveling in before dark," said Rosalee, getting more anxious now that she saw they were getting nearer to her father, knowing also that her father was in as much peril as she and Jack Bell.

"No," said Bell, "let's keep our heads and continue on the way we have been. We'll catch up to your father real soon — probably tomorrow, with any luck. Meanwhile, this is a good place to be if that cat comes calling in the night. We'll tend a fire and take turns keeping watch."

Rosalee's eyes went to the opening of the overhang. "Do you think it might have gotten distracted, given up on us and gone away by now?"

"That would be good," said Bell, "but we can't afford to count on it. Until we know otherwise, we best just figure that cat's waiting around every turn in the trail."

"I hate to think of my father being out there," Rosalee said, "with us being so close yet unable to do anything for him if something terrible were to happen. . . ." Her words trailed as her eyes welled with tears. She turned her face away to hide her emotions, and instead of finishing her sentence, she stepped quietly away. Bell watched her stoop down and busily rake up a small pile of dried brush her father had left lying near the campfire. "I better help you get a camp pitched," she said as if dismissing the subject of her father. "Tomorrow will be another long day."

Bell could think of nothing more to say that might console her. With a breath of resolve, he tipped his hat brim back and looked down, considering the size of the paw prints in the dirt. This was a big male cat, perhaps bigger than any he'd ever seen. A cat this size would have learned to fear nothing up here in this country. Bell tightened his grip on the rifle stock and led the horses to the rear wall of the overhang.

"Easy, boys," he whispered as both horses shied back a step from the dark streak of cat urine on the rocks. With a gloved hand, he settled the animals and wrapped their reins around an upthrust of jagged stone. He stood for a moment letting the horses get used to their new surroundings as he gazed out past the entrance to the overhang and onto the distant slopes reaching upward across the land.

Rosalee was right, he reminded himself: They could have traveled another hour before nightfall. Maybe, for Ben Finley's sake, they should have. But staying here for the night was the smart thing to do. He wasn't about to risk Rosalee's life in an attempt to find her father. Wherever Ben Finley was up there, Bell was sure the old man would agree.

In moments a campfire glowed inside the shadowed belly of the mountain. After graining and watering the horses with snow Rosalee melted over the fire, Jack Bell wiped the animals down with a rag he carried in his saddlebags. By the time he'd inspected their hooves and forelegs and settled them in for the night, the smell of fresh coffee and warm beef and beans drew

Bell to the fireside.

"Are you feeling better?" Bell asked gently as he filled two plates of food and set Rosalee's over beside her.

"Yes, thank you," Rosalee replied while she raised the coffeepot, using the cuff of her coat sleeve around the hot handle. She poured steaming coffee into the two tin cups sitting beside the fire. "I know we can only do what this land and weather allow us to do. I haven't lived in this country my entire life, but I have lived here long enough to know it doesn't pay to get in too big a hurry in these mountains."

Bell nodded in silence, knowing there was nothing more he needed to say. Rosalee understood this land and what it demanded of a person as well as he did. It was within their power to find her father, and there was little doubt they would do so provided they remained cautious and used their heads and their experience. But it went without saying that whether or not they found Ben Finley *alive* depended on many things . . . things beyond their control.

As darkness set in, Bell and Rosalee cleaned the tin plates and eating utensils and put them away. But they kept a pot of strong coffee simmering on the outside edge of the fire. They had gathered plenty of brush and deadfall limbs for firewood, and Bell stoked the fire higher than he ordinarily would have to ward off the cat. While Rosalee slept, Bell sat with a blanket around his shoulders, his rifle across his lap, attending to any sound from beyond the entrance to the overhang.

Throughout the evening, the wind had gradually lessened until finally it had stopped altogether. But with darkness came a resurgence. By midnight a low whir rose and fell sporadically across the land. Bell finished a cup of coffee and, standing up quietly, walked outside the glow of light and into the cutting cold outside the shelter of rock. He looked upward at a turbulent, cloud-streaked sky for a moment to judge the cast of the coming day. There was snow coming. Not a lot, he decided, studying the sky to the west, where the clouds lay thicker and inched slowly toward him, but enough to cover Ben Finley's prints if they didn't reach him by tomorrow afternoon.

No sooner had he predicted snow to himself than he felt a cold wisp of it touch his cheek. Then, as he turned to walk back to the fire, he either heard or sensed a faint, rattling purr of breath from the underbrush to the left of the trail. He spun toward the sound, his rifle coming up instinctively. He listened, frozen in place until he heard it again, this time followed by the slightest snapping of dried brush. He backed a step farther inside the overhang, then another, before halting and standing as still as stone. Beneath the thickness of night and the growing whir of wind came soft, encroaching steps through the stiff snow and brush.

Jack Bell moved his thumb back to cock the rifle, meanwhile steadying the butt to his shoulder and drawing a bead on the darkness, aiming toward the sound. Behind him came a low, frightened nickering, and he knew the horses had picked up the scent of cat on the wind. The sound moved ever closer as he braced himself for the shot. But then the sound he'd heard in front of him suddenly shifted somehow, and the hair on his neck raised as he heard the footsteps come upon his back before he even had time to turn around.

"Jack!" Rosalee rasped, her hand coming to rest on his shoulder as she found him in the darkness. "The horses are going crazy! What's going on?"

A weakness ran the length of him as Bell felt his knees turn rubbery for a second. But then he caught control of himself and, clutching Rosalee's forearm, said in a hoarse whisper, "Keep still! It's out there! I just heard it." Turning loose of her arm, Bell turned back with his rifle toward the darkness.

They stood in dead silence, listening. But the sound was gone. It had stopped cold at what Jack Bell gauged to be no more than thirty yards away. There had been no sound of it retreating through the brush at the sound of their voices, yet Bell was certain the cat had heard them. In his mind, Bell pictured the big animal simply hunkering down out there, close, very close, its superior night vision taking full advantage.

"Back away slowly," Bell whispered over his shoulder to Rosalee. He suddenly felt the cat's advantage over them and wanted nothing more for the moment than to get back on equal standing. "He's seeing every move we make." Behind Bell there was precious light — firelight that would expose this deadly foe to him.

They backed step after step, slowly at first, then hurriedly as Jack thought he heard a rush of padded paws moving quickly across crunching snow. At the fire, Bell faced the front of the overhang with his rifle ready and aimed. Rosalee frantically piled brush onto the licking flames. From the rear wall the horses broke into a nervous round of nickering. "Go settle them down," Bell said, not turning his face from the dark slice of rock and dirt before him.

Rosalee turned from the licking fire and hurried toward the horses a few feet away. Whiskey stood tugging at his reins with his head lowered, slamming his hoof on the dirt floor. But beside Whiskey, the roan had gone out of control. At the sight of Rosalee moving quickly in the flicker of firelight, the horse spooked even worse. It reared upward in spite of its tied reins and in doing so caused the upthrust of stone to snap off from the rock wall.

"Jack, look out!" Rosalee shouted as the roan came down onto its hooves and bolted across the dirt. Jack turned but had time to do nothing more than hurl himself out of the roan's way as the animal veered to keep from trampling him. The terrified horse shot out from beneath the overhang into the perilous night, the piece of rock tangled in its reins and batting its sides, goading it on.

Bare-headed and without even the benefit of the blanket that had fallen from around him, Jack Bell raced out behind the roan, hoping against all wisdom to catch the horse before it disappeared into the darkness. But a few feet past the outer edge of the overhang, Bell stopped short, his breath pounding in his chest, his rifle gripped tight in his hands. He heard the roan's hooves pounding downward along the icy trail and caught a fleeting glimpse of the big cat swishing its tail as it spun as if in midair and disappeared in pursuit.

Rosalee ran out into the cold, shouting aloud at the roan, calling it back. She tried to follow the sound of the roan's hoofbeats, but Bell grabbed her with his free hand and held her back. Somehow in the rush of things Rosalee had grabbed Bell's coat lying beside the fire. She'd thrown it across her shoulders as she ran from the overhang. "Get back inside with Whiskey!" Bell demanded, grabbing his coat from around her and throwing it on himself quickly. "Get that LeMat pistol! Make sure it's loaded, and keep it handy! I'm going after the horse!"

"Yes! Please! Hurry, Jack!" Rosalee pleaded tearfully. She retreated back to the safety of the overhang, already feeling the cold through her wool shirt. From the edge of the glowing firelight, she watched Bell run along the thick trail of snow until the darkness overtook him.

CHAPTER 10

The roan's race with fear was over quickly. As if knowing the outcome beforehand, the big cat anticipated the hysterical animal's every move and bounded along behind it easily. Throughout the chase, the cat moved as silent and sure as death. With speed and deliberation, its body swayed in rhythm to the roll of the terrain, the thick tail working instinctively as a counterbalance. A predator in a predator's world. But the poor horse, a mammal gifted and armed only to flee across an open plain, found itself suddenly bested in this hostile terrain, of which the cat was ancient lord.

Its powerful body faltering as it ran, the horse struggled against the rocky elements unseen beneath the blanket of deep snow. Near the end of the roan's fifty-yard dash, the cat swung up off the trail behind it and seemed to skim along fluidly from rock to ledge, flanking and gaining ground above it as if gliding on a ribbon of silk.

The horse whinnied long and wildly, its peripheral vision catching quick glimpses overhead of streaking tawny fur and a billowing wake of crystalline white spray as the cat closed the gap between them. Where the trail turned sharply for the horse, the rocky slope above it ran out entirely for the cat. Yet the cat seemed to expect it, and at the very instant the substance of earth vanished from beneath its pounding paws, the cat spread all fours, going airborne in a long swirl of steaming breath.

Plunging downward through the cold air, its claws spread, its whole body tensed, the big panther wrapped itself around the horse's neck, sank its claws and clung there as the horse stumbled and rolled forward. Snow billowed; the horse rolled screaming off the trail and down a steep, rocky slope, the cat never losing its grip for a second. Jack Bell heard the melee and quickened his pace, whispering a fast, silent prayer but already preparing himself for what he would find as the horse's wild nickering came to a sudden halt in the darkness ahead of him.

At the spot where the panther had swooped down and made its attack, Bell saw the disheveled snow, the struggle of hoof and limb leading off the edge of the trail and down into the black night. He stared down and listened, but he could neither see nor hear anything above the low whir of wind and slow beginnings of falling

162

snow. Having to accept the finality of what had happened, along with his inability to stop it, he clenched his teeth and raised the rifle butt to his shoulder. He imagined the cat standing crouched over its kill at that very second.

"Damn you!" Bell shouted in rage and defeat. His shot rang out, shattering the silence around him . . . yet only for a brief instant in the enormity of the cold, rugged land. Then he lowered the rifle, levered a fresh round into the chamber, turned and walked back along the trail to the glow of light beneath the rock ledge. Far down the steep side of the mountain, the cat lay as silent as stone atop the warm carcass, its eyes fixed in the direction of the man's voice and the rifle shot. Warm blood steamed in the fur around its mouth. After a moment had passed with no further sound from the ridge above, the cat mopped its tongue around its mouth and went back to its feeding.

Back inside the shelter beneath the snow-covered cliff, Bell called out to Rosalee from the outer edge of firelight before walking in. She lowered the big LeMat pistol and stood to one side as he walked past her to where Whiskey stood tied to another upthrust of rock. Rosalee watched without speaking as

Bell tested the strength of the rock and the reins.

"The roan?" Rosalee asked softly, already knowing there was no good news to come of it. She watched Bell walk back beside her at the fire.

Bell laid his rifle down and held both hands out above the licking flames, warming his palms and rubbing his hands together. Without facing her, he said in a solemn tone, "He got the roan."

Rosalee let out a slight gasp but offered no more.

After a moment of staring deep into the fire in dark contemplation, Bell said, "I thought about trying to slip down the mountainside and killing that panther . . . but that wouldn't have been wise: not in the dark, not in this kind of weather. That was just my anger getting the better of me. Nobody likes to lose a good horse that way."

"You did right coming back here," said Rosalee. She reached out and laid a comforting hand on his forearm. Bell looked at her hand, then brought his eyes up to her face. He saw her eyes glistening wet with tears, and he drew her to him gently, putting his free arm around her.

"I'm sorry about your horse, Rosalee," he

whispered to her, feeling her hair against his cheek.

"I know," she whispered in reply. She composed herself quickly and stood back from him. "We can't blame the cougar. It's only doing what it must to survive. I — I'm just sorry I brought you into all this, Jack." Although she had stepped back, she still stood close, her hands on his forearms. "If it wasn't for me and my father, you would be back in Nolan's Gap right now —"

"Shhh, don't say that," Jack said gently, cutting her off. "I'm here because I wanted to be here. You didn't know we'd run into a big cat . . . it just happened. But we're still here. We've still got to reach your father." He thought about the snow starting to fall and added, "Now that we're down to one horse, we better rest awhile and get moving before daylight. At least that cat won't be bothering us now that he's . . ." His words trailed. "That is, now that he's been appeased for the time being."

"I understand how these things work, Jack," said Rosalee, composing herself even more, stepping back farther from him and turning her eyes away. "You needn't worry about me. I'm terribly sorry for the horse, but my father's safety is all that's important to me."

"Of course," said Bell, stepping back himself. "I figure with any luck, we'll be seeing him sometime today."

Even though Ben Finley's fire had burned down low when the distant rifle shot awakened him, the campsite remained comfortably warm. As Ben stirred upward onto his elbows, he heard something rush across the dirt on the other side of the fire. He caught a glimpse of something scurrying out of sight around the edge of a rock. It caused him to bolt up quickly under his blanket and grab the shotgun lying close at hand. Standing, Ben took a second, rubbing a hand up and down his face to clear sleep from his eyes. Had he really heard something? Had he really seen something? Lately he'd begun questioning himself more and more. But of this he had no doubt. Yes, something had just fled from his campsite. He was certain of it.

Cautiously, he circled the fire, the single-barreled shotgun in his hands, the weak hammer cocked beneath his thumb. When he'd made his camp earlier in the evening, as always Ben Finley had chosen this spot wisely. He'd found a tall, flat-sided boulder that stood back into the side of the mountain and tilted forward at its top, providing a lean-to effect against the elements. No snow lay on the clearing beneath the leaning boulder. Other, smaller rocks formed a half circle back out of the hard press of the wind.

Finley had built his large campfire in the center of the half circle, knowing the rocks would absorb the heat and radiate it in response, keeping him dry and warm throughout the night. He listened closely for a moment, not as concerned with the distant rifle shot as he was with what had just happened here in his own camp. He walked to the edge of the firelight and looked out across the dark, narrow trail, seeing nothing. But then his eyes went down to where the snow started at his feet, and his breath drew tight in his chest. He stared down at what he considered to be the largest set of canine prints he'd ever seen.

"Wolves! Lord God almighty," Ben Finley said aloud amid the first sprinkling of falling snow. His hands trembled tensely around the shotgun stock. He backed up, his eyes scanning the darkness in the direction of the vanishing paw prints. At the farthest reach of the firelight's glow, two red eyes gleamed at him. "Stay back, you devils!" he shouted, raising the shotgun. He pulled the gun's trigger, but the weak hammer fell without firing. "I'm warning yas!" Ben shrieked, his voice sounding shaky to him.

As if seeing or perhaps sensing Ben Finley's helplessness, the red gleaming eyes moved forward toward him across the night. Ben Finley hurried backward, closer to the fire, recocking the shotgun as he went. He pulled the trigger again, seeing the dark image begin to form as the big animal moved in more boldly. Again the weak hammer refused to do its job. Ben Finley cursed the defective gun under his quickened breath and shook it, as if that would fix the problem. He threw the butt to his shoulder, recocked it and tried again, seeing the dark form draw closer with each bounding step.

"Get back, you devil!" Ben Finley screamed at the dark, shadowy creature. This time when the battered shotgun failed, Ben saw he had no time to recock the hammer. Instead, he grabbed the gun by its barrel and wielded it like a club, swinging it back and forth in desperation. Seeing the big animal stop and shy down on its haunches ten feet away, he noted that this was no wolf at all, but rather a big, rough-coated wild dog. The look of fear in the big mongrel's eyes as Ben Finley shouted and swung the shotgun at it told Finley instantly that this dog was as frightened of him as he was of it.

The dog growled low and menacingly, its hackles raised, but still it cowered back. Finley stopped swinging the shotgun but kept it drawn back over his shoulder just in case. "Growl, you big, stinking heathen! But keep your distance if you know what's good for you!"

The big dog fell silent, its ragged tail tucked down between its hind legs. As Finley stared, the dog slinked further down and inched forward, lowering its hackles and offering a soft whine of submission. For a second, the big dog's gesture took Ben Finley by surprise. He eased his grip on the shotgun stock with a puzzled expression on his face. He glanced quickly over his shoulder at the fire, then returned his gaze to the dog. "I see. You've come begging for a warm spot, eh?"

The dog whined even more and inched forward on its belly as if in reply.

"Blasted cur. I'm probably lucky you didn't rip my throat out in my sleep!" He kept the shotgun drawn back but with less conviction. The dog seemed to sense it. Finley looked over his shoulder at the little mule and said, "And you . . . you worthless pile of ears and hide. You could've told me something had snuck in on me."

The mule paid no attention to man or dog as it stood sleepily near the warm rock wall.

Ben Finley backed farther across the small campsite, allowing the dog in closer to the fire's heat. The big cur crawled around to the spot where Finley had first thought he'd seen it when he'd awakened and scared it away. The dog kept its wary eyes on Finley as it shivered and settled in close to the fire. Outside the shelter of the large tilted boulder, Ben Finley saw the falling snow grow thicker, a few flakes drifting in and dissolving on the rising heat.

"What kind of a wild dog goes looking for a campfire to keep it warm?" Ben asked, lowering the shotgun stock and letting it rest on his shoulder. "I know what kind," he answered for the dog. "The kind that hasn't always been *wild*." He looked the dog over good. It was thin but not starved. Its hair was coarse but only medium-length — not thick enough for this climate, he thought. "No wonder you came at the sight of a fire. You're a *fair-weather* cur, is what you are."

Ben Finley stepped around to where his blanket lay on the ground. The dog perked its ears up, watching him curiously. Ben continued to talk idly as he picked the blanket up and spread it across his shoulders. Cradling the shotgun in one arm now,

170

he squatted down near the fire, picked up a short, thick pine log and burrowed it down into the glowing bed of embers. He stared through the flames at the dog lying across the fire from him. All of a sudden he sensed something familiar about the animal, and his lost memories began coming back to him.

"Have I seen you before?" he murmured, watching the dog look back at him through the licking flames.

Once again he saw himself through the watery veil. He stood as before at the small mouth of a cave hidden by brush, his rifle cocked in his hands. Again he saw the blood trail he had followed there, and again he knew there was something clinging to the side of the mountain that he was supposed to see. But still he could not identify it.

"Is that you up there, following me? Looking down from the ridge above?" He stared through the fire, searching for pieces of his scattered memories. While no more pictures came to his mind, he did hear the sound of the dog's long, deep growl, so real that he had to blink his eyes and look even closer at the big cur to assure himself that the sound came only from within his shattered recollection.

"What am I suppose to see?" he asked, as

if the dog might reveal it to him. "Were you there last time? Have I seen you before? I feel like I have . . . but where?"

The dog only gazed back at him, the firelight flickering in its eyes.

"Damn it to hell!" Finley shouted, burying his face in his hands in frustration.

The dog half-rose at the furious sound of his voice. But Ben Finley saw what he'd done and said in a soothing tone, "It's all right, dog. Lay back down — it ain't your fault I'm losing my mind."

The dog judged the softened tone of the man's voice and settled back down onto his spot. Ben Finley managed to shake his piecemeal memories from his mind lest he dwell too long and hard and lose them altogether. He stood up and shook his head and walked to the supplies atop the pack mule. The dog watched, wary but curious, as Ben Finley took out the jerked meat and carved a chunk from it and put the rest away.

"I bet you can eat something, can't you, dog?" he said. Walking halfway around the fire toward the animal, Ben reached out and pitched the piece of jerky over near the dog's front paws. Again the dog looked startled by the gesture and half-rose up. But his nose was quick to catch the smell of the dried beef, and he grabbed it and downed it in one snap of his hungry jaws. He licked his wet flews and looked longingly at Ben Finley for more.

"Naw, that's all for now, big boy," Ben said, squatting back down with his blanket across his shoulders. "I wasn't counting on any dinner company this trip." He ran the knife blade back and forth through the flames to clean it. "You look hungry enough to eat a whole beef in one sitting if I had one to throw at you."

The big dog whined and stared at him in anxious anticipation.

Ben wiped the knife blade across his shirt sleeve and slipped it back into the sheath on his belt. No sooner had he put the knife away than a rush of memory swept over him again, this time so strong he almost swooned under the weight of it. Throughout the day he'd veered off one path onto another, simply trying to satisfy any wisp of familiarity. At times these paths had looked right to him . . . the way a certain rock reached upward and stood positioned between his path and the sky.

Yet at the end of the day, he couldn't honestly say that he'd seen any landmarks, rocks or pathways that had sparked any remembrance for him. *My God, what have you done?* he had asked himself at one point as he'd gathered wood and made camp. Yet now, seeing this dog had given him a new sense of hope somehow. He was on the right path now; he knew it. This dog was no stranger to him; he was sure of that. He pictured this dog running upward along a rocky path, himself right behind it, running to keep up beneath the hot summer sun. Suddenly the memory burned crystal-clear in his mind.

"Don't lose it! Don't lose it!" he demanded aloud of himself, pounding his fist on his knee.

There was the glistening blood trail on the ground at his feet. He stopped for a moment on that hot, steep path and looked back over his shoulder as the dog disappeared downward into the brush-covered mouth of the cave. He saw his horse and mule back there where he'd left them by the cottonwood tree, only now he saw them more clearly than he had ever seen them before. "My God! It's coming back to me!" he cried out, tears streaming down his cheeks. He stood up and began pacing back and forth, looking up at the rocks and mountainside in the darkness, seeing it so clearly now that he recognized this spot even under a blanket of snow.

From the mouth of the brush-covered

cave he heard the voice. It was an old voice. It spoke to him in a language foreign to him, and yet he knew what it was saying. He stopped pacing and stared across at the dog again. In his mind he heard the pistol shot but not before he felt the impact of the arrow slice deep into him. He swayed in place standing at the fire, feeling the pain in the old wound as if it had just happened. Sweat beaded his brow, and he ran a trembling hand across his forehead. "You killed him!" his own voice said through that watery veil.

"Killed who?" he asked aloud, looking first at the dog, then up into the black sky, then back at the dancing firelight. But as quickly as the memory had come upon him, it was gone, as if a hand had reached out from some dark place in his mind and slammed a door shut.

Ben Finley took a deep breath and let it out slowly. He had to stay calm. He had to let this work itself out. He was on the right path. It would come to him; he knew it would. He looked over at the big dog and said in a tortured voice, "Tomorrow I'll find it! I believe you're going to lead me to it."

CHAPTER 11

Leading Whiskey and traveling on foot, Jack Bell and Rosalee Finley left camp before daylight in the falling snow and climbed steadily upward along the thin path. The wind was not fierce, but the snowfall had grown heavier. As the tracks of the mule and Ben Finley became less and less visible, Bell watched the skyline for any sign of campfire smoke, knowing even as he did so that old Ben was not the kind of man to linger in camp while the day slipped away from him. By the time the two had reached the spot where Ben had once again changed paths, the prints they followed were barely more than a trace of an indention beneath the covering of new snow.

When they stopped off the path in the semishelter of a tall, earth-stuck boulder, Rosalee looked forward up the ever-steeper path and said in a breath of steam, "We're getting closer — I can feel it." She took a step forward, cupped her hands to her mouth and called out, "Father! Father, can you hear me?" The echo resounded, the words seeming to slip into every crevice and hidden pass, seeking out the recipient of her question. Rosalee and Bell stood listening for a moment but heard no reply.

"He should have heard me," Rosalee said. "We're close enough he should have heard me."

Seeing the look of despair come upon her face, Jack Bell said quickly, "Yes, and maybe he did. Maybe he's just being stubborn."

"Yes, perhaps that's it," Rosalee said. She leaned back against the boulder and lowered her eyes.

To keep her spirits up, Bell said, "You know, I've been giving some thought to your father and this search of his. He's a smart old man, judging by the way I see him going about this."

"Oh?" said Rosalee.

Bell nodded. "Yep. The way I see it, he's backtracking himself in a way . . . going from one most likely spot to the next, hoping he was there before and trying to pick up any reminder of his last trip up through here."

Rosalee gave him a curious look, not seeing the sense in what he said.

"Haven't you laid something down and later on can't remember where you left it?" Bell said, keeping her attention.

"Yes," said Rosalee, offering a tired smile, "only instead of this being a lost thimble, it's a lost cache of gold."

"But still the same principle," said Bell.

"If there ever even *was* such a mysterious cave, with an even more mysterious cache of gold in it," said Rosalee, "what are the chances of him ever finding it again?" She gestured a gloved hand, taking in all of the endless mountain range.

"Pretty slim when you first think of it," said Bell. "But if you really look at it closely, it might not be as long on odds as you think."

She looked at him a bit skeptically.

"Hear me out," said Bell. "You said yourself that your father always looks around for the best campsites along the paths and trails. If you know that about him, I'm sure he knows it too. So if he's picking the best right now as he goes along, wouldn't these campsites be the same ones he would have picked last year?"

Rosalee considered it for a second, then said, "Yes, I suppose they would. But that's still playing some long odds."

"Yes, but everything in life has its odds. The trick to success is a matter of trimming the odds any way you can. Suppose old Ben goes along choosing the paths he would

178

have most likely taken the last time. Suppose he picks the most likely campsites. At some point, won't the odds tip into his favor of ending up back on the same spot he did the last time?"

Rosalee offered a patient smile. "Now you're starting to sound like my father. That worries me."

Bell returned her smile. "I'm not saying there *is* a cave, a cache of gold or anything else up there awaiting your father. But *if there is,* the odds against him finding it might not be as long as we think."

Rosalee only nodded and looked away for a moment, her eyes scanning the upward trail lying all but buried beneath the blanketing snow. "Perhaps you're right, Jack," she said after a while. "If there is a cave full of gold, I hope for my father's sake he finds it. It's time my father had a lucky break. I can't remember the last time anything good came his way."

"Oh really?" Seeing her somberness, Bell said, looking her up and down, "I can. He has a beautiful daughter who loves him very much."

"Thank you," she said almost in a whisper. Then, as if to change the subject, she looked back along the trail beneath them, seeing their tracks snake down until they fell out of sight. "I hope we've seen the last of that cougar," she said. "Will killing the horse keep him fed for a while?"

Bell was surprised at how easily she brought the subject up. "Yes, I think so. He'll hang around the carcass as long as he can. It's not often a cat kills something as large as a horse. He'll stay close to it." Bell also looked back along the trail. "It was only an unlucky twist of fate on the horse's part. The cat just happened to be at the right place at the right time." He shrugged, then added, "But maybe that's as much as fate ever gives any of us. One event happens, and it causes another." As he spoke, he thought of the snow slide and the men he'd dragged out of it — men who had been there to do him harm, to kill him even. "If we're lucky enough, we just happen to be standing in the right spot when the events unfold . . . like the cat last night."

"I hope there is more to life than that," said Rosalee, straightening up from against the boulder and tugging her hat down tighter onto her head, preparing for the trail.

"Don't mind me; I'm sure there is." Bell smiled to himself, also preparing for the trail, straightening his collar against the falling snow.

The air had grown thinner, colder and harder to breathe, Ben Finley thought, loosening his coat collar and beneath it the collar button of his wool shirt. Beneath his shirt and his wool long johns he felt sweat moisten his chest and the small of his back as he trudged upward on the rocky path, using the shotgun as a walking stick. Behind him the mule balked now and then in protest against the deep snow and the rough footing. Throughout the night Ben had kept the fire burning high. He'd shunned deep sleep, preferring to doze on and off, allowing himself to probe his memory and at the same time remain aware of the dog's presence right across the fire.

After feeding himself and giving the dog another cut of jerked beef, this time warming it over the fire first, Ben broke his camp at the crack of dawn and let the dog take the lead. At first the dog had no idea what Ben was asking of him, but after a hundred yards, looking back and seeing the man and the mule staying behind him, the dog settled his pace and kept the old man in sight. Ben Finley had chopped up a few small cuts of the jerked beef and carried them in the leather satchel. Every now and then he coaxed the dog back to him with a piece. The big cur learned quickly. Within an hour it would have appeared that the two had traveled together for years.

"Take care of me, you mangy cur, and I'll make you a full partner," Ben said, tossing a bite of the jerked beef to the dog as they stopped long enough for Ben to catch his breath and look around for any familiar sign that might further jog his memory. The dog caught the piece of beef, downed it and looped forward around a turn in the trail. In a moment, when Ben Finley hadn't caught up to him, the dog reappeared, cocking his head curiously.

"Don't worry, I'm coming," said Ben, adjusting the satchel on his shoulder, then jerking the mule forward by the lead rope. "If they all called me crazy before, what on earth would they say about me now?" He chuckled and wheezed. "Here I am following a big, mangy stray dog . . . expecting him to lead me to a cave full of gold."

As he started forward, he looked back down the steep trail and at the endless deep canyons and crevices between rolling mountaintops. He whispered to himself, "This time maybe I really am losing my mind."

Earlier he thought he'd heard his daughter's voice calling out to him, but after looking back and waiting for a moment and not hearing the voice again, he decided it had been his imagination playing tricks on him — his exhaustion overtaking his senses. He jerked the lead rope to the mule and trudged on. By noon he stood on a narrow ledge looking out across a deep canyon over three hundred feet below. A few feet ahead of him, the dog came loping down the steep trail, then stopped and looked at him, having doubled back again as if to see what was taking the old man so long.

"Take it easy on me, you ragged cur," Ben rasped, speaking aloud to the dog, his breathing labored, his heart pounding inside his chest. "I'm not as young as I used to be."

The dog came closer, expecting another piece of beef, but as Ben reached inside the satchel, he swayed sideways and almost lost his balance, tightly gripping the lead rope to the mule for support. "I've got to . . . rest for a minute," Ben said in a weak voice. He pulled the mule over to the side of the trail, where a wall of rock reached upward. Sliding down with his back to the wall, Ben let the lead rope dangle in his hand and bowed his head for a moment, knowing the danger of letting himself fall asleep in this high cold.

The big cur whined and barked and

poked its wet nose against the side of his face, causing Ben Finley to swipe an exhausted hand at it. "Get away. I'll be along in a minute," he murmured.

But the big dog would have none of it. He continued to pester and scratch at Ben Finley and at the leather satchel until at length Ben pushed himself up from the wall and rubbed his face with both hands. "All right, all right! We'll go on; I just needed to rest for a second." He looked down at the dog and fished a piece of jerked beef from the leather satchel hanging from his shoulder. He tossed the piece of beef down. "You're right — this is no place for me to sit down and fall asleep. Not in this weather. Not if I ever expect to wake up again."

Once again Ben Finley led the mule forward. In moments the two had followed the dog upward around a sharp turn so thin that a misstep to the right would have sent both man and beast plunging five hundred feet onto the pointed tops of pine and spruce. But immediately after ascending that treacherous turn, Ben led the mule into a small, round clearing where the path appeared to have stopped at the base of a high-reaching wall of rock. Ben slumped as he looked all around, realizing the trail had come to an end.

His labored breath steaming, Ben said aloud to the mule behind him, "Well, this is as far as we'll make it today." He looked upward along a steep, snow-streaked ledge of rock, judging where to best make a camp out of the direct force of the wind. The dog's paw prints led upward between two rocks and disappeared around the jutting lip of a cliff. Ben Finley heard the dog bark up there out of sight above him, as if calling upon him to follow.

Looking back at the wind-blown, swirling snow behind him, Ben only hesitated for a second, seeing that whatever awaited him above could be no less hospitable than where he stood. Then he tied the mule's lead rope around a spur of rock and climbed hand and foot upward on all fours until he pulled himself up onto the flat cliff surface and saw the dog standing there at face level, awaiting him with its tail wagging.

Ben stood up, brushing himself off, out of breath and staggering in place, exhausted. But now, looking around the flat clearing, his expression took on a renewed energy as he saw the blackened remnants of an old campfire tucked back inside a narrow crevice. "Good dog," he whispered, idly reaching inside the satchel and taking out a piece of beef. He dropped it into the dog's waiting jaws as he stepped forward. This spot felt familiar to him all of a sudden.

The crevice was no more than two feet wide, causing Ben to have to step over the blackened campfire remains in order to gain entrance. In the darkness of that narrow space, Ben had no idea how far back it reached into the bosom of the earth. He stopped long enough to take out the tin of sulphur matches he carried inside his coat. Taking out a single match, he closed the tin and put it away. Striking the match down the side of the rock crevice, he held it out before him and took a step farther into the flaring light, looking quickly while he had light to see by.

At his leg, Ben felt the dog standing against him. He lowered his free hand and scratched the shaggy head, hearing the dog's panting breath. "I knew you'd show me something," Ben rasped, out of breath himself, the cold air seeming to slice deep into his lungs. In the flicker of the fading match light, Ben's eyes moved quickly along the floor, seeing the scraps of kindling and firewood, a tin cup and a spoon that he remembered having carried in his supplies for years. They'd been a part of the provisions he'd lost that fateful trip, the memory of which was still locked so securely inside his head.

"My goodness," Ben whispered, stepping forward as the match burned short between his fingers. Stooping down to pick up the dust-covered spoon, he caught a quick blink of recollection, a flash of having been here before. But it vanished as quickly as it had arrived. Ben stepped back and shook out the hot match before the encroaching flames bit his fingertips. "Might as well get a fire going and settle in." Glancing around at the dog, he added, "Looks like I'll be spending some time here."

Ben built a fire and rested while a pot of coffee boiled. After a hot cup of coffee and a portion of stiff beef jerky he warmed for himself and the dog, he rose to his feet, stretched and walked to the front of the crevice, where the mule stood barely out of the weather inside the narrow shelter of rock. Ben Finley had to shove the mule backward and work his way around it in order to leave the crevice and step out into the falling snow. "Don't worry," he said, noting the resistance on the mule's part as he pressed past it toward the cutting draft of cold outside air. "You get to sit this one out."

Back along the path, the tracks of both mule and man were hardly visible now, the snow having erased both from the face of this crystalline white world. The only tracks showing clearly were those of the dog, who had left the crevice only a moment earlier. Ben walked along the dog's tracks, pulling his gloves from his coat pocket and putting them on. He followed the paw prints upward as they climbed the steep mountainside. "I can climb anything a dog can climb," he said to himself, his words gushing steam, sounding raspy yet confident.

But forty yards up, his foot slipped, and he clung to a snow-covered rock for a moment, his breath heaving in his chest. He ventured a look back and realized how close he'd just come to plunging down to his death. The narrow plateau below was nothing more than a sliver of flatland on an almost unhampered drop into a thin gray swirl of clouds. Obscure tips of hundred-foot pine looked like pinpoints below. "Lord . . . be careful," Ben warned himself, his words and breath halting and tight. Above him he heard the dog whining low, and looking up, he saw it standing on another ledge gazing down at him.

"Don't count me out," Ben said almost in a whisper. "I'm still right behind you."

CHAPTER 12

In the early evening, Jack Bell and Rosalee Finley stood at the spot on the trail where Ben Finley had coaxed the mule upward toward the narrow ledge where he'd made his camp. Unfortunately, the new snow had already wiped out Ben's tracks. The trail ahead lay smooth and untelling as the steep path Ben Finley had taken upward into the steep mountainside. "The snow beat us to him," Rosalee said in dismay, staring ahead. "We'll have to wait until the snow ends and start searching for his trail all over again."

They had walked the horse past the point where Ben Finley had left this trail and started upward. "Maybe not," said Bell, stopping and gazing upward at a thin curl of smoke and wavering heat that seemed to rise out of the earth above them. His voice dropped to almost a whisper. "One door swings shut . . . another door swings open."

They turned and walked back, their eyes on the wisps of smoke, to the point on the trail where it looked most likely a person would have turned off and climbed to an extending ledge. "Would your father recognize the sound of his own pistol?" Bell asked, gesturing a nod toward the big LeMat revolver in Rosalee's holster, then looking up along the ridgeline, judging the impact a shot might have on the mantle of snow lying there.

"I — I can't say, Jack," she replied. "But if he does, he might just take off and try hiding from us."

"You were calling out to him earlier," Bell reminded her.

"I know, but that was a mistake," Rosalee replied. "I realize it now. If we're this close, I don't want to run the risk of him not wanting us to find him."

Jack Bell looked at her, considering her words. Then he let out a breath. "It's just as well. I don't know if I trust that snow up there." He turned a patient smile to her to show he meant no sarcasm, and said, "Besides, I almost forgot, we're saving a man who might not want us saving him. You and the horse can rest here while I go up there."

"No, Jack," said Rosalee. "That's not fair on you. You're as tired as I am. That's *my* father up there. I should be the one going."

Jack took a moment judging the steep mountainside, seeing the slimmest imprint of a narrow path winding among the snow-covered rocks. "Whiskey can make it up there," he said finally. "We'll both go." He turned the horse to the mountainside and said to Rosalee, "I want you in front of me in case one of us slips."

"I'm perfectly capable of climbing without falling," she said indignantly.

"I wasn't talking about you, Rosalee," Bell said quietly. "I meant me or Whiskey. I don't want you behind this horse if he happens to lose his footing."

"Oh, I see," Rosalee said, a bit embarrassed. "I'm sorry."

Bell nodded, guiding her in front of him and the horse with a hand gently closed around her forearm. "No need to apologize. It's easy to misunderstand things in conditions like this. Cold weather and thin air can make things sound strange until you get used to it." He tugged the horse's reins slightly, and the three began their climb, snow still falling steadily around them from a low, swollen sky.

As Bell and Rosalee climbed the path toward Ben Finley's campfire inside the rock crevice, high above them Ben Finley struggled up over the lip of another protruding cliff and lay flat on his back for a second, staring straight up and gasping for breath. The climb had stretched his physical ability to its limits. The last few yards he'd had to stretch from one thin rock ledge to the next, snow and ice crunching and showering down around him.

"But . . . I made it," he gasped to himself. The dog stepped in and licked his face, its tail wagging in excitement. "Here now, cut that out!" Finley spit and rubbed his wet face. He had to shove the animal back, gently but firmly, before he could rise up onto his knees and look around the narrow rock ledge. As he looked, he slapped himself all over with his hat to free himself of snow and ice.

"My . . . what have we here?" He rose the rest of the way to his feet, panting, his breath still shallow, steaming wildly. He stared awestruck at the dog's paw prints leading into a high wall of what appeared to be solid rock. Beside him, the dog stood wagging its tail, as if pleased to have shown him the way. Ben Finley stepped forward to where the surface of the ledge curved downward beneath the rock wall. At the base of the rock he saw where the dog had dug away the snow, revealing a short crawl space of an entranceway.

"The cave!" Finley said, his heart suddenly leaping in his tired chest. He flung himself back down onto his knees in front of the black slice of darkness. His hands trembled as he pulled out his tin of matches and drew one from it. Before lying down flat to strike the match and see inside, he glanced back over his shoulder, then took on a puzzled expression. "But is this *the* cave?" he asked aloud. "The one I've been seeing?"

The dog cocked his head sideways in curiosity.

Ben Finley saw nothing familiar, nothing from the flashes and pieces of memories that had been taunting him all this time. But this was no time to stop. He turned back to the dark opening, lowered himself to his belly and crawled forward, the match out before him. When he'd crawled half of his body length into the darkness, he struck the match against the flat rock only inches above his head and almost reeled back in fright at what greeted him. Less than three feet from his face lay a human skeleton stretched out on its side, staring at him through empty black eye sockets.

"Scare the bejesus out of a fellow!" Ben Finley said softly to the dead calcium remnants. He only looked at the skeleton a second longer, noting the bits of rawhide and rags still clinging to the bare rib cage. One bony hand lay as if reaching forward toward the outside world, struggling toward the light of day. The other bony hand lay clasped to the breast bone, balled in a fist.

While he still had the light of the match, Ben Finley looked past the skeleton, seeing countless overlapping dog paw prints lead away into the pitch darkness. "That big cur has had his run of this place for a long time." Seeing the light of the match begin to dim as it drew closer to his fingers, Ben scooted backward out of the opening, shaking the match out as he went.

He sat in silence, looking at the dog, then glancing down at the opening where he knew there lay a dead man. He tried to get a picture of what had happened, but nothing came to him. "Was that your master, boy?" he asked the big cur. "Is that it? Something happened to your master, and you've been on your own out here ever since?" The dog only continued to stare curiously.

But in recalling the looks of the skeleton, Finley realized the man had been dead since long before this dog was born. It might have been the remains of some ancient Indian, Ben thought, pushing himself to his feet. He'd have to find out more when he went back inside. As he thought about it, he looked all around through the falling snow, judging how much daylight he had left. He would have to climb down to his campsite and prepare himself for what might be a long crawl deep into the belly of the mountain.

"Come on, dog," Ben said, trudging forward. But beside him the dog only whined quietly and appeared to want to linger near the entrance to the cave. Ben stopped and turned to where the dog stood, saying, "There's nothing here for you anymore, boy. You best come on with me."

But the dog would have none of it. He moved off away from the entrance and whined, coaxing Ben Finley to follow him. "Whatever you're trying to show me will have to wait till tomorrow, boy. I'm freezing my old bones up here." He turned once again and trudged through the snow. In a moment, when he didn't hear the dog's panting breath, he looked back over his shoulder. But the dog seemed to have vanished. Ben made a long, searching scan of the area but saw nothing of the animal. With the day slipping away from him, Ben knew he had to get down to the camp and warm himself. The dog, the cave and the treasure would have to wait.

On the ledge where Ben Finley had made his campsite, Rosalee wept to herself and gave silent thanks at the sight of the little mule's tail swishing back and forth just inside the crevice. "Father!" she called out as they walked closer, Jack leading Whiskey by the reins. "Father, it's us . . . Rosalee and Jack Bell!"

When no response came from the crevice, Bell stopped and took Rosalee by the arm. "You wait here; hold Whiskey for me while I make sure everything's all right." He put the reins in her gloved hand.

Rosalee stood tense, looking concerned as Bell walked forward and said, "Ben . . . it's me, Jack Bell. Rosalee and I came to make sure you're all right up here. Are you going to answer me?"

As Bell spoke, he looked all around the narrow ledge, laying his hand on his pistol butt. For all he knew, someone could have waylaid Ben Finley since the last time they'd seen his telltale boot print. Bell wanted to take no chances.

Pressing past the mule and into the crevice where the flames of the fire stood low but still flickering strong, Bell looked all around — enough to see that Ben Finley's supplies were there, but Ben wasn't. Then Bell backed outside. "It's his camp all right," said Bell. "But he's not in there. Looks like he's been gone for a while. The fire's just starting to burn itself down. I'd say he's been gone over an hour." He looked all around. "But which direction?"

"There's his tracks," said Rosalee, pointing over to a single boot print at the edge of the path leading up into the steep mountainside. She hurried over, letting Whiskey's reins fall to the snow. Jack Bell joined her, looking first down at the boot print then at another farther up the steep grade. "My goodness, what's he doing up there in all this snow?" Rosalee asked in a despondent tone, not looking for any reply.

"I don't know, Rosalee," Bell replied all the same, "but this time I am going alone. I need you to stay here with Whiskey and the mule and keep the fire going. I don't think we need to worry about that cat . . . but keep your pistol ready just in case."

"Yes, I understand. But please hurry, Jack," she said.

"Don't worry, Rosalee. I'm not planning on spending any more time on this mountainside than I have to, believe me." Bell looked at the steep slope, then shook his head. "Your father must have some mountain goat in him." He snuggled up his gloves and tugged his hat down tighter on his head.

Rosalee held her coat collar closed at the throat and watched Jack step up onto the deeply covered path. She remained in the same spot, staring after him in the falling snow until he'd climbed upward and disappeared around a steep turn. Then she turned and led Whiskey to the narrow crevice, where heat from the fire wavered in the cold air.

Before Bell had gone fifty yards, he saw a thin powder of snow sliding down from among the rocks above him. He stopped long enough to hear deep, heavy breathing a few feet up. "Ben," he called out. "Is that you?"

There was a silent pause, then Ben Finley said, "Yeah, it's me, Jack. What brings you up here?"

Bell noted a wariness to the old man's voice. "What do you think brings me up here, Ben? I'm looking for you." He smiled to himself and stepped upward toward the sound of Ben's voice.

"I'm not going back, if that's what you're thinking," Ben said.

"Sorry, Ben, but that is exactly what I'm thinking. No need in me beating around the bush about it. You've got no business up here."

Bell pulled himself up the path and stood against a snowcapped rock. He looked at where Ben Finley lay at the end of a three-foot slide in the snow. The old man struggled to right himself upward onto his knees.

"Dang it all!" Ben said, his breath rapidly pumping a trail of steam. "I made it this far. It'd be worse trying to turn back now than it would to go forward." As he spoke, he brushed snow from the seat of his trousers and from the leather satchel hanging from his shoulder.

Bell stepped forward, reached a hand out to the old man. Ben took his hand and pulled himself to his feet. "Rosalee is down at your camp, Ben. Let's get on down there and get warmed up some. Get ourselves some hot food and coffee. Then we can talk this over."

"Rosalee's down there?" said Ben. "What on earth did you mean bringing my daughter up here? This ain't no fit place for a young woman!"

Looking around at the snow and the rough, rocky terrain, Bell said, "This ain't no fit place for anybody, in case you haven't noticed. But I didn't bring her up here, Ben. She brought herself; I came with her. If I hadn't, she was going to come by herself all the same. Would that have suited you any better?"

Ben grumbled an answer under his breath. Then he looked back at Bell and said, "I expect she told you everything? About what happened to me up here last year? About the — ?" His words stopped short.

"About the gold?" Bell asked, finishing the old man's words for him. Seeing the instant look of concern in Ben's eyes, Bell added quickly, "Don't worry, Ben, I have no interest in your gold, if there is any."

"Oh?" Ben eyed him suspiciously. "Well, what if I was to tell you that there danged sure is gold? That I just found the very spot where I stood last year when I first found it?"

Bell studied his eyes, seeing the old man was serious. "I'd still say we need to get some hot coffee and food in us, Ben," said Bell.

"See? You don't believe me, do you?" Ben snapped.

"Take it easy, Ben," said Bell. "Right now, I don't know if I believe you or not. But I do know that if we freeze to the side of this mountain, it's not going to matter whether or not you've found any gold."

"But I did find it! I did!" Ben grabbed the front of Jack Bell's coat, desperate to be believed. "Don't you see? If I leave here this time, I might never find it again!"

"Settle down," said Bell, peeling the old man's hands from his coat. "You mean to tell me that you just came right up here, went straight to the spot you'd found before? After all this time, not having any idea where it was? How did you manage such a thing, Ben?"

"I'll tell you how," said Ben. "A big wild dog showed me the way!" As soon as Ben said it, he glanced around for any sign of the dog, knowing that without the dog, his whole story sounded like the ravings of a madman.

"A wild dog, huh?" said Bell, looking around with him. When Bell looked back at the old man's face, he remained respectful but couldn't conceal his doubt. "Where is this dog, Ben?"

"Well . . . he just ain't here right now. But he'll be coming directly. He likes to sleep close to a fire at night."

"A wild dog who likes to sleep in a campsite?" Bell asked, still being respectful.

Ben Finley raised his hat and ran his hand back nervously through his gray hair. "I know how this sounds. I know how bad this looks on me. But you'll see! There is a dog around here!" Once again he searched the steep mountainside, then desperately scanned the snowy ground for any prints. A confused look came to his face, as if he might be doubting himself.

Bell saw what he was doing and said

gently, "This dog you're talking about doesn't leave much sign, does he, Ben?"

Ben looked all around again, then said, "The snow already covered what few tracks he left! He came up here ahead of me; then the snow got worse!" Wide-eyed, he pointed off across the steep slope, saying, "There's tracks out there though . . . if the snow hasn't already got to them. I swear there are!"

Jack Bell felt sorry for the old man and placed a gloved hand on his shoulder as he replied to him. "That's all right, Ben. Don't worry about it right now."

"But it's true, Jack. I haven't lost my mind. I saw the dog plain as day," said Ben.

"I'm not disputing your word, Ben," said Bell. "Right now, the most important thing for us to do is get down to your campsite, out of this snow. Come on, Rosalee's stoking up the fire. She's waiting for us."

But Ben stood firm. "All right then. I'll go to the campsite, but I'm not leaving this mountainside. Not now. I've found the place where I was last year, Jack. I know I have. I can feel it in my bones."

"Ben, I hope you have," said Bell. "But I came with Rosalee to find you and bring you home. If Rosalee wants to stay up here and help you search for your gold, I'll stay too.

That's a promise. But this is a family matter between the two of you. It's not my place to butt in."

"You're not mad at me for taking your mule?" Ben studied his eyes for a second. Seeing that Jack harbored no ill feelings, he said, "I knew you was a fair man the first time I laid eyes on you, Jack. I'll tell Rosalee what I've found up there. She and I will have to work this out on our own." He stepped forward in the falling snow. Before following the path downward, he added, "Jack, I'm grateful you came along with Rosalee. I won't forget you for it."

Jack Bell only nodded. "Come on, let's go get warm."

CHAPTER 13

Halfway down the side of the mountain, the smell of boiling coffee rose up to them. The aroma, and the thought of hot food and coffee awaiting them, seemed to make Ben Finley move a little faster. By the time he and Jack Bell had climbed down to the campsite, Rosalee had put Whiskey close to the side of the mountain, out of the cold air and falling snow. She'd grained and watered the horse and slipped his saddle from his back. The saddle lay inside the crevice near the fire. Rosalee had taken off her gun belt and laid it against the saddle. She sat stooped beside the fire, stirring beans she'd cooked in a pot from her father's supplies.

The mule had moved farther inside the crevice to escape the falling snow on its rump. But now that the fire was burning higher and the snowfall had all but stopped, the mule had backed away from the heat. At the sound of Jack Bell's voice outside, Rosalee left the big spoon in the pot and hurried, pushing the mule to one side enough for her to get past it. As soon as she saw Jack Bell and her father trudging toward her, she ran to them.

Bell stood to the side and watched her wipe tears from her eyes and throw her arms around her father. Then Bell moved away from them and over to where Whiskey stood against the rock wall. He looked the horse over, hearing Rosalee chastise her father soundly for slipping away and causing so much trouble. Bell busied himself with the horse rather than have Ben Finley embarrassed by seeing him standing nearby, listening.

"It's a family matter," Jack whispered to the horse, turning its head back to him when it tried to look toward the sound of Rosalee's raised voice twenty yards away. "Let's tend to our own business." He ran a gloved hand on Whiskey's jaw and kept his head turned away from the Finleys.

Rosalee sounded firm with her father but not harsh or abusive, Jack Bell noted to himself. Ben Finley had committed a thoughtless act. He deserved to be told what his actions had cost. A good horse was dead because of him. It could have been a human, Jack reminded himself. It could even have been Ben's own daughter. But it wasn't, Bell said to himself, and he managed a thin smile. He was glad to hear that Rosalee wasn't being too hard on the old man. Ben

Finley's intentions had been honorable, if foolish.

Bell stayed beside his horse until after Rosalee and her father had walked inside the crevice. A moment passed. Then Rosalee stuck her head out and called to him, "Jack, come get some food and coffee. Aren't you hungry?"

"Thought you'd never ask," Bell whispered under his breath. Before going inside to eat though, Bell led Whiskey over to the crevice, backed the mule out, put the horse in its place, then crowded the mule in behind it. The mule brayed in protest and nosed forward until it managed to get squeezed in almost as far as it had been, only now it stood pressed between a horse and the rock wall. "Gripe all you want to," Bell said to the mule. "Just don't fight."

Inside the small, cramped campsite, the three ate and drank hot coffee. Ben Finley gulped his food and hurriedly told Rosalee and Jack Bell everything that had happened. Bell watched how Rosalee listened respectfully yet remained detached as her father grew more and more excited. As he'd told her the part about the wild dog, Rosalee shot Bell a guarded glance, then returned her attention to her father.

Ben Finley had risen to his feet when he

finished his story. He paced back and forth restlessly on the few narrow feet of dirt. Finally he stopped and firmly slapped his hand against the rock wall. "I know if I had just gone down in that cave with some light, I would be standing in the midst of that fortune right this minute!"

"Father," said Rosalee in a gentle but firm tone, "we're going home. First thing in the morning, after a good night's sleep, we're going back to Nolan's Gap and put this incident out of our minds. Mr. Bell was kind enough to come along and help me. We shan't impose on him any further."

Both Rosalee and her father turned their eyes to Jack Bell. He lowered his coffee cup from his lips and said, "It's no imposition on me one way or the other. I told you I'd help you find your father . . . and we have found him. Whether or not we go right back to Nolan's Gap or spend a little extra time here is up to you two."

"Jack, that's not very helpful," said Rosalee. "It sounds almost as if you're encouraging him to stay up here!"

"No," said Bell. "I'm not encouraging him to stay. I'm just saying that whatever you two decide, I'll abide with. He's right for wanting to stay and find his lost treasure. You're right, wanting him to come home where it's safe and warm."

Rosalee and Ben Finley stared at Bell in silence for a moment. Then, turning to her father, Rosalee said in quiet resolve, "If I thought for a moment that you'd found your lost treasure up there, don't you think I'd want you to go back for it, Father?" Before Ben could answer, Rosalee said, "Yes, of course I would — I know how much this means to you." She stepped over closer to her father and ran her hand back across his disheveled hair. Her voice became soothing. "This is all in your mind, Father. There was no mysterious wild dog . . . no cave beneath the snow. I don't mean to sound cruel, but you have to realize: This is something that you've created instead of facing the fact that it's all a fantasy."

"No," Ben Finley said. "There is a cave up there. There was a wild dog too." But his voice had begun to lack conviction. Looking down, ashamed, his confidence slipping away from him until he began even doubting himself, he said meekly, "How can a person's mind see something so clear . . . only to find out it's all a made-up thing?"

In the following silence, Rosalee turned to Jack Bell as if he might know what would help. "Jack, am I being unreasonable?"

Rosalee asked, her eyes glistening with tears.

Jack stood up slowly and finished the last drink from his cup of coffee. "I told you, I think both of you are right in what you want. If I were King Solomon, I'd say leave it up to the wild dog."

"What?" Ben Finley and Rosalee both looked at him.

"Ben, you're convinced a dog was up there with you," Bell continued. "But nobody besides you has seen it." Bell looked from Ben to Rosalee, then said, "If there is a dog, then there's also a chance the rest of what he's told you really happened."

"All right," Rosalee agreed, "but then what? How will we know there's a dog?"

"If this dog shows up between now and morning, when we're ready to head down, then you agree to Ben and me going back up there and having a look around. Fair enough?"

"Well, yes. I suppose so," Rosalee replied, still seeming to consider it.

Bell turned to Ben Finley. "If no dog shows up by then, will you agree to go back to Nolan's Gap and never do something like this again?"

Ben Finley wasn't ready to give in. "But what if something has happened to the dog, and he can't make it back down here? I still saw the cave in the ground! I can't walk away from this."

"Sorry, Ben. That's the deal. Rosalee agreed to her side of it," said Bell.

Ben Finley rubbed his neck in exasperation, then said, "All right, all right, I'll go along with it. Either the dog shows up before we leave in the morning or else we go home and I forget about it." Now he looked back and forth between Rosalee and Jack Bell. "Satisfied now?" he asked them both. Then, to Rosalee, he said, "It ain't as if I want this treasure for myself, you know. This is for you, Daughter . . . to make life a little easier on you. To buy you those pretty things like all young women want."

"Father, wait," said Rosalee, seeing Ben turn away from the fire and walk outside, pressing his back to the rock wall to get past the mule.

When Ben didn't look back or acknowledge her, Rosalee started forward after him. But Jack Bell stopped her with a hand on her forearm. "Give him a few minutes alone, Rosalee," he said. "He'll see that this is the only fair way to do it. Dreams can be hard to turn loose."

"I hope we've done the right thing," Rosalee said. "He's going to be so disap-

210

pointed when we start back home in the morning."

"Yes, but at least we turned it into a gentleman's agreement. He's an honorable man; he'll want to keep his end of the deal. Any other way it would have just been you and me forcing our will on him. This doesn't take away his self-respect."

"Yes," said Rosalee, "I saw what you were doing when you presented the idea. One thing I can say for my father: If he gives his word, he will keep it. I'm the same way." She offered a thin smile. "It must be true: The apple doesn't fall far from the tree."

Jack Bell didn't respond. Instead, he sat back down and poured himself more coffee, then gave Rosalee a curious look as he settled back against his saddle on the ground.

The dog moved sleek and easy through the night, his senses electrified by the darkness. The deathlike quiet surrounding him endowed him with a power akin to the supernatural. He heard through the silence the soft brush of hooves against the stiff snow as an elk ventured into the moonlight. He heard the strong, quiet batting of wings as an owl swooped down in search of small prey. These things he heard above his own panting breath, above his running, above the pounding of his heart.

His body was well-fueled, not only by the food the man had given him earlier, but also from the fresh kill of a rabbit. Tonight he ran with more reckless abandon than usual. Being with the man had piqued his senses and made him restless and unsettled. For many months now, he'd gone without the fresh scent of humankind either on or near him. He had not felt the touch of man's hand or heard the command of man's voice or bathed himself in the luxury of man's warming fire. Man had become vague in his memory. He did not even realize that he'd missed these things, for his intellect afforded him no such perception.

The dog had no knowledge of the countless thousand years past that had bonded his species to man. He did not think about man these months on his own as he'd prowled and ranged, reclaimed by the elements of the wild. He did not recognize the ache and the longing inside him for those things to which he'd grown accustomed as if in some distant life altogether. He only felt drawn to the man who came upon his mountain bearing familiar scent and sound and animation. Without realizing, he ran tonight to purge himself, to free himself of what he'd become and prepare himself somehow in anticipation of where destiny would lead.

On the upper ledge, he stopped and toed gracefully but warily forward to a point where he caught the rising scent of wood smoke and humans: of their foods, their animals and all vestiges of their being. He was drawn to these scents, and yet he hesitated. Here he reigned, the sole leader of his solitary realm. Without the ability to reason it, he knew instinctively, as all of his pack ancestors had known, that to live with man he must become supplicant to man.

As he stood on the high ledge looking down upon the glow of firelight shining through the thin top of the rock crevice, he caught another scent, this one distant yet strong and full of foreboding. The scent came adrift on the air from across the breast of the mountainside, and upon breathing it in, the dog lowered slightly in his shoulders, turning in its direction. Although the big cat was over a mile away, the dog's senses brought clearly into his mind the fierce padded paws rising and falling across the snow and the night like the steady oncoming certainty of death.

The dog's hackles rose. Pale moonlight shone on his bared fangs as he growled low and menacing toward the scent of the cat.

With no further hesitancy, the big cur spun from the jagged rock edge in a flurry of fur and snow and raced downward from his lofty perch toward the glowing campsite far beneath him.

An hour later, inside the campsite, Jack Bell awakened as he felt the shadow of Ben Finley fall across him then slip away into the night. Rising from his blanket, Bell looked over at Rosalee's sleeping face in the flicker of firelight. Then he pulled on his boots and wrapped the blanket around his shoulders. Picking up his hat and rifle, he eased out alongside Whiskey and squeezed his way past the mule.

"What's the matter?" Ben Finley asked, seeing Bell emerge into the moonlight and walk toward him. "Afraid I'd take off in the middle of the night?"

"Not at all, Ben," said Bell, his rifle cradled in his arm. "I know you're a man of your word. I just walked out for a breath of air, same as you."

"I'll be honest about it," said Ben. "I didn't come out for a breath of air. I came out looking for that dog." He offered Jack Bell a tired smile.

"That's what I figured," Bell said, returning the smile. "I'll be honest too — I came out hoping you'd find him."

"But you're betting I won't, aren't you?" Ben asked.

"I'm not betting either way, Ben," said Bell. "Nothing would make me happier than to see you and Rosalee walk back to Nolan's Gap with a mule loaded down with gold."

"That's me and Rosalee," said Ben. "But what about you? If you're along when we find it, far as I'm concerned you're in for a part."

"No thanks," said Bell. He looked away across the night, the dark land below.

"No? Just like that?" Ben asked. "You turn down what could be a fortune in gold? I'm afraid you'll have to explain that kind of thinking to me, Jack Bell. I don't understand it at all." Ben shook his head. "They call me crazy, but danged if you don't sound about as —"

"All right, I'm in for a part," said Jack Bell, cutting him off with a smile. Rather than have to explain himself, Bell shrugged and said, "You're right. I'd be a fool to turn it down."

Ben gave him a wizened, curious look. "Now you're just going along with me, ain't ya?"

Bell started to reply, but then he stopped. Something had caught his attention near the edge of the trail, and he tried focusing on it in the darkness. From the crevice, Whiskey let out a low nicker as if in warning. Bell gave a quick glance at the glow of light where the horse and mule stood. The mule stood silent, but with his long ears peaked. Whiskey stomped a hoof and crowded closer to the mule. Bell's eyes went back to the darkness at the edge of the trail.

"What is it?" Ben whispered. He moved closer beside Jack Bell and added, "I knew I should have carried that LeMat with me."

Above the trail, the dog stood in dead silence, but with his hackles high and his teeth slightly bared. He'd felt the scent of the cat grow closer as he'd made his way down the mountainside. When he'd neared the flat ledge where the campsite glowed, he'd swung wide and silent around the crouching cat that sat staring at the two men on the ledge. The dog had made the circle, openly giving the cat his scent, making ready for battle with no regard for the element of surprise. His style would be canine: savage, brutal, swift and straightforward.

With a flick of its tail, the cat spun to face the dog, still crouched, poised for battle but not welcoming it. The cat had not come to fight, but rather to feed. What the cat discerned from the dog was something foreign and confusing to the nature of the feline. The dog was here to fight for the sake of fighting, to defend for the sake of defense. The smell of both the dog and the aroused fury within the dog spoke clearly the dog's intention.

The cat gave no ground yet was by no means game for battle. The dog sensed it. It was not fear the dog sensed. It was reluctance, and he knew through instinct to play upon that reluctance. He stepped forward, staying low on his front paws. He stopped again and this time growled so low under his breath that the cat almost sensed the sound rather than heard it.

The cat arose out of its crouch, taking a backward step. Its head cocked low to one side, a sign of submission that the dog understood. A low purr oozed from the cat's chest.

The dog froze midstep and allowed the big cat to back away silent and slow until at length, with the flick of its tail, the night swallowed it. The dog looped along in the cat's path, partly following, partly ushering it away from the campsite below.

"Did you hear it, Ben?" Jack Bell whispered. He kept his thumb across the rifle hammer.

"No," Ben whispered hoarsely, "I never

heard a thing. What's it sound like? It's not the dog, is it? Lord, I hope it is!"

Bell didn't answer right away. He stared at the mountainside above the campsite. Finally he said, "I think it might be best if we keep a guard posted the rest of the night. I just had one of them strange feelings."

"What kind of feeling?" Ben asked.

Still studying the mountainside and the wild terrain surrounding them, Jack Bell said, "The kind of feeling like something just stepped over my grave."

CHAPTER 14

Throughout the night, the two men shared guard duty between them without waking Rosalee. Bell spent the night on the cusp of sleep but never fully gave into it. Even while Ben Finley kept watch over the campsite and the animals, Bell found himself opening his eyes every few minutes just to keep tabs on the old man. He trusted Ben Finley but not completely — certainly not enough to go soundly to sleep while Ben stood guard. There were few men Jack Bell would trust that much.

He liked Ben, yet the fact remained that the man had stolen his mule and run away from town with no word to anyone. With a big killing cat out there prowling somewhere, trust was something Jack Bell couldn't afford right then. When he heard Ben's lowered voice, Bell opened his eyes and looked at him, seeing that the old man was talking to himself.

"Come on, boy. I know you're out there. I know you want to come in here where it's warm." Sitting beside the fire but facing away from it toward the outside darkness past the horse and the mule, Ben Finley whispered aloud as if the dog could hear him across the frozen earth.

Without making any movement or sound, Bell looked around the crowded area, making a check for his own satisfaction. Upon seeing Whiskey and the mule crowded into the front of the crevice, and seeing Rosalee fast asleep across the fire from him, Bell closed his eyes once again and dozed lightly. The next time he opened his eyes, he saw that Ben Finley was no longer sitting by the fire. He rose quickly to his feet, this time with his boots still on from when he'd gone outside earlier. Putting on his hat and picking up his rifle, he snatched his blanket from the dirt and wrapped it around himself as he went. He pushed his way past the animals, not knowing what to expect outside in the cold hour before dawn.

As Bell stepped out into the freezing air, Ben Finley turned toward him from where he stood looking out longingly across the night. In the thin gray of morning, Ben saw the expression on Bell's face and said, "I'm still here, Jack. I just came out to fill the coffeepot and get myself some fresh air is all." He nodded down at the coffeepot sitting in the snow, but then his eyes couldn't keep from searching the darkness up along the ridges above them.

Bell settled even more and let out a breath. "Looking for the dog?" Bell stepped over, stooped down and picked up the coffeepot. Ben had already filled the pot with packed-down snow.

"Well . . . can you blame me?" asked Ben, still scanning the grainy darkness.

"No, I suppose not," said Bell. "If I was in your situation, I reckon I'd be feeling the same way."

"I thought I heard something far off a while ago," said Ben Finley. "That's really why I came out here." His eyes searched the upper ledges as he spoke. "I couldn't make out if it was the dog or a pack of wolves. Whatever it was sounded like it was in trouble. I hope nothing's happened to that dog."

Jack Bell only stared at him, wondering if this was his way to try to buy some extra time.

Ben turned his eyes to Bell. Seeing the look on Bell's face, he said with a touch of desperation in his voice, "Oh, he'll show up. I know he will."

Bell studied his face for a moment longer, then said, "It's going to be daylight pretty soon, Ben. Time to get under way. Is everything going to be all right?"

"I gave you and Rosalee my word," Ben said indignantly. "Of course everything is going to be all right. I might be old. I might even be a little bit crazy . . . but my word is still worth as much as the next man's."

"I know it, Ben," Jack Bell said. "Just checking." He closed the lid on the coffeepot with finality. As he turned back to the crevice, he said over his shoulder, "I'll get a pot of coffee started and wake Rosalee. Are you coming in?"

"I'll be right along," Ben said. "I'll go break us up some wood first." He nodded at a twisted pile of snow-covered brush along the icy ledge. Turning back toward the wide, grainy darkness, Ben's eyes searched even more intently as he whispered low under his breath, "Where are you, boy?" Silence loomed.

Inside the crevice, moments later, Rosalee sat up with her blanket wrapped around her and saw Jack Bell hunkered down, stoking up the fire with fresh kindling. He looked at her as he poked the kindling into a bed of glowing coals beneath the snow-filled coffeepot.

"Morning," said Jack, touching his fingertips to his wide hat brim.

"Morning," Rosalee replied. Immediately her eyes darted around the crevice.

"Where's my father?"

"Don't worry; he's fine," said Bell. He watched fire flare upward from the glowing coals and spring to life on the kindling. "I take it there hasn't been any dog showing up?" Rosalee said.

"Nope," said Bell. "No dog. I don't think that surprises you any."

Rosalee sighed. "Poor Father. Does he seem too awfully disappointed?"

"Ben's doing all right," said Bell. "He knows he gave his word, and he's prepared to keep it. Can't ask more than that from a man, can we?"

"No, we can't," Rosalee said quietly.

Having taken his gloves off, Bell rubbed his hands together above the flames and said, "Your father is a very lucky man, having somebody care about him the way you do."

Rosalee detected a loneliness in his voice, and for a second she didn't reply. Finally she said, "Yes, he and I are fortunate to have one another." She wrapped her blanket around her shoulders and moved close to the fire, beside Bell. She wanted to ask him about himself, realizing just how little she actually knew about this man. Did he have family? A wife, children perhaps? She studied his profile in the flickering firelight as he warmed his hands above the low, dancing flames. Just as she was about to ask him, he began speaking as if having heard the questions in her mind.

"My folks died when I was only a kid. I was too young to remember them," he said. "I grew up in an orphanage."

"Oh, I'm sorry," Rosalee said.

"Ah, it wasn't so bad. We got enough to eat most times. The Jesuits ran the place. They were hard but fair enough, I suppose. No different than life's been." He gave a thin smile, looking into the fire as he spoke. "So I've got no complaints." He stirred a short stick in the coals. "I used to wonder how it would be though, having a dad, a mom, maybe some brothers and sisters that were truly kin to me, not just some other kids that landed on the same spot as me, needing a home."

There was something in his words and voice that melted the rigid, no-nonsense appearance she tried so hard to maintain about herself. For a moment she felt compelled to reach out and lay her hand on his forearm. She almost did. But then at the last second she caught herself and lowered her hand. "What about other family?" she asked. "Do you have a family waiting somewhere for you?"

"No," Bell said quietly, shaking his head

slowly as he continued gazing into the fire. "It's just me." He glanced at her, then back to the fire. "If I had a woman and children waiting for me somewhere, do you think I'd be out here? Living on the trail, from pillar to post?"

"Well . . . I just meant that perhaps you were out here seeking your place in the world, as men often do for a time." His words seemed to unsettle Rosalee a bit. She raised a hand to her hair nervously as if checking to see if it were properly in place. "I hope you don't think I meant to imply that you are some sort of shiftless, misguided drifter —"

"No, ma'am, Rosalee," Bell said, cutting her off. "I didn't think that at all." His gaze returned to the fire.

"I do realize that a man must often go off in search of his fortune," Rosalee added.

"Yes, I understood what you meant," said Bell. "But if I ever had a wife and family, believe me, Rosalee, that would be my fortune in itself. I wouldn't need to go running off looking for any more in life."

Quietly, as if reflecting, Rosalee said, "Many men say that, Jack. But I wonder how many really mean it. Sometimes I think it a man's nature to always want to go see what's beyond the next horizon. If that's so, how can a woman and children compete with something so strong?"

"I don't know about other men, but it's not my nature," said Bell. "I know it must look like it. I have a reputation for being a drifter . . . but it wasn't my choosing. It just seemed to happen to me." His trace of a smile appeared again. "Strange, I suppose, how some men want to chase off after whatever's around the next turn, but they never get to do it. Me, I never cared about it . . . yet it seems like that's all I ever do."

Rosalee seemed to consider the irony of what he said, then offered in a gentle tone, "Well, someday you'll get to settle down, Jack . . . and have a family of your own, a home of your own. It just takes longer for some men to find themselves than it does others."

"Find myself?" A short silence passed. Then he said, "I never considered myself lost."

Before Rosalee could answer, Ben Finley came pushing his way past the animals, carrying an armload of dried twigs and short pieces of juniper and spruce deadfall. Dropping the wood close to the fire, Ben said, "I could have sworn I heard a dog last night. It sounded like it was in pain."

Rosalee and Bell both gave him a dubious

look. "All right," Ben said. "I know what you're thinking, but I swear I heard it."

"Father, we're going home," said Rosalee.

Ben relented, stooping down beside Bell and warming his hands over the fire. "I know . . . we're going home," he repeated in defeat.

Rosalee and Bell passed one another a guarded glance. "Why don't I just warm us up some beef," said Bell. "We'll have ourselves a short breakfast and get a good early start."

As Jack Bell reached for the tin skillet, at the front of the crevice the mule began braying loudly and kicking its rear hooves high. Whiskey neighed and pressed against the rock wall, also ready to do some kicking. Bell dropped the skillet and snatched up his rifle. He advanced on the kicking mule, cocking his rifle hammer and looking for the cause of all the trouble. A flurry of fur rolled beneath the mule's hooves and let out a yelp, trying to avoid being trampled. Ben Finley heard the sound and came running up beside Bell. "Don't shoot!" he cried and shoved Bell's rifle upward. "It's the dog!"

Bell caught himself in time and held his shot. He eased the hammer down with his thumb, seeing the dog limp forward a step then fall gasping against the rock wall, still too close to the mule but unable to do anything about it. Ben Finley ran forward and grabbed the mule by its lead rope. "Whoa now," he called out, taking a firm hand with the frightened animal, calming it. The mule settled quickly. Ben shoved it away with a hand on its bony rump. Bell had started to step forward and pick the injured dog up, but Ben cautioned him back. "He doesn't know you, Jack. You best let me get him."

"Sure thing, Ben." Bell watched, his rifle hanging loose in his hand.

Ben scooped the dog up in his arms and ran back to the fireside with it. "He's hurt pretty bad!" he said.

"I'll say he is," Bell replied. He winced at the sight of the dog's ribs glistening white along his side where four claws had sliced him to the bone. Blood had matted in the dog's fur, then frozen, stopping the flow enough to prolong his life. "Put him here near the fire, Ben." As Bell spoke, he jerked up his spare blanket and spread it on the dirt.

Rosalee stood back, but only for a second, watching over Bell and her father's shoulder as they examined the dog's wounds. The dog shivered uncontrollably and whined low and pitifully. "I'll get some snow for hot water," Rosalee said. She picked up the tin skillet and hurried out of the crevice. The animals had settled, but the mule still brayed in protest as she shoved her way past him. Whiskey stood watching calmly.

"So this is the dog, Ben?" Bell said, probing a finger to a thick layer of dark blood on the dog's head. The dog lowered its head, wary of this strange man yet knowing it needed help.

"Yep, it's him," Ben said. "How many other wild dogs do you suppose are running loose up here?" He managed a smile, running a hand along the dog's bloody head. "See, I told you both I'm not imagining things." Seeing the dog's uneasiness at their excited voices, and at being in their hands and at their mercy, Ben lowered his voice and said to the dog, "Don't worry, boy. We're not going to hurt you. We're going to fix you up and make you feel better."

"Looks like the cat got him," Bell said, also lowering his voice as he checked the shivering dog over for any more wounds. He'd already told Ben about the incident with the cat and the horse.

"That must have been what I heard," said Ben, still comforting the dog as he spoke. "I bet he would have come on in last night like I said if he hadn't tangled with that panther and got himself hurt."

"No doubt you're right, Ben," said Bell, happy for the old man, hearing the difference in his tone of voice, seeing a renewed spark of confidence in his aging eyes. "Who knows? Your friend here might be the only thing kept that cat from making a run at us and our animals last night. There's no telling what this boy might have saved us."

"Is he going to be all right, you think?" Ben asked with a concerned look.

"I think he'll make it," said Bell. "He lost some blood before his fur matted up. That helped him some. He's pretty cold. Probably came mighty near to just laying down somewhere and freezing to death."

"He likes fire," said Ben. "That's what kept him coming. He knew if he could make it to this campsite he'd be all right."

Rosalee came back in carrying the snow-filled skillet. She sat it down over the hot coals and looked at the shivering animal. Flecks of ice and snow had melted on the dog's face, giving it a sad, miserable appearance. "I carry a needle and some thread in my saddlebags," she said. "I'll get them."

As the snow in the skillet quickly melted above the hot coals, Rosalee went to the saddlebags sitting in the dirt beside Jack's saddle. Along with the needle and thread, she brought back a white cotton cloth that she had neatly folded and placed in the bags for just such an emergency. Jack Bell and Ben Finley worked on the dog, carefully cleaning and inspecting the four slashes on his ribs, a long, fierce cut that had left his right ear separated down the middle and a lesser cut across the top of his right foot. The dog lay docile and obliging, watching the two men attend him.

"That panther showed you no mercy," Jack said aloud to the dog, swabbing his foot with the cloth dipped in warm water. "I'd like to think you killed him before it was over, but I expect that's not the case."

The dog whined as if in agreement. Rosalee kneeled and stroked the animal's wet, scraggly head. The dog settled down and seemed more at ease beneath the woman's touch. Soon the shivering subsided. When Bell and the old man had finished cleaning the dog's wounds and fresh blood began to ooze freely from the gashes on the dog's side, Jack looked up at the other two with a threaded needle between his thumb and finger. "You might have to hold him down while I do this."

"I'll hold him for you, Jack," Ben volunteered. He gave his daughter a quick glance, a satisfied smile coming to his weathered face. "If this ole boy hadn't showed up when he did, I might never have been able to search for my treasure."

Rosalee sighed and leaned in closer, taking a good look at the wounded dog. "All right, Father. I admit it. You weren't imagining it. You did meet a big wild dog up there. But that doesn't mean you're going to find any gold."

"No, it doesn't," Ben said. "But this dog showing up when he did means I at least get a chance to go look." He looked back and forth between the two of them as Jack prepared himself for the task of sewing up the dog's wounds. "After all, I kept my end of our agreement. I was ready to leave here this morning and not look back if things hadn't turned out the way they have. A deal is a deal."

"You're right, Father: A deal is a deal," said Rosalee. She gave Jack Bell a glance. "I gave my word, and I'll keep it. We'll go back up and search for your gold."

"It might be a while before this fellow does any climbing on those high ridges," said Bell. He reached down and patted the wounded dog's head. Then he nodded for Ben to hold the animal so he could begin his needlework.

Rosalee and her father both watched

closely, Rosalee noting how steady Jack Bell's hand remained throughout the procedure. Holding the warm, wet cloth, Rosalee reached in every few minutes and blotted blood out of the way so Bell could see what he was doing. The dog tried to rise up at the first sting of the needle, but Ben held him down gently yet firmly. The loss of blood had already weakened the animal and to a great extent even dulled the sensation of pain. In moments the dog lay still and allowed Bell to go about his work. "You're a brave ole cur," Bell said, patting the dog's side gently.

Once he'd finished stitching the dog's side wounds, Rosalee held the split ear in place while Bell sewed it together. "That'll have to do," said Jack Bell, wiping sweat from his forehead. "He'll never win a prize for looks, but I don't think he'll worry about that." As weak and sore as the dog was, he still managed to roll up off his side and stand shakily, looking at the three faces gathered over him.

They watched, holding their breath as the dog found his balance and struggled in place for a second. Then he stepped over closer to the fire, lay down stiffly and curled up into a ball. The stitches showed fresh and fierce in the glow of firelight. "See?"

said Ben Finley. "He likes a warm fire. He hasn't always been wild."

Seeing the look of contentment on the old man's face as he reached forward and patted the dog's head, Bell and Rosalee gave one another a guarded smile.

PART 2

CHAPTER 15

Max Brumfield and Dolly Lisko had just returned from eating a hot supper at the only restaurant in Nolan's Gap when Black Moe Bainbridge led the riders in off the trail. The heavily armed, grim-looking procession lined their horses along both hitch rails out front of the Western Palace. Three days earlier, they had made camp at the place where Delbert Hanks had thrown snow over Fleetus Gibbs' body the day he'd killed him. But hungry wolves had followed the scent of blood as soon as Delbert Hanks had ridden out of sight. With little effort, the wolves had dug up Gibbs' body and devoured it on the spot, leaving only torn bits of clothing, a hat and one chewed-up boot.

"I've seen all I want to see," Black Moe Bainbridge had said to the others, standing in a circle of beaten-down, bloodstained snow where the feeding frenzy had taken place. Staring long and hard in the direction of Nolan's Gap, he added, "Even Fleetus deserved better than this." Bloody paw prints led off in every direction. Bainbridge had carried the grizzly scene in his mind from there to Nolan's Gap, paying almost no attention to the spot where Delbert had buried Rance Hardaway.

"If that murdering sumbitch is here, boys," Black Moe said to the line of dismounting riders, "I want the first taste of his blood myself." He stepped down from his saddle carrying Fleetus Gibbs' ragged hat wadded up in his left hand. Inside the hat he'd stuffed a short remnant of one of Gibbs' badly gnawed arm bones.

At the sight of the riders, Dolly Lisko slipped around behind the bar to help Stanley Barger serve the oncoming clientele. Max Brumfield stood smoking a cigar as Black Moe and the others crowded in through the doors. "Welcome to the Western Palace, gentlemen," Brumfield said, making an obliging gesture with his hand. "Where your pleasure is *our* pleasure."

"Save your welcomes for somebody who really gives a blue flying damn, Brumfield," said Black Moe, stopping at the bar rail, looking all around and pitching Gibbs' hat and arm bone onto the bar. He pulled off his leather gloves one finger at a time while the rest of the men lined along the bar on either side of him.

Before Max Brumfield could respond,

Dewey Sadlo, standing beside Bainbridge, said, "In case you don't know it, Brumfield, this is Black Moe Bainbridge."

"Oh?" Max said coolly, looking Black Moe up and down. "I've never had the honor of meeting you, but I've heard a lot about you."

"Who do I have to smack upside the head to get some whiskey flowing in this dump?" Gannerd Woodsworth said, leaning slightly across the bar toward big Stanley Barger. The big bartender didn't back an inch. He stood poised with a whiskey bottle ready to pour.

"You can start with me," said Stanley, "but you ain't going to like the outcome."

"Boys, boys," said Dolly, stepping in and setting shot glasses along the bar. "All this does is keep everybody waiting." She passed a quick glance along the cold, pinched faces of the men.

"Come on, Gannerd. She's right. Leave the man alone and let him pour!" Red Tony called out.

As Gannerd relented and settled down, Stanley eyed him closely and filled his shot glass. Then Stanley filled the glass in front of Black Moe Bainbridge and moved along behind the bar pouring shot after shot in turn. Bainbridge tossed back his shot of whiskey, then turned back to Max Brumfield. "You'll find we're a spirited bunch, Brumfield. But well-mannered so long as you don't cross us."

"I wouldn't dream of crossing you, sir" — Max Brumfield smiled, still cool, taking a long draw on his cigar — "so long as you're spending lots of money. You'll find me most accommodating."

"Good then," said Bainbridge, pushing his shot glass forward for a refill. "Because I'm here to kill one no-good murdering sumbitch name of Jack Bell." He drew his big Walker Colt from his holster and checked it as he spoke. "So without any further ado, where the hell is he?"

Max Brumfield's expression turned serious. "I don't know where he is," he lied. "He's been gone for a long time. Fact is, I heard him say something about going to San Francisco. Knows a woman who runs a boardinghouse there, he said."

"Oh, I see. A boardinghouse, huh?" Black Moe gave him a doubtful look. "Boys," he said over his shoulder, "finish your drinks and go turn this town upside down. Bring me anybody that looks like he *might* be Jack Bell." He looked back at Max Brumfield and said, "If you say he's gone, he better be gone. I hate a liar." All the men left except

Delbert Hanks, who still stood at the end of the bar.

"I told you Jack Bell is gone, and I meant it," said Brumfield.

Black Moe studied Brumfield's eyes for a second. "Gone where?" he asked bluntly. "Don't say San Francisco again, or I'll get awfully cross." The big Colt relaxed sideways in Brumfield's direction. Bainbridge's thumb lay across the hammer, showing Brumfield he was ready to cock it if need be. "Ain't nothing I hate worse than hearing the same lie twice in a row."

"What makes you think I try to keep up with every ragged-assed miner who happens through here with a plug mule on the end of a string?" said Brumfield.

"Don't get yourself started off on a bad note with me, Brumfield," said Bainbridge. "Early Philpot told me this man Bell is a poker player. That means you know something about him and his comings and goings."

"Philpot, huh?" said Brumfield. "I might have guessed his greasy handprints were on this thing. I know that Bell won some money off him. I suppose that's all it takes to get a man killed these days. You call that a fair shake?"

"I don't call it one way or the other," said

Black Moe, relaxing the Colt, letting its barrel drift down away from Brumfield's chest. "Philpot's got trouble with the man, that's true enough. But there's more to it than that. Bell killed one of us, a detective, in cold blood."

"What? You're out of your mind," said Brumfield. "Jack Bell is no killer."

"I've got a live witness to it," said Bainbridge. He raised a hand and waved Delbert to him from the far end of the bar. As Delbert Hanks came forward reluctantly, Moe Bainbridge nodded toward him, saying, "This man watched Jack Bell do the hateful deed. We even found the spot where he left our pal's body to the wolves. I tell you, it weren't no gentle sight."

"You saw the whole thing, is that right?" Brumfield asked Delbert Hanks.

"Yep, I saw it all," said Delbert.

"Then you better hope you saw the same thing Billy Freeman saw," said Brumfield, "because if you didn't, there's going to be a big problem between the two of you." He eyed Delbert Hanks closely.

"Billy Freeman," said Delbert, his eyes darting all around the saloon. "What do you know about Billy Freeman? He's dead."

"No, he's not dead," said Brumfield. "He's alive and well right here in Nolan's

Gap. Just aching to tell his side of the story to anybody who'll listen."

"Yeah?" said Delbert, his brow suddenly taking on a worried look. "What story is he telling? Not that it matters to me. I know what I saw out there."

"Since it doesn't matter to you," Brumfield replied, "we'll wait and let him tell us. He's right across street in the new jail. I have him chained to an anvil in one of the cells. Second night here, he tried to steal a horse and make a run for it." Brumfield grinned. "The damned fool stole a blind horse. He spurred it, trying to make a getaway, but the horse ran straight through the front window of the mercantile store. Billy's working off the window repairs at half a dollar a day. Looks like he'll be here most of the winter."

Black Moe looked Delbert up and down skeptically and said, "A friend of yours, huh?"

"I wouldn't exactly say he's my friend, but we've known one another awhile," Delbert offered, still looking worried.

Black Moe gave Brumfield a sly smile as he replied to Delbert Hanks. "Well, friend or no friend, I'm curious to hear his side of the story. I believe Delbert here would lie to God almighty, knowing the truth is all that'd save him."

"You've no right to talk to me like that," Delbert hissed.

"I know it," said Black Moe, the big Walker Colt still in his hand. "That's what makes me enjoy it all the more." He turned once again to Max Brumfield and said, "I hate thinking about poor ole Fleetus Gibbs running all over the place in some wolf's belly. I owe it to him to kill the sumbitch who did him in. What say just us three go visit this Billy Freeman whilst the boys are all busy looking around for Jack Bell?"

"Suits me," said Brumfield, his gaze boring a hole into Delbert Hanks. He took a long draw on his cigar and blew the smoke out slowly in Delbert's direction. Delbert's face took on a grave, sickly sheen.

Billy Freeman carried the heavy anvil out through the open cell doorway and set it down on the floor with a heavy thud. A ten-foot length of chain bolted the one hundred and fifty pound solid slab of steel to his right ankle. Billy stood bent over the anvil, resting for a second. Then he stepped over to the corner of the office, his chain dragging behind him like a large snake, picked up a broom and began sweeping the rough wooden floor when the sound of the door

244

opening drew his attention.

"Billy, we brought you a visitor," said Max Brumfield, stepping through the door first, followed by Delbert Hanks, then Black Moe Bainbridge. At the sight of Delbert Hanks, Billy Freeman's eyes widened. Brumfield couldn't tell if he saw surprise or fear on the young man's face.

Billy's jaw dropped for a second, but then he blinked hard, recovered and turned his eyes to Max Brumfield. "A visitor? You make it sound like I'm a prisoner here."

Brumfield and Black Moe looked at the anvil on the floor, then at each other. Brumfield shrugged. "Well, Billy, call it what you want to. You're here until the mercantile owner says you've squared accounts with him."

"Do you know this man?" Black Moe cut in impatiently, asking Billy Freeman as he swung a finger at Delbert Hanks.

"Well, uh . . ." Billy stalled, looking Delbert up and down.

"Yeah, he knows me," said Delbert, taking the lead. "And yeah, he was with me and Rance Hardaway and Stoy Manlon when Jack Bell ambushed us. Right, Billy?"

"Yep," said Billy Freeman, "that's right. Just like he said."

Max Brumfield watched and listened

closely. Billy Freeman hadn't spoken a half-dozen words about what had happened since he'd been in Nolan's Gap. Now that Delbert Hanks was here to instruct him in what he should or shouldn't say, Brumfield saw a whole different attitude starting to form. "What exactly happened out there, Billy?" he asked. "Tell us without looking to Delbert here for advice."

"Well, I —" Billy stammered.

"Hold it, Billy," said Delbert. "You don't have to do what this saloonkeeper says." He glared at Max Brumfield. "He got covered with snow when Bell started shooting at us. But I bet he must've seen Jack Bell kill Rance Hardaway first — right, Billy?"

"Yeah," said Billy, his voice sounding more sure of himself now that Delbert guided him. "Bell shot Rance for sure. Stoy too." He shot a glance at Delbert as if for approval.

"So there you have it," said Delbert. "Don't go trying to change what we've told you. Bell is a murdering, ambushing sumbitch whether anybody here likes hearing it or not." He jutted his chin toward Brumfield. "You're no lawman. You've got no right holding this man here . . . chained to an anvil like some kind of varmint. What kind of tinhorn jail is this anyway?" He

246

looked all around.

"Right now it's under construction," said Brumfield. "Until wc get a blacksmith to make some cell doors, we're using that anvil as sort of a dry-land anchor." He grinned and puffed his cigar.

Black Moe Bainbridge had stood quietly observing, taking it all in. He enjoyed seeing Delbert Hanks in a tight spot, squirming like a bug on a griddle. But now, hearing heavy boots come across the boardwalk to the door of the jail, Black Moe knew the fun was over. Red Tony and Ellis Dill shoved the door open and walked inside. "We've turned this fleabitten town on its ear, Moe," said Ellis Dill. "Nobody can tell us anything about Jack Bell except that he might've left here a few nights back with an old man and his daughter. They headed up into the high passes, in all this snow . . . if you can believe that."

"The high passes, you say?" Black Moe gave a sly grin, looking back at Max Brumfield. "Reckon they must know a short cut to San Francisco?"

"Listen to me, Bainbridge," said Brumfield. "Bell is innocent."

"Innocent of what?" said Red Tony with a grim smile.

Black Moe gave a casual nod to Ellis Dill

and Red Tony. "You two go on over to the saloon." He waited for a second as the two men turned and left.

Once Red Tony and Ellis Dill were gone, Max Brumfield stood firm as Black Moe turned a cold stare into his eyes. "Bainbridge, these two men are lying," said Brumfield, his fists gripped tight at his sides. "You're a detective, for God sakes: Question them! Squeeze the truth out of them if you have to. Jack Bell is a good man! He's no killer."

Black Moe Bainbridge looked bored with it. "Brumfield, that's as good as we're going to get from these two lying yardbirds. I can see they're lying. But then again, so are you. San Francisco? A boardinghouse? Why not New Orleans? A gin parlor?" He raised his pistol from his holster slowly, cocking it on the way. "I hate saying it, but I'm about to lose faith in anything you might tell me from now on."

Max Brumfield still held his ground, ignoring the big Walker Colt. "That's right, I made up San Francisco! What of it? I'm only trying to save the life of an innocent man, damn it!"

"Like Red Tony said, innocent of what?" Bainbridge's thin smile widened. He turned the big Walker toward Billy Freeman and said to him, "Pick that anvil up and get out of here with it, boy."

"Huh? What?" Billy looked back and forth, bewildered.

"That's right, you heard me. I'm cutting you loose. This is your lucky day, boy," said Black Moe Bainbridge, the Walker Colt still cocked, looming among the men like the shadow of death.

"What should I do, Delbert?" Billy Freeman asked, a frantic ring to his voice.

"If I was you, Billy," said Delbert, "I'd pick up that anvil and make tracks."

"Go on, boy," said Black Moe. "That's the best advice you're likely to get around here today."

Billy reluctantly stooped down, picked up the heavy anvil and turned to Max Brumfield. "You sumbitch, you caused all this! I'd have been halfway to Denver by now, snow or no snow, hadn't been for you!"

"Now, now," said Black Moe, opening the door and waving Billy outside with the barrel of his Colt. "I hate hearing a man blame all his troubles on somebody else. Get on out of here before I lose my temper."

"You — you're not going to — to shoot me in the back, are you?" Billy Freeman asked, almost in tears.

"Not if you can run quick enough to get out of my gun sight, I won't," said Bainbridge. "Now hurry up!"

Billy stumbled forward through the open door, the weight of the anvil already pulling him down in the knees. "But I can't run! Not carrying this! Please, mister, this ain't right! It ain't fair at all!"

"True, this is not a perfect world," said Black Moe, giving Billy a shove to get him started. "I'm using you to illustrate a point." Billy screamed, running hard down off the boardwalk into the snow-filled street, his knees trembling and buckling beneath the load.

"My God, Bainbridge!" said Max Brumfield. "Don't kill that poor fool."

"I'm afraid I must, Brumfield," said Black Moe, raising the big Colt. "You can see for yourself, that boy is trying to escape."

"No, Bainbridge, please!" said Brumfield.

But his words cut short beneath three loud blasts from Black Moe's big Walker Colt. Billy Freeman flew forward, the bullets punching him, the anvil leaving his arms and falling heavily to the ground as he continued on until he ran out of chain. Then he slapped facedown in the snow and mud amid crisscrossing wagon and horse tracks. Black Moe chuckled, amused by the spectacle. "I swear I never figured he could make it that far, that fast . . . carrying that big chunk of iron."

"Billy always was stronger than he looked," said Delbert Hanks, stepping forward in curiosity to gaze out at the bloody body lying dead and still in the cold.

"How about you, Delbert, boy?" asked Black Moe, the Walker Colt still smoking in his hand, the sound of it still ringing in the room. "Are you stronger than you look? How far and fast do you expect you can tote an anvil?"

Delbert gave Black Moe a defiant look.

Max Brumfield stood watching the two, uncertain what might come next.

But then Black Moe turned his attention away from Delbert and faced Brumfield, opening the Walker Colt, punching out the three spent cartridge casings and replacing them as he spoke.

"Just think, Brumfield," he said. "That could have been you lying out there looking straight down." Once again he offered a sly grin. "It still could, far as that goes." He gave a nudge of his head toward Billy Freeman's body. "I did that to get your attention."

"If you killed that poor fool just to scare

me, Bainbridge, you've taken his life for nothing. You've already learned as much as I can tell you," said Max Brumfield, still standing firm. "Jack Bell left here with an old man and his daughter. If you want to know where, I guess you'll just have to follow their tracks in the snow."

"Some men follow tracks," said Black Moe. "Others like to know where they're going to begin with. I bet before I leave here, you'll tell me everything you ever knew about this killer, Jack Bell."

"Jack Bell is no killer. That's one thing you'll never get me to say," said Brumfield. "I've got a feeling you know he's innocent, Bainbridge."

"Innocent . . . guilty." Black Moe wagged his big Walker Colt in his hand. "Who can say about any of us? Delbert sees him as a bad man. You see him as a good man. I believe your vision of the man is clouded by friendship, barkeep."

"Jack Bell is a friend of mine, I'm not denying it," said Brumfield.

"There, you see?" Black Moe grinned, raising a long finger for emphasis. "It's hard to find what you'd call a *clear and unsubjective* opinion these days. Your opinion is clouded by friendship; mine is clouded by making money. You say your friend never killed anybody, but then you weren't there. Neither was I. Delbert and Billy Freeman were there, but now Billy's dead, and you can't believe nothing Delbert says." Black Moe grinned.

"Like hell," Delbert Hanks bristled. "I'm a bona fide eyewitness."

"Shut up, boy," Black Moe growled. Then he continued, saying to Max Brumfield, "In a moral issue such as this, I always say go with what profits you the most. Early Philpot swears the man is guilty as hell. That's good enough for me."

As they stood staring at one another, three pistol shots exploded from the direction of the Western Palace. "Now, that would be ole Gannerd Woodsworth, I bet — him and the boys starting to make themselves to home in your saloon." Black Moe wagged the pistol toward the door. "Let's get over there, see what kind of mischief they've gotten into."

CHAPTER 16

Walking along the hastily vacated street toward the Western Palace, Brumfield, Black Moe and Delbert Hanks heard more shots ring out, followed by loud laughter and cursing. From storefronts, Brumfield saw faces peep out behind drawn window blinds, then disappear. The small town had bolted its doors and taken cover as if to sit out a terrible storm. Ahead of him, Brumfield saw a horse come racing out of his saloon, leaving the doors flapping so hard in its wake that one tore loose from its hinges and fell to the boardwalk. The horse leaped out into the street and ran in short circles, splashing up ice and mud.

"It always pleases me to see a bunch of spirited ole boys having a good time," said Black Moe. "What about you, barkeep?"

"Go to hell," Brumfield hissed over his shoulder.

Erie "the Swede" Olaffson ran out of the Western Palace and chased the horse back and forth until he caught its dangling reins and managed to throw himself up into the saddle. But the horse wasn't ready to settle down. In its wild thrashing, it reared up high, slipped in the icy mud and plunged down backward, sending up a spray of brown slush. The Swede threw himself clear without a second to spare. No sooner did the horse rise dripping and covered with mud than the big man threw himself back into the saddle and took control, forcing the horse to the crowded hitch rail.

"Swede, when you get through playing with the horses," said Black Moe in passing, "I want you to show Brumfield here that same trick you did in that saloon over in Wakely."

"You mean raising the bar up from the floor?" asked the Swede, working hard at keeping his English crisp.

"Yep, that's the one." Black Moe grinned.

"Save yourself the trouble, Bainbridge," said Max Brumfield. "My bar is fastened down tight with steel bolts and hex nuts."

"Really?" Black Moe chuckled. "So was the one in Wakely. That's what made it so interesting. I believe that big, yellow-haired polecat could lift hell out of Texas if he could get both arms around it."

Delbert Hanks laughed out loud, seeing Brumfield look back over his shoulder at Black Moe. "You oughta see the look on your face, Brumfield," Delbert said. "I bet the last time you ever had to take any guff off anybody —"

"Shut up, boy!" Black Moe snapped, coming to a halt out front of the Western Palace. "I hate having to keep telling you to keep your stupid mouth shut. Keep it up, I'll get some pig rings and pin your lips together."

Delbert fell silent, the laughter disappearing abruptly as he realized by the look on Black Moe's face that the man was dead serious. Still, Delbert wasn't going to be talked down to without talking back. "I got a right to say what suits me. Don't forget, I work for Early Philpot too. Matter of fact, I'm his right-hand man." He thumbed himself on the chest.

"Just this one time," said Black Moe, "I'm going to remind myself that you're too big an idiot to realize that I'm in complete control here." He took a step toward Delbert, his hand wrapping around the big Walker butt in its holster.

"I ain't some lackey you can keep on pushing around." But Delbert took a begrudging step backward, trying hard to maintain a show of courage.

"You ain't seen *pushing* yet," said Black Moe. "Let's see if you've got enough sense to follow an order when I give you one."

Black Moe pointed past Delbert at the body of Billy Freeman lying in the street. "Get yourself out there and bring that anvil and chain back here to me. Looks like we'll be needing them both before long."

"Let him go get it," Delbert said, nodding at Max Brumfield. "He's the one who'll be wearing it."

"How do you know he's the one?" Black Moe asked bluntly, his eyes riveted onto Delbert's.

"Who else?" Delbert gave a smirking grin. "He's the one who knows where Bell is. He's the one who'll —" His words stopped short as realization set in. "Hey! Wait a damn minute! I ain't about to wear no anvil chained to my ankle!"

"You will be, if you don't go get it and bring it back here like I told you."

Seeing where he stood with Black Moe, Delbert swallowed an angry response and settled down. Still, he resisted following Black Moe's order. "I don't have no wrench. I'd need a wrench to loosen the bolt holding the chain."

"Why you telling me?" Black Moe growled at him. "Do I look like I've got a wrench up my sleeve?" He darted his eyes to Max Brumfield. "Do you have a wrench up your sleeve?"

Brumfield shook his head in silence.

Delbert shrugged. "How the hell am I supposed to get it off his ankle?"

"You've got a boot knife, don't you, punk?" said Black Moe.

"A knife?" Delbert looked sick. "Lord God, I can't just go cut his foot off right out in the middle of the street."

"Are you sure you can't?" Black Moe raised the big Colt slowly, cocking it.

Delbert had taken all the abuse he was going to take off the man. To hell with it, he thought. He was no kid. He was fast; he was deadly. His hand streaked down and snatched his pistol. But behind him, the Swede's big, cold, wet hand clamped around his wrist and held the pistol pinned down in its holster.

"See what I mean about how stupid you are?" said Black Moe. Delbert stared wide-eyed down the black, vacant bore of the big Walker Colt.

"I wasn't going to shoot you, Black Moe! I swear to God I wasn't," Delbert pleaded.

"Then what were you going to do?" Black Moe asked quietly.

Delbert's eyes darted to Brumfield in panic, then back to Black Moe. "I — I —" he stammered. Then, breaking down into a sob, he said, shaking his bowed head, "I

258

don't know. I was just doing all I know to do."

"That's not the answer I'm looking for," Black Moe whispered close to Delbert's ear, holding the tip of the barrel jammed up against Delbert's nose. "I was hoping you'd say you was just on your way to get that anvil and chain the way I asked you to in the first place."

Delbert recovered, raising his tear-filled eyes suddenly. "I was. So help me God, I was!"

Black Moe eased the big Colt back from Delbert's nose and patted his shoulder. "I knew you was all along," he said in a soothing voice. He nodded at the Swede. "Turn him loose, big fellow. He's a changed man."

"Do you want for me to box his jaws?" asked the Swede in his stiff English.

"No, I don't think he'll need any slapping around," Black Moe said with the patience of a benevolent father.

"What about his gun belt?" asked the Swede.

"What about it?" asked Black Moe.

"Want for me to take it off from him?" asked the Swede, struggling with his newly acquired language.

"Naw," said Black Moe. "He needs that

gun belt to keep his shirttail from flying up over his head." Black Moe grinned in Delbert's tear-streaked face. "You ain't going to disappoint me again, are you?"

Delbert sniffled and shook his head without looking up.

"Good," said Black Moe. "You hurry up now. Don't make the Swede have to come looking for you." He gave Delbert a nudge and watched him back away, turn and walk quickly toward Billy Freeman's body.

"He's been just like a young mustang pony ever since I took him under my wing," Black Moe said to the Swede and Max Brumfield, the three of them turning to walk through the doors of the Western Palace. "But now I've just about got him to where he knows who's holding the reins."

Inside the Western Palace, Brumfield stopped abruptly and stared at the men lined along the bar. Two bullet holes stared back at him from the large mirror on the wall. A broken table lay upside down near the roaring potbellied stove; the stove's door hung open. Nate Reardon stood poking one of the table's broken legs into the flames. "Here comes some more, Nate," said Floyd Finch, raising a chair high over his head and crashing it down on the edge of an ornate billiard table.

Max Brumfield winced to himself and tried to keep from showing his feelings.

"They'll have this place warmed up in no time," Black Moe laughed.

"It doesn't make any difference what you do, Bainbridge," said Max Brumfield. "There's nothing more I can tell you about Jack Bell!"

Walking forward to the bar, Black Moe threw an arm across Brumfield's shoulders and hugged him close to his side. "Hell, don't worry about it, Mr. Max," he said. "To tell the truth, as much fun as the boys are having, I'd just as soon you not tell us anything. My, my! But look what a rowdy bunch they are! I'm very surprised they ain't all took out after that woman bartender by now." He gestured a hand toward Dolly Lisko, who was hurriedly helping Stanley Barger fill beer mugs and set up fresh bottles of whiskey in front of the drinkers.

At the end of the bar, Gannerd Woodsworth stood with a rack of antlers atop his head. At his feet lay a deer head he'd jerked down from the wall. As Brumfield, Black Moe and the Swede walked over to the bar, Gannerd raised his pistol and shot a whiskey bottle into a spray of glass against the wall just as Dolly Lisko reached for it. "Come here, little darling,"

Gannerd shouted at Dolly above the roar of drunken laughter, cursing and heated words among the men. "I want you to look me over good, see if one leg looks shorter than the other."

"Go shoot yourself in the ear, you idiot sumbitch!" Dolly shrieked at him, clasping her hand and looking it over for any damage.

"She likes me, I can tell!" Gannerd Woodsworth said with a wide grin. He started to climb over the bar, but before he could, Black Moe raised his pistol and fired three shots straight up to get everybody's attention. Splinters showered down onto Brumfield's shoulders. He took a deep breath and let it out slowly.

"Everybody listen up!" shouted Black Moe, the big Colt smoking in his hand. "The Swede is going to show us a little exhibition of raw, *Herculean* strength. Any of you haven't seen this before, you're in for one hell of a treat, is all I can say."

A murmur rippled along the line of drinkers.

"Now all of you step back from the bar a little, so's the Swede can look it over real good," said Black Moe.

"Look it over for what?" asked Red Tony Harpe.

Beside him, Dewey Sadlo said, "Red, you weren't around in Wakely when he did this. Ole Swede there will rip this bar right off the floor and roll it over on its side!"

Red Tony Harpe looked confused. "Why?"

"Why? Because, by God, he can do it, *that's why*," Dewey Sadlo laughed. "Don't you like seeing something done just as a test of strength?"

"I reckon." Red Tony shrugged, still not seeming too sure. He took a last draw on a thin cigarette and flipped it away onto the floor. "But as far as lifting this bar goes, that ain't nothing. I can do that myself."

"Uh oh," said Dewey Sadlo. "We've got ourselves a challenger here!"

As the men all booed Red Tony and scoffed at him, Max Brumfield moved around behind the bar and stopped beside Dolly Lisko and Stanley Barger. "Max, we've got to do something quick," Dolly whispered. "They'll tear this place to the ground if we don't stop them."

"I know, Dolly," Brumfield replied, "but there's nothing we *can* do to stop them. I just watched Black Moe kill that poor, stupid Billy Freeman for no reason. Don't say anything to provoke him or any of the others. They're all ready to turn the least little thing into a bloodbath."

"Say the word, Boss," said Stanley Barger. "I'll start busting heads until they stop me."

"No, Stanley," said Brumfield. "I don't want you or Dolly either one hurt. While they're all busy watching this ape turn my bar over, I want both of you to clear out of here."

As Brumfield spoke, the three watched the Swede strip off his muddy shirt and throw it aside. The drinkers hooted and cheered and stomped their boots on the floor.

"I'm not leaving you here alone," said Dolly.

"Don't argue with me over this, Dolly!" Brumfield whispered between the three. "Stanley, make sure she gets out of here, if you have to knock her out and carry her."

"When I leave here she'll be under my arm, Boss, I promise," said Stanley.

Brumfield looked all around sadly and shook his head. "I never would've believed this happening. I could understand an Indian attack or something like that . . . but not a bunch of detectives putting me out of business just because I won't tell them what they want to hear."

"What is it they want to hear?" Dolly asked.

"Never mind," said Brumfield. "It wouldn't make any difference anyway. Black Moe wants to destroy something."

"Tell me what is it they want to hear," Dolly persisted, searching Brumfield's face. "Stanley and I have a right to know, as long as we've been with you." But before Brumfield could even try to answer, she said, "This is about Jack Bell's whereabouts, isn't it?"

"I told you it makes no difference," said Brumfield. "These men are ruthless. Now keep your voice down and get ready to go."

Outside in the street, Delbert Hanks kneeled down in the snow over Billy Freeman's body, the dead man's big boot gripped tight in his shaking hand. "Damn it, Billy, this ain't my idea, you know! I sure didn't wake up this morning itching for a chance to cut off somebody's damn, dirty, stinking foot!" He raged at the body, hoping to raise his temper to a point where he wouldn't mind cutting and hacking through soft flesh and hard bone in order to free up the chain. "How did I get into this?" he growled to himself.

Delbert looked back and forth frantically along the deserted street, his breath steaming, wishing someone would come running out carrying a wrench he could use. Maybe he could go find a wrench somewhere, he thought. But then, hearing the laughter and gunshots coming from the Western Palace, he knew that it wouldn't do for him to go find a wrench. Somehow the whole point of him doing this had to do with whether or not he'd cut off a man's foot if asked to do so. He gritted his teeth. *All right then, to hell with it; here goes . . .*

He sawed the big blade back and forth through Billy Freeman's boot top where the leather had been bunched up by the steel shackle clamped around it. Hearing the coarse sound of steel slicing through leather reminded Delbert of what it was going to sound like cutting through Billy's leg. The thought of it turned his stomach queasy.

Wait a damn minute. Delbert stopped and looked at his trembling knife hand. He ran his coat sleeve across his forehead and looked back and forth, making sure no one was watching. "God almighty," he whispered.

Who was he kidding? He wasn't about to do this. Killing a man meant nothing to him. But something like this? *Huh-uh.* He had better things to do than cut the foot off of a corpse. This was demeaning to him. He dropped Billy Freeman's foot and moved back away from the body.

Across the street he spotted an old man sneaking along the boardwalk toward the mercantile where the front window was boarded up owing to Billy Freeman plunging through it on the blind stolen horse the other day. "Hey you!" Delbert shouted. When the old man stopped and pointed a finger to his thin chest, Delbert called out, "Yeah, that's right, I'm talking to you! Get over here — I need you to give me a hand with something." The old man hesitated, and Delbert shouted, "Damn it to hell, don't make me come drag you out here!"

Delbert stood up, snatched the pistol from his holster, cocked it and pointed it at the old man, all the while keeping an eye on the Western Palace Saloon to make sure Black Moe or one of the others didn't happen out and see what he was up to. "All right, I'm coming!" the old man cried out. "Don't shoot!"

"Hurry it up!" Delbert demanded, getting anxious.

When the old man stopped a few feet away, staring at Billy Freeman's body, Delbert pitched the knife onto the ground at his feet and said, "I need you to take that knife and whack his foot off so I can take that chain loose."

"Why not just loosen the bolt?" the old man asked.

"Damn it *to hell!*" Delbert shrieked, losing control. "Because that ain't the way I want to do it!" The pistol trembled in his hand.

"Sorry then," the old man said. "I ain't cutting his foot off. It's bad luck to maim the dead. You want it cut off, I'd advise you to do it yourself."

"Mister," Delbert said with stone-cold finality, "pick that knife up and get to cutting, or I will shoot you graveyard dead! Do you understand me?"

"Yep, I understand clear as day." The old man nodded. "But I ain't cutting his damned foot off, and that's that."

"All right then, you old sumbitch!" Delbert tightened his grip on the pistol butt. He started to pull the trigger, but then, glancing toward the saloon, he thought better of it, not wanting the gunshot to attract attention. "Damn it!" He lowered the pistol and stomped his boot in the muddy slush. "Get out of here then! Go on, get!" he screamed. The old man backed away a step, then turned and ran, slipping and stumbling until he disappeared around the corner of an alley.

"Now what?" Delbert asked himself aloud, his breath steaming as he looked down at Billy Freeman, then over at the loud voices resounding from the Western Palace. He didn't owe Black Moe a damn thing, he thought, and he wasn't about to cut a man's foot off just because Black Moe told him to. He didn't have to take this kind of overbearing treatment. He could go after Jack Bell all by himself. Get on the trail while those idiots were busy getting drunk. He looked over at the mercantile store again. All he needed was some supplies.

Without another moment's thought on the matter, Delbert walked over to the hitch rail out front of the Western Palace, slipped his horse's reins free and led it away quickly. At the first alleyway he came to, Delbert pulled the horse out of sight, walked to the back of the buildings facing the street and found the rear door to the mercantile store. Looking all around as he wrapped the reins around a telegraph pole, he kicked the door open and slipped inside. From now on, he wasn't taking orders from anybody. Why should he? he asked himself. Delbert Hanks knew what he was doing.

CHAPTER 17

Inside the Western Palace, all Max Brumfield could do was watch in silence as Black Moe and his men reduced the well-kept saloon's furniture and fixtures to a broken heap of rubble. This wasn't about Brumfield telling these detectives where to find Jack Bell. Black Moe and his men were doing this simply because they could get away with it. Brumfield resigned himself to the fact that he was powerless against them. He would keep himself in check until they moved on. Then, like any man had to do in the wake of a terrible storm, he would repair, clean up and start anew.

"All right now, all of yas gather around close!" shouted Black Moe. "Red Tony's about to show us what he's made of!"

From the middle of the floor, Gannerd Woodsworth called out with a loud laugh, "If he ain't careful, he'll show us what he had for breakfast!" On the floor at Gannerd's feet lay Nate Reardon, passed out drunk. Someone had taken the long picture of a nude woman from the wall behind the bar, cut her face out with a knife and slipped the painting over Reardon's head. Reardon's mouth lay agape, appearing to rest in the woman's hand.

At the end of the bar, Red Tony stood rolling up his shirt sleeves. Angered by Gannerd's words, Tony said, "If you're so damn strong, Gannerd, don't be bashful, step on over here yourself. We'll make room for you."

"I'm saving myself!" Gannerd replied, a bottle of whiskey hanging from his hand.

"Yeah? Saving yourself for what?" Red Tony asked in a sarcastic tone.

"Saving myself for her!" Gannerd responded, reaching out with his boot toe and tapping it against the naked woman wearing Nate Reardon's drunken face. Laughter rose up from the men. "She's ugly as hell," Gannerd went on saying, "but I heard she cooks like the devil himself."

On the far side of the room, the Swede stood alone, not joining in the laughter and drinking with the other men. He stared at the long, heavy bar as if it were some living opponent whose doom he would soon bring about. He flexed and unflexed his bare arms and broad shoulders beneath his wide galluses, loosening up. His big wool shirt lay on the floor against the wall.

"Look at the Swede over there, boys,"

Black Moe called out to the men. "This ain't no joking matter to him. He aims to rip this damn bar up and sling it aside like a dead grizzly bear! Eh, Erie?"

The Swede nodded grimly in reply, his eyes still riveted to the bar as if his cold stare might intimidate it. "Let us get on with it," he said in a tense, thick voice.

"Hey, don't rush me, Swede," said Red Tony. "I go when I'm damn good and ready, not a minute before." Yet even as he spoke defiantly, Red Tony moved closer to the end of the bar. He tried to give the Swede a harsh glare, but the big man never cut his gaze away from the bar to acknowledge Red Tony in the least. This contest of strength was strictly between the Swede and the long, heavy, polished slab of wood.

Red Tony spit into both palms, rubbed them together and squatted down with his back against the end of the bar. "Here goes," he said.

"Don't forget: Lift with your back, Tony, not your arms," Floyd Finch called out. "The back is where a man's strength is."

"Where the hell did you ever hear that, Finch?" Dewey Sadlo asked, standing beside him. "That's the craziest damn notion I ever heard!"

"It's the truth," said Finch. "They've

studied it over in England. Never lift with your legs or arms. Always use your back."

"No way in hell," said Sadlo, shaking his head. "You've got that all backward. You'd get somebody hurt bad if they listened to you."

"No I wouldn't. It's a fact of science," said Finch.

"You idiots shut up!" shouted Red Tony. "I'm the one doing the lifting!"

"Then get at it!" Black Moe shouted at Red Tony. "So far all you've lifted is your lip!"

"I'm ready," said Red Tony. He reached both arms out behind him and ran his hands along the bottom of the bar, searching for a place to get a grip. On the front of the bar he found a good grip beneath a recessed lower edge six inches off the floor. On the rear of the bar he found a thick length of the bar's frame about the same height off the floor as the front edge. He squeezed both hands tight and pulled upward a bit, just testing. He inhaled and exhaled quickly: three deep puffs of air. Then his face went tight and blank as he held his breath and put his strength against the heavy weight of the bolted-down bar.

"Lord God, look what a face!" said Ellis Dill.

"Redder than a billy goat's ass," remarked Gannerd Woodsworth, stepping closer now that the contest had started. On the floor, the naked woman wearing Nate Reardon's face snored loudly.

A deep, rumbling growl came up from Red Tony's chest as his arms and legs quivered with strain. A low popping sound arose from the floor where the bolts held the bar in place. Red Tony grunted and pushed upward with his legs, his back flat against the smooth wooden end of the bar. But with all his strength against it, the bar refused to rise. After a long, hard moment, Red Tony collapsed, his breath expelling loudly.

"There you are, boys," said Black Moe. "Red Tony's done in. He ain't moved a damn thing."

"Hold on," Red Tony gasped, slumped against the end of the bar, still squatting there. "I just . . . turned loose . . . to get a better hold on it. I ain't . . . through yet."

"All right then," said Black Moe, "but you best get to doing something. Bets are waiting to be settled."

"I'm doing something." Red Tony put his back to the end of the bar again and began taking short quick breaths, getting ready.

Beside Max Brumfield, Stanley Barger had slipped in quietly and said in a guarded tone, "Damn it, Boss, this ain't right. We

274

can't let this bunch put us out of business."

Max Brumfield looked at Stanley in surprise. "What are you doing back here? Didn't you and Dolly get out like I told you?" As he spoke, he looked around quickly for any sign of Dolly Lisko.

"Don't worry; Dolly's gone," said Stanley Barger. "We got out like you wanted us to. But I couldn't leave you here alone. Running from a fight just ain't in me, Boss. I'm sorry."

"So am I, Stanley," Brumfield said in a lowered voice. "This is not a fight, and I'm trying to keep it from turning into one. Let them do whatever it takes to get them out of here. We can fix whatever they ruin."

"I know, Boss," said Stanley, "but I figure I can't leave you here without me standing beside you. That just ain't the way one friend does another where I come from. I just ain't made that way."

"All right, Stanley." Max Brumfield relented a bit, even managed a trace of a smile. "But let's keep our heads and not try to be heroes. This will all pass —"

Brumfield's words were cut short by the sudden shrill scream of pain that tore itself loose from Red Tony's chest. Snapping their attention in the direction of the bar, they saw Red Tony rise screaming into a crouch and limp around in a short circle, dragging his left foot behind him as if he had no control of it. "What the hell has he done now?" said Black Moe, staring in disbelief at the twisted, limping, screaming Red Tony as the man circled past him.

"Oh, my back! My God! My back!" Tears streaked down Red Tony's distorted face. "I've broke my back! God help me, it's broke plumb to hell!"

"Somebody grab him, get him down," shouted Black Moe, hurrying in closer to Red Tony. Three men rushed in and grabbed Red Tony. They threw him screaming to the hard plank floor. "Hold him still until he settles down," Black Moe demanded.

Max Brumfield shot a quick glance at the Swede and saw the thin cruel smile on his face. The Swede's eyes seemed to brighten at the sound of Red Tony's screams. Stanley whispered near Brumfield's ear, "Serves him right, the bastard. I hope they have to ride him out of here on a board."

"Maybe this will be enough for them," said Brumfield.

"No, Boss, this won't satisfy them," said Stanley Barger. "I've been behind a bar long enough to know. These men ain't gonna stop until there's blood spilled. I just don't want it to be yours."

"Or yours either," said Brumfield quickly. "I want your word that you won't do something stupid."

"Damn it, all right," said Stanley, giving in. "I won't do nothing stupid. I swear I won't."

The men dragged Red Tony away from the bar screaming and laid him along the back wall of the saloon. One of them helped him down half a bottle of whiskey in one long, gurgling drink. When Red Tony lowered the bottle from his lips his screams had turned to low, whimpering sobs. He collapsed on the floor, hugging the whiskey bottle against his chest, gritting his teeth in pain.

"This was all Early Philpot's doing," Max Brumfield whispered to Stanley Barger. "Someday I hope he gets what's coming to him."

"He will," said Stanley with finality. "That goes without saying."

Brumfield just looked at him.

"Boys, let's all give Red Tony a little hurrah here," said Black Moe. "You have to admit, the man gave it his best."

The men clapped and whistled, but only for a moment. Then money changed hands and the Swede stepped forward and looked back and forth across the waiting faces. He spread a smug grin of superiority and tilted his chin up. His huge chest swelled even larger beneath his wide galluses. "Now I will show to all of you how this is done," he boasted.

"That big tub of horseshit," Stanley Barger whispered. "I hope I can keep from going over there and busting his yellow head open."

"You better," said Max. "You gave me your word."

"I know, Boss. I'm just wishing out loud," said Stanley.

A hushed silence fell upon the men, prompted by the Swede stepping up to the bar and looking it over closely in appraisal. He took his time, rubbed his hands together and did some short knee bends, his eyes never leaving the bar. Then he turned his back to the end of the bar and said to the gaping faces, "I am ready to make this thing done."

A spirited cheer went up until Black Moe raised his hands toward the crowd and silenced them. "Make all bets quickly, boys. The Swede is ready to do battle with this big wooden sucker!"

The Swede squatted down in the same position Red Tony had taken. He put his arms back behind him and locked a death grip on the same edges Red Tony had used. But instead of inhaling and exhaling several times, he took one long, deep, breath, held it, closed his eyes and put all of his weight and the bar's weight against the slow upward push of his powerful legs. Immediately, a long creaking sound ran the length of the floor beneath the bar.

"Jesus, Lord God!" said Black Moe. "He's gonna lift this whole place, him and us all inside it!"

The men stared in awe, seeing the floor bulge upward, the bolts holding the bar fast to the floor but the floor itself and the thick joists beneath it groaning and rising slowly. The Swede stopped and held the bar, rising floor and all, and took a fresh deep breath, once again holding it as he went back to his task. He put all of his power back into motion. This time the floor seemed to surrender itself to the Swede's thick legs. The long groaning sound turned into the sound of wood being ripped lengthwise. Boards split where the bolts held the bar in place. Nails shot up out of the floor and fell all around the Swede's big boots. Men backed away as if the nails were out to get them.

"Whoooie! My God, what a pull!" shouted Black Moe.

"I can't watch this," Brumfield whispered to himself. He closed his eyes and kept his face expressionless, pretending not to hear the boards splitting or the bolts breaking loose.

Following the sound of wood being ripped apart, a gasp went up from the men. Brumfield kept his eyes closed until a tremendous thud caused the entire building to rumble and shudder on its foundation. Then a deathlike silence set in. Opening his eyes, Brumfield saw an updraft of dust in the air and the bar laid over on its front in the middle of the floor. "Anybody tells me they ever saw anything like that is a lying sumbitch," Black Moe said, sounding awed by the spectacle.

Max Brumfield turned to Stanley Barger and, seeing the enraged look on the big bartender's face, said in a calm tone, "Stanley, go home right now. Put this out of your mind, and stay away from here until these men are gone."

"I can't do it, Boss," Stanley said, shaking his head slowly, taking a step toward the Swede. "I think of all the time and trouble you and I went to in building this place. Then to stand back and watch these turds ruin it . . ." His words trailed.

"You gave me your word, Stanley," said

280

Brumfield, grabbing Stanley by his shirt, trying to hold him back.

"I swore I wouldn't do nothing stupid, Boss," said Stanley, reaching down and twisting Brumfield's hand away from his shirt sleeve. "I can't see nothing stupid about cracking that big yellow monkey's head on the corner of that bar he just tore all to hell."

"Damn it, Stanley!" said Brumfield.

"Take off, Boss," said Stanley. "You'll have time to get away before I'm finished with this big sucker."

Max Brumfield saw there was no stopping Stanley Barger. Glancing back and forth wildly, he spotted the sawed-off shotgun they kept under the bar. When the Swede turned the bar over, the shotgun had spilled out onto the floor. Apparently no one had paid any attention to it lying there. Brumfield inched his way toward it as Stanley approached the Swede.

"Hey you!" said Stanley Barger, advancing on the Swede, his shoulders leveled, his big fists hanging freely at his sides.

"Yah, me?" the Swede looked curiously at Stanley.

"That's right, you!" said Stanley, making sure the Swede saw his displeasure. "Did you ever wonder how long it takes a couple of regular working men like me and Brumfield to rebuild something like this after some big idiot like you tears it up?"

The men standing around the Swede cleared a path for Stanley and stepped back into a circle, seeing what was coming.

Now the Swede saw it too. He unhooked his big thumbs from his galluses and spread his feet shoulder width apart. "I have not even an idea," he said. "Why don't you tell me then: How long does it take?"

"Too long," said Stanley Barger.

The Swede saw the big right hand coming at him but wasn't fast enough to get out of the way. He took the blow full on the chin, the sound of knuckle against bone resounding loudly, causing the men to wince a bit. The Swede staggered back a step but recovered and tried to block Stanley's hard left jab. But again he wasn't quick enough. The jab put a deep gash on the Swede's cheekbone and set his cheek on fire. But the big man's head only snapped back, his long blond hair flying up wildly for a second then settling as he shook off the blow and gave Stanley a strange, cruel grin.

"I didn't want you to go down too quick," said Stanley. "The fact is, I've got all night." He leveled his guard and stood balanced, his feet spread apart beneath him, ready for the Swede to make his move.

Back behind the circle of men, Black Moe raised his pistol from his holster and started to take a step forward, his thumb cocking the pistol's hammer as he went. "Let's see how this bartender fights with a bullet or two in his ass!" But the sound of the shotgun cocking behind him, followed by the feel of the double barrels jamming into his back, caused him to stop short.

"Bring it down and holster it, Bainbridge," said Max Brumfield in a lowered voice, seeing some of the men turn their attention from the fistfight and stare at him. Their hands had already wrapped around their pistol butts, ready to draw. "Tell them this is going to be a fair fight, Bainbridge," Brumfield commanded.

"You're crazy, Brumfield," said Black Moe. "When this is over, what're you going to do?"

"I haven't got that far ahead in my planning yet," said Brumfield. "But right now I'm seeing to it that Stanley gets a fair shake. Tell your men to leave him alone, or I'll decorate the wall with your innards."

Black Moe saw the men advance a step, poised and ready. Past the men, Stanley Barger and the Swede were going at it toe-to-toe, trading blows that would have staggered a field ox. Black Moe swallowed the knot in his throat and said, "You heard him, boys! Let's keep this as fair as we can. The Swede knows how to handle himself!"

The men turned back toward the fistfight. Stanley Barger stood battering the Swede with a flurry of body shots, each punch sounding like someone beating dust from a carpet with an ax handle. But the Swede took the blows without losing ground. Bowing only slightly at the waist, he managed to reach through Stanley's guard with both big hands and grab the bartender around the throat. He lifted him straight up in the air, Stanley still punching him relentlessly, the blows traveling up from the Swede's body to his broad face.

Blood flew from the Swede's nose and from both of his deeply gashed cheeks. With a loud, long snarl, he turned one hand loose from Stanley's throat, grabbed him by the crotch and raised him above his head like a sack of feed. Stanley's fists never stopped swinging, only now there was nothing for him to hit. Taking a step back onto his right foot for balance, the Swede suddenly lunged forward and hurled Stanley across the width of the saloon.

"Lord God, have you *ever?*" said Black Moe, seeing the bartender pass overhead like a rag doll. Stanley landed sidelong against the big potbellied stove, knocking it over in a spray of soot from the falling tin pipes. Fiery embers and flaming chunks of wood spilled out and rolled in all directions. Seeing fire lying scattered all about the floor, Max Brumfield uncocked the shotgun and ran for a bucket of water sitting against the wall behind the spot where the bar had stood.

"You men help me! Please! Before this place burns to the ground!" Brumfield shouted at Black Moe and his men as he ran, dropping the shotgun to the floor. Snatching up the oaken bucket, he raced back among the burning embers and doused water back and forth as Stanley Barger and the Swede continued their fight.

Black Moe reached down, picked up the shotgun and cradled it in his arms. He kicked a burning ember away from his boots. "What's wrong, Brumfield?" Black Moe said with a dark laugh. "You wanted to see a fair fight. None of us is going to lift a finger till this is over." He grinned at the men gathered around him.

"Damn it!" Seeing smoke begin to curl from the stack of firewood against the wall where a hot coal had rolled, Brumfield tossed the rest of the water from the bucket.

Looking all around wildly, seeing the hopelessness of his situation grow by the second, he turned with the empty bucket and ran toward the front door. But a boot stretched out in front of him and tripped him, sending him sprawling. Laughter roared among the men. Locked in battle with the Swede, Stanley Barger saw Brumfield's plight but was powerless to help him.

"Slow down, Brumfield. Take it easy," said Black Moe. "I bet right now if I was to ask you where Jack Bell is, you'd no doubt tell me, wouldn't you?"

"Go to hell, Bainbridge!" Brumfield shouted, blood trickling from a fresh cut on his forehead where his head had hit the edge of a floor plank. "I'd rather watch this place burn to the ground than to give up a friend." He spit toward Black Moe's boots. "But a rotten bastard like you wouldn't understand that!"

Black Moe grinned, turning the shotgun toward Brumfield and cocking it. "But I understand this." He braced himself for the recoil.

"Wait! Don't shoot!" Dolly Lisko shrieked, coming through the door. "I'll tell you where Jack Bell is!"

"Dolly, shut up!" shouted Max Brumfield. "Get out of here right now!"

"Jack Bell *really* is up in the high passes," Dolly said hurriedly, in spite of Brumfield's warning. "It's the truth! He and a young woman from town went up there looking for her father! Her father thinks there's a cave full of lost gold up there! Now lower the gun!"

But Black Moe kept the shotgun leveled at Brumfield. "Lost gold, huh? In this kind of weather? You must think I'm a fool, little lady."

"No, it is the truth, so help me God!" Dolly said, her voice taking on a pleading tone as Black Moe slowly turned the shotgun in her direction. "I wouldn't lie for Jack Bell . . . risk my neck for him. I'm telling you what you've been asking. Please listen to me —"

But Dolly's words cut short beneath the roar of the shotgun. Black Moe stared in surprise. "My God," he whispered. The blast picked Dolly up off the floor and hurled her backward. She slammed into the wall beside the front door and sank like a stone, her stylish lady's hat cocked down low on her forehead. Her head fell to one side, bobbed limply for a second, then hung there.

"Dolly, no!" Brumfield screamed, trying to crawl quickly to her. But Dewey Sadlo and Ellis Dill stepped into his path and took a firm stance, their tall dirty boots stopping him. Smoke rose from the plank floor where hot coals had begun to ignite the dry wood.

"Boss!" shouted Stanley Barger, seeing what was going on. He tried shoving the Swede away in order to get over to Max Brumfield. Out the corner of his eye he saw flames lick up the wall from a pile of charred and glowing wood. He wanted to call a halt to the fight, but the Swede would have none of it. Stanley tried to turn and run to Brumfield, but two big arms locked around him from behind, lifted him in a fierce bear hug, then slammed him to the floor.

"Boys, believe it or not, I never meant to shoot her," said Black Moe. "This damn thing has the worse jackrabbit hair trigger I ever seen." He examined the shotgun in his hands as if still surprised by what he'd done.

"It don't matter," said Dewey Sadlo, stepping away from Brumfield on the floor and turning to Black Moe. "You still kilt her. That's all a judge is going to look at." Ellis Dill planted a boot on Brumfield's back and pinned him down to the rough plank floor. With his face pressed to the floor, Brumfield saw flames lick higher up the back wall.

"What are you saying, Dewey?" Black

288

Moe asked, already knowing the answer.

"I'm saying we better clean up after ourselves right here, right now . . . or this thing is going come back upon us sure as hell loves a backsliding sinner!"

Black Moe looked down at Max Brumfield on the floor, then turned his eyes to the two big men still fighting like gladiators from a time long past, smoke curling up around them as they stood in mortal combat. Black Moe turned his gaze back to Dewey Sadlo and said in a lowered voice, "I'm afraid you're right. We best handle this our own way while we can."

Dewey Sadlo got the message. He raised his pistol from his holster and said down to Max Brumfield, "Goodbye, barkeep."

CHAPTER 18

Stanley Barger tried to tear away from the Swede at the sound of three pistol shots exploding in the smoke-filled saloon. But the Swede wasn't about to let him go. While Stanley had dangled in the air, he'd battered the big man with his boot heels until the Swede was forced to release him from the bear hug. Still, the Swede had managed to keep a grip on Stanley with his right hand. His big left fist pounded Stanley mercilessly.

Nate Reardon had stuck his head out the front door and looked back and forth along the street, making sure no crowd had formed against them. Two townsmen came slipping cautiously along the opposite boardwalk with buckets in their hands. Reardon fired two shots at them, shouting, "Get out of here, you nosy sumbitches!" The townsmen dropped the buckets and ran. Reardon laughed to himself. Then, seeing Billy Freeman's body lying in the street with the anvil still chained to his leg, Reardon turned to Black Moe and said, "Hey, Delbert ain't done what you told him to. That man's still laying where you dropped him."

"I'm not surprised," Black Moe replied calmly.

"I see no sign of Delbert's skinny ass out there," Reardon added, coming over beside Black Moe.

"That doesn't surprise me either," said Black Moe. "In fact, I was hoping he'd get some rabbit in him, run on ahead of us, clear the trail so to speak." He grinned slightly. Standing over Max Brumfield's body, he called out through the smoke and licking flames that had grown steadily higher, "Finish that peckerwood off, Erie! Let's get the hell out of here!" A half circle of flames stood dancing upward between him and the two combatants, keeping him from venturing any closer.

"I will . . . be along . . . in a . . . moment," the Swede replied, his words punctuated by the powerful blows striking Stanley's chest and face. His pride didn't want to admit to Black Moe and the others that this bartender was not the kind of man he could finish off anytime he felt like doing it. Stanley Barger had taken everything the Swede had thrown at him and thrown back plenty of his own. Nor was Stanley done yet. With both hands free, his fists swung windmill fashion, leaving gash upon gash on the big man's exposed cheeks.

The skin beneath the Swede's left eye had been ripped loose and lay stuck downward in the thick blood and mangled flesh on his cheekbone. His right eye was nearly closed. Both men were bare-chested now and covered with blood. Dewey Sadlo aimed his pistol and cocked it toward the fighters. Black Moe shoved his arm up before he could fire a shot. "What the hell is wrong with you, Dewey? You want to kill the Swede?" said Black Moe.

Dewey uncocked his pistol and let it hang in his hand, staring through the fire at the fighters. "If he don't get a move on, he's got more than getting shot to worry about."

Black Moe shrugged. "I don't know what to tell you. I've heard of men who'd rather fight than eat. Damned if these boys don't beat all I've ever seen."

"What're we going to do?" Reardon asked.

"If you want to go through fire to break those big suckers up, you go right on," said Black Moe. "I'm leaving." He called out to the Swede, "You hurry up and come on quick as you can now, you hear? Me and the boys will leave you a horse."

"I . . . won't . . . be . . . long!" the Swede

shouted in reply.

"Die! You . . . bastard!" bellowed Stanley Barger.

"See? He's doing fine," Black Moe said to the others. He turned and walked out the front door, the others following, two of them with Red Tony's arms looped across their shoulders, helping him along stiffly. "God, I never hurt so bad in my life," Red Tony sobbed drunkenly.

"Should've lifted with your back like I told you," said Floyd Finch.

Some of the men gave last looks over their shoulders toward Stanley Barger and the Swede. "God almighty *damn!*" said Ellis Dill, the last one to leave the burning saloon.

Even as the sound of horses' hooves rumbled away on the hard, frozen ground, Stanley Barger and the Swede fought on. Stanley had battered the man's face until his arms gave out. Then the Swede slung blood from his face and long hair and came at Stanley with a new burst of strength. He lunged, bowed at the waist, plowed his head into Stanley's stomach, and lifted him in the air once again. This time, instead of throwing Stanley, he slammed him down onto the plank floor again, this time landing atop him. Stanley managed to keep his head from taking the impact, but the rest of his body wasn't as lucky. His lungs emptied in a blast of breath. He lay limp, drained, helpless.

The weight of the Swede crushed down on him. "Now . . . the killing blow . . . what no man ever saw . . . and lived to tell about," the Swede said, his own breath scarce, his chest heaving in the smoke. He raised his big, bloody right fist for Stanley to see.

Stanley Barger lay helpless, near death, almost welcoming it, the full weight of the Swede pressing him into the floor. "Bring it down then . . . you yellow-headed . . . son of a —"

A loud, animal-like yell cut Stanley's words short as the raging Swede drew his big fist back past his broad shoulders and hurled it down with full force at Stanley's face. Stanley, although having accepted his death in his conscious mind, at that last split second instinctively felt his head jerk to one side, no more than a couple of inches. But a couple of inches was all it took to send the Swede's fist slicing past his ear and crashing straight down through a weak spot in the plank floor where a knot had long since dried and turned brittle.

The Swede's killing yell turned into a long grunt of pain. The impact of his punch thrust him downward. Stanley was thrown from beneath him as the big man's arm disappeared into the smoking floor. "Jesus Christ!" Stanley managed to say in his exhaustion, having struggled halfway to his feet and standing with both hands still on the floor, steadying himself. The Swede looked back and forth wild-eyed at Stanley hovering near him and at the fire creeping closer all around him. Frantically, he jerked his arm upward, but it stopped at the elbow as if being held by some demon beneath the floor. "I'm stuck!" he shouted to no one in particular.

"I bet you are," said Stanley, his strength coming back quickly at the sight of his opponent's new predicament. "How bad?"

The Swede tried again to jerk his arm free. Again the demon held it tight. "I can't get loose!" Now his bloody eyes turned to Stanley above him, looking for mercy from the man he'd tried to kill. "Whatever will I do?" he pleaded, his eyes moving from Stanley to the licking flames and boiling black smoke as it grew heavier and drew closer around them.

"Don't panic," said Stanley. He coughed and patted a bloody, exhausted hand on the Swede's slick, wet shoulder. He also looked all around, at the fire, at the smoke, as if searching for something to use as leverage. His eyes came to the burning stack of firewood against the wall. Flames roared upward from it. Then he looked back down at the Swede's face and asked, "Are you sure you're stuck tight?"

"Yes, I'm sure! I am not lying!" said the Swede, his voice pleading.

"All right, that's good enough for me." Stanley patted his broad shoulder again. He staggered through the smoke, coughing, until he reached the pile of firewood. He raised a boot and kicked the pile over, causing flames to flare up.

"Hurry!" said the Swede.

Stanley coughed as his eyes searched through the smoke until he found a two-foot length. He reached in and grabbed it. Smoke rose from the end of it. He staggered back to the Swede, holding the length of wood with both hands.

"Please hurry!" said the Swede, still jerking on his stuck arm, the floor still holding it tight.

"Hold your head up," said Stanley.

The Swede obeyed, coughing, his eyes watering. "Hurry!"

Stanley looked down at the floor and the stuck arm once more as he drew back the firewood with both hands. "Here we go, you big bastard!" Before the Swede could duck, Stanley swung the firewood back and forth, batting the Swede's head from shoulder to shoulder four times, until his tired arms gave out again and hung heavily down in front of him. He coughed and pitched the piece of firewood away. "Weren't so tough . . . after all . . . were you?" Stanley said. The Swede lay limp and unconscious in his own blood, bits of tree bark buried in his bloody cheeks and forehead.

Stanley coughed more violently, staggering back and forth, falling almost to his knees before catching himself. "And now," he said, righting himself, backing toward the small window on the rear wall, "I must . . . bid you *adieu.*" He touched a bloody hand to his bare forehead as if tipping a hat.

At the rear window, Stanley reached for the latch. Before opening the window, he looked back at the Swede lying helpless on the floor, barely visible now through the encroaching smoke and fire. "Serves you right," Stanley said. Turning back to the window latch, he started once again to open it. But once again he stopped. "Well shit," he whispered in a raspy voice. Then he turned and staggered back to where the Swede lay. "I hope you're not going to . . . get me killed, fooling with you."

Stanley saw the big man try to turn his head with a low moan. Squatting down, feeling the intense heat lick at his naked back, Stanley reached in with both hands, forcing his fingers down between the Swede's forearm and the jagged edge of wood. Taking a good tight grip he heaved upward until the plank broke off, leaving a larger opening. He grabbed the Swede's limp arm and pulled, to no avail. "What the hell is holding you?" he asked the dazed Swede. He tore off a larger length of flooring as the fire raged closer and licked upward, the flames growing bolder now, spreading out across the ceiling.

Stanley coughed but found breathing easier down close to the floor. "You better come loose this time, or I'm leaving you here," he said. He reached down and found the Swede's fist jammed down against the ground and doubled back on itself. "You're more trouble . . . than you're worth," he said, starting to choke. Keeping calm, he turned the big fist around to where he could get its fingers to open up. Then he drew his arm out of the hole and said, "All right, now let's . . . see what happens."

This time Stanley stood crouched over the Swede, holding his breath, his back feeling scorched, burning hot. He put both arms around the man and pulled upward. The stuck arm came up and flopped onto the floor just as Stanley needed to lower himself and take another breath. "That's more like it . . . you stubborn sumbitch," Stanley said to the Swede's bloody face. "Damn . . . it's hot in here." He stayed low and dragged the Swede to the floor beneath the window. Looking up through watery eyes, he said, "Let's see if I can open that window now without burning us both up."

The Swede moaned, his blood-slick hand managing to grip Stanley's forearm. Stanley looked down at him, thinking he smelled burnt hair and flesh. "Don't worry, you sonsabitch. I ain't left you. I never left nobody in my life."

From a ridge atop Nolan's Gap, Delbert Hanks stopped his horse and looked back over his raised coat collar at the smudge of black smoke drifting upward and out across the hilltops. He stood in his stirrups for a better look, but from this distance the streets and rooftops of the town were hidden from his sight. He could not see the rushing townsmen running back and forth from the water trough, throwing bucket after bucket upon the raging fire. *Well, so much for that,* he thought to himself. So

Black Moe had burned the town down. It meant nothing to him. He was just glad to get away. Now he intended to stay away.

Delbert had heard gunshots as soon as he'd rode upward off of the main trail. At first he'd thought it might be some townsmen firing at him. After all, he had kicked in the rear door of the mercantile store and taken what supplies he might need from the stockroom. But once he'd thought about it, he'd realized that nobody was going to be shooting at him. Whoever owned the mercantile had long since taken cover, afraid of what Black Moe and the rest of the detectives were going to do to the town.

"Well, there you have it, gentlemen," he said to himself, addressing the townsmen. Readjusting his coat collar up beneath his hat brim until his cheeks and face were completely shielded from the cold, he spit and took a deep breath. To hell with all of them. He had a good head start. He'd stay ahead of them. He'd get to Jack Bell, kill him, then collect not only the bounty money from Early Philpot but the reputation he'd long wanted for being a cold-blooded shootist. That's what it all meant to him. He nudged the horse forward on the narrow, snow-filled path.

Three miles farther back, on the main trail, Black Moe led the line of horsemen upward. "If we ever have to make an answer for what happened back there," said Dewey Sadlo, "we better all have the same story."

"Yeah," said Black Moe, "I'd hate being a lawman my whole life, then end up swinging for murder on the end of a rope."

"Boys, it can sure as hell happen," said Sadlo, shaking his head in regret. "The best I can tell you is for us to all say it was a case of self-defense."

"Self-defense? Good luck," said Ellis Dill, riding in front of Red Tony Harpe, leading Tony's horse for him while Red Tony sobbed and made short little screams of pain with each step of his horse. "We can say *self-defense*. But we all know how hard it is for this many men to tell the same story without getting it balled up some way."

"Damn it to hell, Ellis," said Dewey Sadlo, reining his horse around hard and glaring at him. "Can't you ever keep from being so damn cynical?"

"It's the truth, and you know it," said Ellis Dill.

"It might be the truth," said Sadlo, "but that doesn't mean you've got to bring it up right now — not at a time when what we need is a strong show of unified support among us."

"Both of yas shut up," said Black Moe, taking over the conversation. "When there's no opposing eyewitnesses, the truth is whatever the majority turns it into. We know damn well no living person saw what happened but us. Max Brumfield came at us with a shotgun; we shot him; he pulled the trigger when he fell." Black Moe shrugged. "Brumfield accidentally shot the woman and killed her. Which is sort of what really happened, except it was me that shot her. But it really was accidental."

"What about the Swede and that big bartender?" asked Floyd Finch.

"What about them?" Black Moe responded, staring ahead.

"How would we ever explain the two of them burning up in a fire like that?" said Finch.

"We don't know for sure that they did," said Black Moe. "If they didn't, then it's up to them to explain it best they can. If they both did burn up, we just say they was fighting and couldn't stop long enough to get out. That's true, ain't it?"

"Yeah, true enough," said Finch. "Unless if that bartender's alive and tells what happened to Brumfield and the woman."

"Don't worry," said Black Moe, "if there's one person I can guarantee ain't alive, it's the bartender. Either the Swede killed him, or he burned up."

Dewey Sadlo and Ellis Dill looked at one another. The others rode with their heads lowered against the cold, their breaths and their horses' breaths steaming behind them.

"God," Red Tony whimpered, "I can't stand this pain! If I don't get no better before long, I hope somebody will please shoot me."

"Keep bellyaching about it," said Black Moe. "I bet you'll get your wish." He gigged his horse forward, looking down at the fresh tracks Delbert Hanks' horse had left in the snow. "Look at ole Delbert here, making fast tracks up this mountain." Black Moe grinned. "Thinks he's going to live forever, I reckon. The dumb sumbitch. You almost have to admire a person like that."

"Yeah," said Dewey Sadlo, giving Ellis Dill a harsh look, "I bet ole Delbert ain't *cynical;* not like some I could mention."

"Keep pulling your big, fancy words on me, Dewey," Ellis Dill warned. "See if we don't end up firing weapons at one another."

Dewey Sadlo continued giving him a harsh stare until Dill booted his horse forward and rode alongside Black Moe on the narrow path.

In Nolan's Gap, the townsmen finally gave up on saving the Western Palace. Instead, they concentrated all their efforts on saving the buildings on either side of the saloon. They'd had to break ice in order to get what little water was left in the troughs along the street. But there was no shortage of snow. By the time the fire had peaked and begun to subside, the townsmen had wet down everything on the windward side of the Western Palace. At length the remaining charred framework crashed down upon itself. Soon the flames grew shorter.

Behind the Western Palace, the townsmen had followed a loud, lingering scream and found Stanley Barger and the Swede lying in snow and mud amid broken window glass. Smoke curled upward from Stanley's burnt hair, from his smoldering trousers and from the burnt, blackened skin on his back and outstretched arms. Two feet in front of his outstretched arms lay the Swede.

Even as some townsmen dragged the two away, others scooped up handfuls of snow and threw it on them. At first the snow melted and slid off. But they continued, hearing Stanley Barger moan through chattering teeth, "Thank God . . . don't stop . . . please don't stop."

At the end of the event-filled day, Stanley lay on his stomach on a cooling bench that the barber, Ralph Smith, used to dress out the dead for a funeral or else to keep their flesh from spoiling until someone claimed the body. For someone in Stanley Barger's burnt condition, the cooling bench was a godsend. The surface was caned wicker; beneath it was a deep, tin-lined tray filled with snow and ice. Stanley's burns caused him to shiver uncontrollably until a strong dose of laudanum and a tall water glass full of whiskey served to dull his pain. Beside him on another cooling bench lay the unconscious Swede in the same condition, all of his long hair singed off the back of his neck.

The barber looked at the Swede for a second, then turned back to Stanley Barger. "God knows they had no cause to beat you like an animal, Stanley. But what I really can't understand is why they turned on one of their own and beat him so unmercifully."

Stanley's battered eyes rolled to the ceiling for a second as he took a deep breath, feeling the effects of laudanum and rye run the length of his spine like soothing warm syrup. "It's a long story, Ralph. You had to be there, is all I can tell you," he whispered

305

in a gravelly drugged voice.

"I see," said the barber, already dismissing the matter. "Well, that's as much as I can do for you right now, Stanley." He reached out to pat a reassuring hand on Stanley but could see no place to do so that wouldn't cause more pain. He dropped his hand to his side. "But Lord willing, you'll be up and around in no time. Burns like these things just take time to heal proper."

"Heal me quick, Ralph," Stanley whispered through his parched throat. "There's something I've got to do." His eyes closed, and his charred face relaxed on the cooling bench.

CHAPTER 19

Jack Bell and Ben Finley climbed the last few feet up to the icy ledge and stood on the same spot the dog had led Ben to four days earlier. The spot had not been hard to find. Fresh snow had blown over the scrapings the dog had made with his claws, but except for the last few feet of the climb, they had followed the meandering path upward around rock and over deadfall. On Jack Bell's shoulder he carried a coiled rope and his empty saddlebags, having taken out the contents before leaving camp that morning. Under his arm he carried two fresh torches they had made the night before while sitting around the campfire.

Looking down at the opening at ground level, Ben Finley trembled with excitement. He caught his breath and wiped the back of his glove across his forehead. When he raised his face, Bell saw tears in his eyes. "I can't believe it," Ben said, also carrying empty saddlebags draped over his shoulder. "All this time I knew it was up here . . . still I can't believe we're standing here, looking at it."

Bell said gently, "Don't get your hopes too high just yet, Ben. There's a big difference between a lost treasure and a hole in the ground. So far all we know we've got for sure is the hole in the ground."

Ben calmed himself, breathing easier. "I know, Jack . . . but it's there. I saw it last night. It's been coming back to me little more at a time. Last night I could almost remember everything that happened to me up here." His eyes turned clouded all of a sudden as if he'd just recalled something unpleasant.

"What is it, Ben?" Bell asked, looking closely at the old man's eyes.

Ben shrugged it off. "Nothing. I reckon I'm just tired. This has been a tiring journey for me." He looked all around as if searching for some clue or sign. "But I'm all right. It'll soon be over. Rosalee will have everything she's ever dreamed of." His eyes sparkled again, the cloud seeming to lift. "That's the main thing, ain't it, Jack?"

Jack spoke as he took the rope down from his shoulder and handed Ben the two torches to hold for him. "It would be for me, I suppose, if she was my daughter. Not to say that Rosalee is the kind of woman who has to have lots of money to make her happy. But I can see how you'd feel good knowing you could give her nice things."

"Yes, that's all I ever wanted: to be able to give Rosalee nice things," said Ben, examining the tips of the torches as Jack Bell looped the rope around his waist and tied it. "Is it wrong for a man to go to extremes in order to provide for his daughter, Jack?"

"No, Ben. You've done nothing wrong that I can see." Jack managed a slight smile, taking one of the torches from Ben's gloved hand. "Searching for lost gold might be a little out of the ordinary, but I wouldn't call it *extreme*." He gestured a nod down at the ground. "Some people might call you foolish, out here looking for lost gold. But if there's gold down there, they won't call you foolish. They'll call you, *sir*."

"I don't care much what they call me one way or the other," said Ben. "Not so long as Rosalee's happy with me."

"I expect Rosalee will be happy with you either way, Ben," said Bell. He kneeled down and brushed snow away from the small opening into the mountain's belly.

"Much obliged, Jack," said Ben. "I've been needing to hear something like that."

With one end of the rope tied around his waist, Jack Bell jerked on it and said, "Don't forget, two hard tugs on this means I'm in trouble . . . start pulling me back. If I tug on it five times, it means for you to come on behind me, I've found something. Are we clear on that?"

"Yes, I understand," said Ben. "Two hard yanks means pull you out, five yanks means follow you." He nodded with finality as if ingraining the information in his mind. "Be careful," he added.

"I'll try," said Bell. "Here goes."

Ben watched Jack Bell take out a tin of sulphur matches. Opening the tin, he took out a match and struck it. Then cupping it in his hand against the wind, he quickly lit the torch.

Ben held the coiled rope and fed it out to him as Jack Bell shoved the torch ahead of himself and belly-crawled into the earth. Having been forewarned about the ancient skeleton lying in the long crawl space, Bell scooted to one side and looked at it in the torchlight as he pulled himself past. He stopped long enough to look closely at the dusty shreds of leather and cloth still clinging to the brittle calcium remains. Then he crawled on.

Thirty feet past the skeleton, Bell stopped when he saw the outer light of the torch in front of him spread out in width. The walls of the narrow opening had opened up into a larger area. Bell breathed in deeply and whispered to himself, "Well, there is something down here . . . that much is right." He crawled forward until his free hand found the edge of an opening. He had reached a large cave; he was certain. But this was no time to get in a hurry. He had no idea how far down it might be from this edge to solid ground.

Bell held the torch out at arm's length and eased forward until he was able to support himself on his elbows. The torchlight spread over the rock walls of a large cavern. Jack Bell looked up in awe at the craggy stone ceiling twenty feet above him, then down at the dust-covered floor four feet below. He eased out through the opening like a mole and stood against the wall, untying the rope from around his waist. He gave five solid jerks on the length of rope, letting Ben know it was all right to come down. As Bell waited for Ben Finley, he drew in a few feet of rope every few seconds, knowing Ben was on his way. Bell waited patiently, looking all around the cavern until he heard Ben Finley scraping along toward him through the small tunnel. "Here's the cavern here, Ben, just like you said it would be."

"Thank God!" said Ben Finley, coming out of the tunnel torch first. Jack Bell gave him a hand of assistance until Ben stepped down onto solid ground beside him. With his hand on Ben Finley's arm, Bell felt the old man tremble at the sight of the large cavern. "It's here, Jack, so help me! It's here!" He hurriedly untied the rope from around his waist.

"Calm down, Ben. I believe you," said Bell. "Let's take it nice and easy. If it's here, you'll find it. That's for sure."

"I am calm," said Ben, his eyes darting back and forth in the flicker of torchlight. "At least, I'm as calm as I can be."

"I understand," said Jack Bell. He held out his burning torch and stepped forward, Ben right behind him, both of them warily examining the cavern. On the walls they saw ancient drawings of stick figures: man, horse, buffalo, antelope. "Looks like this was a busy place at some time over the past few hundred years," said Bell, holding his torch out near the wall.

"It's had its share of comings and goings all right," Ben agreed, scraping his boot back and forth across the floor, seeing broken animal bones, a stone scraping tool and a small pedestal work stone. In the dust on the earth floor, dog tracks ran in all directions, all of the same size, apparently all from the same animal. "Looks like my friend the dog has been the most recent one to live here."

"Yep," Bell agreed. He glanced to their side at a metal-trimmed shipping trunk that lay covered with dust, its lid open. "We know this didn't belong to whoever made those drawings." He stepped over to the shipping trunk and stooped down for a closer look. Running his hand along the open lid through a fine, thin coat of dust, he said, "This doesn't appear to have been here long."

"No, it hasn't," said Ben Finley. He stood staring at the trunk, his memory becoming more and more clear, a grim expression on his face.

Bell reached down inside the trunk and pulled up a small drawstring bag. He shook it slightly to remove the dust in order to make out the words printed on it. "West Track Mining Company," he read aloud, turning, holding the empty bag up for Ben Finley to see. At the same time, his eyes searched back and forth on the ground, looking for more. "This is bringing back some recollection for you?" he asked.

"Yes, it is," said Ben Finley, his voice taking on a grave tone. "And I don't like what I'm recalling." He backed up a step, turned and looked all around the cavern until his eyes followed the dog's paw prints into the deeper darkness of another entranceway twenty feet away. Without another word to Jack Bell, Ben began following the paw prints.

"Ben, wait up," said Bell. "Let's not get separated from one another down here."

Jack Bell might just as well have been talking to the stone walls surrounding them. Ben Finley walked on like a man in a trance. Bell followed, quickening his pace as the circling light of Ben's torch reached farther ahead into the darkness away from him.

"There was a robbery four years back," said Ben, his voice sounding different somehow. There was a strange new clarity about him now in both his voice and his demeanor. He stared straight ahead as he ventured onward. "Three men stole a shipment of gold on its way to Wakely. The men were never caught, and the gold was never recovered. It was over a hundred thousand dollars worth of nuggets," Ben continued, his voice going a bit lower as Jack Bell caught up and walked alongside him.

"But this is not something you've just now remembered, is it, Ben? This is something you already knew," said Jack Bell.

Ben Finley stopped in his tracks. Still staring straight ahead into the darkness beyond the torchlight, he said, "That's right, Jack. I already knew all that."

"And you know what we're going to find up ahead, don't you, Ben?" said Bell, probing as he tried to help the old man sort out whatever dark images had come upon him.

"Yes," Ben said grimly. "I know what we're going to find up ahead. We're going to find the body of a man I killed. Unless someone or something has moved him, he'll still be there with a bullet hole in his chest."

Ben Finley's words stunned Jack Bell for a second. He almost came to a halt. But seeing Ben continue steadily on, Bell kept up with him. "You killed one of the men who robbed the mining company?"

"No . . . I killed somebody else. Somebody I wish to God I'd never killed. You'll see when we get there."

Bell studied his fixed stare in the flicker of torchlight. "And you had forgotten all this until we came down that tunnel? That's hard to believe, Ben."

"You've got to believe me, Jack," said Ben. "Some of it was coming back to me in bits and pieces, but for the most part I didn't remember it until I looked at that gold bag you picked up back there.

Somehow, seeing that empty gold bag made all the pieces fall back into place." He stopped abruptly and shook his head. His voice trembled against a tide of remorse. "I took a man's life, Jack . . . and I haven't allowed myself to face up to that fact until today."

Jack Bell followed him, a step behind, down a long corridor that gradually lessened in height until, by the time it opened into another cavern, they were walking slightly crouched with their heads bowed beneath a low ceiling. Once inside the new cavern, the musty, lingering smell of death filled the thin air and the light of their torches glowed upon a dried corpse lying propped up against a large stone. Jack Bell waved his torch back and forth slowly, hoping the fire would help dissipate the foul, looming smell.

The corpse wore a rawhide shirt with a bullet hole in the chest surrounded by a black bloodstain. From the long braided hair and knee-length moccasins, it was plain to Jack Bell that this was the corpse of an Indian. An elderly Indian, he thought to himself, observing closely. A lizard sat perched on the corpse's shoulder. It looked at the two newcomers to this lower realm, then darted down inside the corpse's rawhide shirt.

"There he is," said Ben Finley, keeping his voice lowered as if it might awaken the man he'd killed, "right where I left him."

Jack Bell walked over to the corpse and looked closer, but Ben stood back, a look of shame and regret on his shadowed face. "What happened here, Ben?" he asked, looking down at a long knife that had fallen from the outstretched fingers of the Indian's dying hand.

Ben said quietly, "I wish I could say it was self-defense. But that ain't so. I never should have come onto his place. It was back in the other cavern where I shot him. I followed him here and watched him die. I might've been able to help him, but I didn't. I was badly wounded myself."

"How does your killing this man tie in with the three men who robbed the mine, Ben?" Bell asked, still looking down at the corpse as the lizard ran across its dried, shrunken belly beneath the rawhide shirt.

A silence passed as Ben Finley summoned up the strength to relive the events of a year ago in his mind.

"Four years ago, I'd been panning the upper streams for nuggets when I came upon the camp of the three men who'd robbed the gold shipment down on the lower trail. They never saw me hiding above them in the rocks while they counted bag after bag of the gold nuggets. At first I had no idea they'd stolen that gold, although I knew they sure didn't look like any prospectors I'd ever met. These were well-dressed men wearing suits and dusters. They rode big horses suited to the teeth with firearms. You know the type, I reckon."

"Yes," said Bell, trying to get a picture of the men.

"Well, the more I listened, the more I come to realize they had stolen that gold. I should have high-tailed right then and got out of there . . . but seeing that much gold does strange things to a man. I lay there and watched and listened, knowing they couldn't see me. And when I heard them say they had to hide that gold and lie low for awhile, I decided then and there to follow them and see where they put it. So I did . . ." His words trailed.

"And once they were gone, you came in here and took it," said Bell, getting the picture now.

"Oh, no, this wasn't where they hid the gold," said Ben. "It was nearly twelve miles from here where they hid it. I took it from there and searched for over a whole day until I came upon this place and decided to hide it here." He shrugged. "See, I knew that I couldn't be caught carrying that stolen gold any more than they could. I decided to leave it buried up here for as long as I needed to. Then one day I'd come get it and take Rosalee away from here."

"What went wrong?" asked Bell, keeping Ben Finley talking, glad to see the old man get all of this terrible burden off his chest.

"Everything worked out fine the first couple of years," said Ben. "I prospected up here, so nobody thought much about me always coming up this way. I came by every few months, keeping an eye on my hidden treasure . . . but it was eating me alive, knowing it was here and not being able to bring it home to my daughter. But soon the robbery talk died down. The mine detectives stopped looking for the robbers. I was all set to make my move. But then I got up here, and an old Ute and his dog had drifted in and taken over this part of the cavern." He nodded at the corpse. "I reckon you can guess the rest of it."

"So the dog belonged to this man?" asked Bell. "You didn't recall ever seeing the dog before?"

"No," said Ben Finley, "and that's the God's-honest truth. I still don't recognize the dog as being from here. But I know it's him . . . and on our way walking back in here a while ago, it dawned on me why that dog has stuck with me. He recognized the scent of his dead master on that leather satchel I carried. That satchel used to belong to this man." He pointed down at the corpse, not allowing himself to look straight at it.

"You think a dog has that kind of memory?" Bell asked quietly.

"Yes, I do," said Ben. "He remembers the feel of a warm fire. He remembers the scent of his master." Ben's voice took on a tone of regret once again. "He wasn't here when I killed this man, or I bet he'd have remembered that too. He brought me here, you know. Was he trying to show me what happened to his master? Did the scent make him think that I was this man?"

Bell saw the dark depression come to Ben's eyes. "That's something you'll never know, Ben . . . so don't torture yourself over it." He looked back at the corpse, then back at Ben, wanting him to continue. It was better for the old man to talk about it than to think about it, Bell decided.

Ben Finley stood lost in dark contemplation for a moment. Then he said, "This old Ute Indian came here because this was the last place in the world left for him . . . the last place where he thought he could find peace for himself. I tried to reason with him, let him know that I had to go through here into the back cavern. I even offered him money, chewing tobacco. He wouldn't budge. I was afraid to tell him what I wanted back there for fear he might want to keep it for himself."

"The Utes place no value on gold," said Bell.

"Yes, I've always known that," said Ben. "But I lost my head. It's hard to think straight when there's a hundred thousand dollars involved. Like I said, the gold was eating me up, Jack. I was a wild man in a wild man's world, thinking with a wild man's mind. I can't excuse myself for it."

Jack Bell studied Ben Finley's tired eyes.

"I waited up in the rocks until I saw the dog leave," said Ben. "Then I snuck in, found the old Indian asleep and tried to slip right past him. But he heard me, I reckon. He woke up and stalked me along the corridor there. He shot me with an arrow, the one that was stuck in my back when they found me. And then —" Ben's voice cracked and weakened. "He came at me with that knife, and God help me, I shot him and watched him die!" He bowed his face in his weathered hand.

Jack Bell gave him a moment of silence.

Then Ben's voice resumed, little more than a whisper. "I grew weak from loss of blood, but I took off my shirt and tried to get the arrow out, only I ended up breaking it. From there it gets foggy again. I must've wrapped the blanket around myself and wandered down from here to where they found me."

"Then the gold is still back there, back where we came in?" Jack Bell asked.

"Yes, unless somebody has found it and taken it, it's still back there. I haven't seen any strange boot prints." He pointed at the dust-thick floor, at some prints that had long since faded beneath fine new layers of dust until they were faint impressions with rounded edges. "Those are all my tracks from the day I killed him," Ben said, pointing down. "Now that all this is coming back to me, I wish I'd never had to lay eyes on it again."

"You don't mean that, Ben," said Jack Bell. "What about Rosalee? What about everything you've been saying about giving her a better life?"

"I suppose you're right," said Ben. "It's just that I feel so low-down awful now. I can't understand how a man can block something like that from his mind for so long. Then all of a sudden it came back to me like a bolt of lightning. I reckon the only right thing for me to do is to go to the law, tell them everything that happened and throw myself on the mercy of the court."

"Let's go see if the gold's there, Ben. We'll take this thing one step at a time. You want to make sure that whatever you do is the right thing for both you and your daughter."

"Thank you, Jack," said Ben Finley. "I can't tell you how good it feels knowing I've got somebody I can trust on my side. If I had a son, I'd want him to be just like you."

Jack thought about it for a second, then said, "If I were your son, Ben, I'd count myself fortunate to have you as a father."

In spite of his low state of remorse for what he'd done, Ben Finley managed a smile. "Come on now. I'll uncover that gold, and we'll get back down the mountain to Rosalee."

CHAPTER 20

They walked through the stone corridor back to the first cavern they'd entered. Once there, Ben Finley walked along the far wall with his torch held out, lighting his way. With no problem at all he followed the drawings on the wall until he came to a spot where a pair of ancient hands had crudely drawn a scene of the sun; beneath it, a stick figure of a man stood throwing a spear into a herd of fleeing buffalo. On the ground beneath the wall, a boulder stuck up from the earth.

"Here, hold this for me," said Ben. He handed Jack Bell his torch and stooped down, wrapping both arms around the center of the boulder.

"Wait, let me help you, Ben," Jack Bell offered. But as he looked around for a place to lay the torches, Ben shook his head and leaned all of his weight against the heavy rock. It turned over onto its side with a jarring thud. Then Ben stepped back, blowing out a breath and wiping his palms together.

"There it is, Jack, right where I hid it." He held out his hand for his torch. Jack handed it to him, and the two stooped down and cast the torchlight over the hole beneath the overturned boulder.

"If I ever doubted you before, Ben, I never would again," said Bell, seeing the pile of small canvas drawstring bags, each the same as the empty one he'd found earlier. Only these weren't empty. These were bulging and tight. Jack and Ben both reached down, each picking up one of the plump, hand-sized gold nugget bags and hefting it in his palm. Ben watched Bell open the drawstring, shake a small mound of tiny nuggets and dust into his hand and look closely at it.

"It's hard to imagine how no more than a thimbleful of that stuff is worth more than the average man owns in this whole wide world," said Ben, awed by the sight of the softly glowing mound of unrefined gold.

"Yes, it is hard to imagine," said Jack Bell, impressed but not ecstatic. "I always wonder how gold came to be what it is. Brass is harder and shines just as well. Copper's more useful —"

"Aw, but there's nothing as pretty or as sought-after as gold," said Ben, cutting him off. With a bittersweet smile, he went on, saying in quiet contemplation, "It's so popular because the streets of heaven are paved with it. Because the Lord's chariot is made of it . . . and because angels play music on harps of solid gold."

"That's as good a reason as any, I expect," said Bell, "and just as real as some I've heard." He poured the small mound of gold carefully back into the bag, drew the string tight and laid the bag gently back where he'd gotten it.

Ben raised his eyes to meet Jack Bell's. A sadness came to his face. "I reckon when a man has spent his entire life in search of a thing the way I have, the last thing he better do is start questioning the value of it." He glanced at the darkness leading back to the other cavern where the corpse lay suspended in endless time. "Gold is what we've turned it into. The only value of anything is the amount we're willing to place on it: no more, no less." He too laid the small bag among the others and stood looking down at it.

A silence passed. Then Jack said, "Looks like it'll be easier going if we take this out through the front. How's the trail out there?"

"It's not bad, the best I recall," said Ben. "We'll come out farther back down on the main trail. It'll get us down to the camp a little quicker."

"We better start packing this gold up and

get ready to go," said Bell. "It's going to be a hefty load in all this snow. Looks like that mule is finally going to start earning his keep."

For the next half hour, the two loaded the bags of gold into the empty saddlebags until the saddlebags bulged at the seams. When they were barely able to close the straps on the heavy saddlebags, there were still several bags of gold left lying in the hole. Ben picked one up and tried stuffing it down into his saddlebags, but Bell stopped him. "We can't get all of them in one trip, Ben. We'll have to take these down and come back tomorrow."

Ben wiped his beaded forehead on his coat sleeve. "We can't leave all this here!" He stripped off his coat and laid it on the ground at his feet. Rolling up his shirt sleeves, he said, "It's too hot down here; I'm burning up."

"Slow down, Ben," Jack Bell cautioned. "You're working yourself into a lather over this. Look at you: A while ago you were talking about turning yourself and the gold in; now you can't stand thinking about leaving some of it behind until we can come back tomorrow and get it."

Ben Finley took a deep breath and let it out slowly. "I'm sorry, Jack. See? See how gold does a man? A while ago I was wishing I'd never laid eyes on it. Now that I'm standing here able to run my fingers through it, I can't get enough of it." He shook his tired head. "I swear, I'm ashamed of myself acting this way, especially with that old man lying in there dead." He got himself in check, then said, "All right, Jack . . . let's do it your way. We know where it is when we want it. This time I won't forget."

Jack Bell smiled. "Don't worry, I wouldn't let you if you tried." They finished strapping their saddlebags shut, rolled the rock back into place over the hole where the few remaining bags lay, and in moments had left the cave to rest in pitch darkness as their torchlights moved away down the stone corridor.

For three days the dog had done little more than limp past the horse and the mule to the front of the crevice and stare out across the sky above the treetops. Today, in the afternoon, he ventured out past the opening and looked up in the direction Jack Bell and Ben Finley had taken up the mountainside. He whined for a moment. Then he turned, facing the trail down the mountain, and a growl rumbled low in his chest. *Like a bad omen,* Rosalee thought. She watched the dog shiver, then limp across the trail, relieve himself and slink back inside the crevice to his warm spot near the fire. The stitches in his side were still tender but healing steadily.

While he went back to sleep, Rosalee walked out into the dimming sunlight with Jack Bell's rifle cradled in her arms. She looked upward herself, along ridgeline after ridgeline, but saw no sign of Bell or her father, only the stirring of the wind and white veils of snow powder drifting from the pine canopy. Higher up, the wind moaned.

"Cat or no cat," Rosalee said aloud to the mountainside, "if you two are not back tonight, first thing tomorrow I'll come looking for you."

Jack Bell and her father had left early in the morning before daybreak. They should have been back by now, Rosalee thought. She had been worried about the two ever since they'd left camp. Now, with the shadows of evening stretching long and dark across the land, her concern grew. A faint sound down the trail drew her attention, and she walked warily toward the first turn where the trail curved and dropped down out of sight.

"Careful, Rosalee; watch your step," she whispered to herself. Knowing the big cat could be anywhere, she lay her thumb over the hammer of the rifle and stepped over to the far edge of the trail, hoping for a better view around the curve. As she crept closer, she heard a horse nicker low under its breath. Relieved that it was not the cat waiting around the turn in the trail, she let her thumb fall loose on the rifle hammer and called out, "Hello the trail! Who's out there?"

Rosalee waited for a second. When no reply came, she walked forward slowly until she'd rounded the turn enough to see a horse standing riderless, staring back at her, its reins dangling in the snow. Fearing the horse's rider might have fallen victim to the cat, she stepped closer, looking the horse over for any blood or signs of an attack. At first the horse shied back a step, but then it stopped and stood still as Rosalee put out a hand and took a hold of its reins.

"What are you doing out here all alone?" Rosalee asked in a whisper, her eyes going past the animal and checking the trail behind it.

No sooner had she looked along the trail than her eyes went to the ground alongside the horse and saw the boot prints in the snow where someone had stepped down from the saddle. She retightened her thumb across the rifle's hammer, seeing that the prints ran right past her feet. But as she turned quickly around in that direction, a strong hand seemed to come out of nowhere and snatch the rifle from her hands, slinging her to the ground in the process.

"Well, well, just look at you!" Delbert Hanks stood over her, wearing a wide, cruel grin, the rifle gripped in his gloved left hand. In his right hand, his pistol was out and cocked, pointed down at her. "I was hoping that horse was going to answer you, ma'am! Just think what he'd be worth if he did something like that."

"What do you want?" Rosalee asked in surprise and fear.

"What do I *want?*" Delbert chuckled, looking her up and down with hungry eyes. His expression caused her to pull her coat closed across her breasts. "Ma'am, you couldn't have picked a worse question at this very moment." He stepped forward, reached down with the rifle barrel and tried to open her coat with it. But Rosalee shoved the rifle barrel away.

"My father is right around this turn!" Rosalee hissed. "You better get out of here, you saddle tramp!"

"Ain't that just like a woman?" Delbert shook his head as if in disappointment. "We ain't known one another five minutes . . . you're already lying to me and calling me bad names."

"Mister, I'm warning you," Rosalee said, trying to bluff her way out. "I'm not alone here."

"Hush now, of course you are," said Delbert, brushing her words away. "I heard Jack Bell came up here with an old man and his daughter. Now that I see you, I reckon Jack wasn't crazy coming out in this weather after all. I figure they're off somewhere, else Jack himself would be out here checking things over instead of you." As Delbert spoke, he tossed the rifle aside and began unbuttoning his coat with his free hand. "And that would have been his bad luck . . . cause I already would have killed him. Whereas I couldn't live with myself if I had killed something as pretty as you . . . especially before we introduced ourselves properlike. Got to know one another." He pulled his coat open, unfastened his gunbelt and let it fall to his feet.

"I don't know what you *think* you're going to do," Rosalee warned, drawing her coat tighter as she scooted backward on the snowy ground, Delbert stepping right along with her, "but if you try laying a hand on me, you better hope you learn to see out your ears. I'm slicing your eyes out before you kill me!" She held her free hand up, her nails spread like claws.

"I like women who talk tough to me," Delbert said, grinning, stalking forward. Rosalee managed to scramble to her feet, running backward at first, then turning, slipping in the snow as she made her way around the turn in the trail, toward the crevice. Delbert stopped and watched her run, cocking his head to one side, studying her as she fled. "My goodness . . . what did I ever do to deserve something this good?"

He allowed Rosalee to get almost to the crevice before he turned to the horse, picked up its reins and led it along behind him, leaving his gun belt where he'd dropped it. Before entering the crevice where smoke curled up from between the rocks, Delbert tied the horse to a jet of snowcapped rock and said to it, "This don't concern you; you wait out here where it's nice and cool." He laughed to himself. "I'll just drop in there by the fire. I shouldn't be over an hour or two!"

At the entrance to the small campsite, Rosalee had slipped on ice and fallen to the ground. She continued slipping and falling as Delbert walked toward her. Then she finally got her footing and pushed her way past the mule and the horse and ran frantically around the fire, searching for something she could use to defend herself. "Hope you're as ready for me as I am for you," Delbert called out, shoving the mule to one side and coming on into the crevice.

As Delbert stepped inside, the wounded dog stood up stiffly at the sound of his voice and the commotion caused by Rosalee rummaging wildly for a weapon. "God almighty, what an ugly dog," said Delbert, cutting a glance at the wounds and the missing fur on the dog's side. The dog growled low and stood staring at Delbert with its hackles raised. Delbert swung his cocked pistol toward the dog. "Don't give me no hard time. You ain't worth a bullet, but I'll sure put one in you." He continued around the fire, avoiding the dog, and headed for Rosalee, seeing her raise the skillet in her hand.

She spun toward him, wielding it like a club. "Stay away from me," she screamed.

A shot from Delbert Hanks' pistol knocked the skillet from her hand. "You'll have to do better than that," Delbert said, grinning. But his grin vanished at the sound of the dog coming at him. Before he could cock the pistol again and swing it around, the big cur shot out across the fire and

334

clamped its jaws on his gun hand just above his wrist.

Delbert screamed for help as he fell. "Please! Get him off me! For God sakes!" With the big wounded cur atop him shaking its head back and forth, its sharp fangs spiked into his bleeding wrist, Delbert's pistol flew from his hand and landed all the way across the fire out of sight beneath the mule's hooves. "Call him off me!"

But Rosalee wasn't about to call the dog off. Not seeing Delbert's gun, she continued slinging supplies back and forth until she closed her fingers tightly around the handle of her father's big hunting knife and turned on Delbert with it. Seeing her coming, Delbert hurriedly crawled away, dragging the dog around the fire with him to avoid the knife. Rosalee lunged at him, stabbing and slashing.

Being dragged too close to the fire, the dog felt the short flames lick at his side. He turned Delbert loose with a loud yelp. Fire singed his thin fur.

"Damn you! Put that knife down!" Delbert screamed at Rosalee, kicking at her with his boot as he scrambled quickly toward his pistol. But Rosalee stabbed at him with no mercy, the blade going deep into his leg beside his shin. As Delbert screamed and jerked his leg away, the knife came loose from her fingers. "I'll kill you!" Delbert raged.

But when Delbert flung himself the last few inches toward his pistol, the excitement overtook the mule and it brayed and stomped and managed to pull Delbert beneath its sharp hooves. He gave up trying for the pistol and concentrated on shielding himself. He wrapped both arms around his head. "God! Get it off me!" Delbert screamed. Blood flew from the gashes on his wrist, from the knife blade sunk deep in his leg, and now from a deep gash the mule's glancing hoof made on his forehead.

Rosalee wasn't about to risk getting trampled making a move for Delbert's pistol. Instead, she returned to her father's supplies, searching for the sawed-off shotgun. Having carried Jack Bell's rifle all day, she'd given no regard to the old shotgun. Now she looked all around for it desperately. Finally she saw it leaning against the rock. She snatched it up while the commotion continued behind her on the other side of the fire. Without even checking to see if it was loaded, she threw it up to her trembling shoulder and advanced around the fire with it cocked and ready.

"On your feet," Rosalee shrieked. "I've

got you covered!"

But Delbert was pinned against the wall by the nonstop fury of the mule's kicking front hooves. The mule brayed loud and long. When Delbert did try to get away from the hooves by scurrying beneath the mule and trying to get out of the small area, the horse nipped at him and turned enough in the tight area to get a solid shot at him with its powerful rear hooves. All Rosalee could do was watch in awe. She couldn't risk pulling the trigger and hitting the animals.

"Come out with your hands raised!" Rosalee shouted, feeling more and more in control, seeing both the horse and the mule taking their turns at kicking and nipping at the man.

"I can't! For God sakes, help — !" Delbert's plea for help cut short in a gasp as Whiskey's hooves landed a blow in his stomach and sent him rolling in a ball on the dirt floor. Rosalee had to jump out of the way to keep Delbert from knocking her down.

"You can raise them now with no excuse," Rosalee said, positioning herself over him with the tip of the shotgun barrel only inches from his face.

It took Delbert a moment before he could utter a word. He still lay in a ball, struggling

337

to catch his breath. "You . . . wouldn't shoot me . . . would you?" he managed to ask in a strained, tortured voice.

"I hope you try something else, mister," said Rosalee, "just so you'll find out." Rosalee was surprised at how steady her voice sounded. Her hands were a bit shaky, but not too shaky. She'd grown out of breath struggling to the crevice through the snow and ice. But now she'd recovered. She'd taken control.

The dog stepped in beside Rosalee and stood with its hackles raised, it fangs bared, ready to hurl itself on Delbert. The horse and the mule had settled as quickly as they had blown up, the mule having to stomp a front hoof and make a few more brays to wind itself down. "I don't know . . . how this . . . got so . . . out of hand," Delbert said, squeezing his words out. "I only wanted to talk to . . . Jack Bell."

"Then you're in luck," said Rosalee, her voice firm, not buying a word this man had to say. "You'll be talking to him the moment he gets back to camp. Until then, if you so much as make one false move, I'll empty this shotgun into you and feed the dog what's left."

CHAPTER 21

Carrying the saddlebags full of gold made the climb back down the mountainside slow and cumbersome. By the time Jack Bell and Ben Finley stepped onto the trail, the sun had slipped down out of sight, leaving only a fiery wreath along the jagged skyline. As soon as they came upon the fresh hoofprints in the snow, they became suspicious. But when they moved forward a few yards and found Delbert's boot prints and Rosalee's footprints in the disheveled snow, Ben almost sobbed aloud.

"Keep a clear head, Ben," Bell cautioned him. A few feet away lay the discarded gun belt and Jack Bell's rifle. Bell reached down and picked up his rifle and ran a gloved hand along the barrel. He checked it quickly, making sure it was loaded.

"Oh my God! Rosalee!" Ben said, no longer able to control himself. His shaky voice resounded in the evening silence. He dropped the heavy bags from his shoulder, ready to bolt toward the crevice. Bell grabbed his arm, stopping him.

"No, Ben, wait!" Bell commanded in a

harsh whisper. "We don't want to announce ourselves from out here. . . . We'll do her more harm than good!"

"You're right." Ben gained control quickly. "Tell me what to do!"

"Follow me," Bell whispered, keeping a close eye toward the crevice and the slow curl of smoke rising from it as he slipped the heavy saddlebags from his shoulder and hurried to the side of the trail. Bell pitched his heavy saddlebags behind a rock. Ben did the same. They turned and hurried alongside the trail in a crouch until they took cover for a moment behind a snowcapped boulder.

Delbert's horse saw them and nickered under its breath. "Here," said Bell, shoving his rifle into Ben's hands. "You get on the other side, near the horse. Let me go in first. If something goes wrong for me, you'll still be out here, able to help her."

Ben realized that Jack Bell had just told him he was willing to be the first to risk his life to save Rosalee. But there was no time to even thank him. Instead, Ben only swallowed the knot in his throat and nodded his head. "I understand," Ben whispered. He hurried toward the lone horse outside the crevice. Jack Bell hurried to the entrance, his pistol drawn and ready. Yet before he got all the way to the entrance, Rosalee came walking out alongside the mule, the shotgun in her hands.

"Father? Jack? Are you two out here?" No sooner had she asked than Jack Bell saw her and came to a halt, lowering his pistol and letting out a tight breath.

Ben Finley ran to his daughter as fast as the slippery ground would allow. "Oh Rosalee! We thought something terrible had happened to you." Before hugging her to his chest, Ben gestured a hand toward the strange horse.

"It almost did, Father," said Rosalee. "But your wild dog protected me." She smiled across his shoulder at Jack Bell.

"See," said Ben, "I told you that's a good dog!" He held Rosalee out at arm's length. "Are you sure you're all right?"

"Yes, Father, I'm all right," said Rosalee. "And don't worry: The man riding that horse is inside with his feet and hands tied. The dog's guarding him." She turned to Jack Bell. "The man said his name is Hanks. He said he came up here to warn you that there are men on your trail. Do you know him?"

"Delbert," said Bell, nodding his head slowly. "Yes, I know him. He's a no-account backshooter. I don't think you can believe anything he tells you. He works for Early Philpot in Elk Horn."

"He said these men are detectives, Jack," said Rosalee, giving Bell a worried look. "He said they're out to collect a bounty on you."

"A bounty?" Bell looked toward the crevice. "I guess I better find out what he's talking about." He turned his gaze to Ben Finley and said, "Ben, while I go talk to this man, why don't you tell Rosalee what we found up there?"

A gleam came to Ben's tired eyes. "You think she really wants to know?"

"I bet she does," said Bell, walking to the crevice with his rifle hanging from his hand.

"All right, Father. What did you find up there?" Rosalee asked with a slight sigh, as if prepared for bad news.

Ben took out one of the small nugget bags as Jack Bell stepped inside the crevice. "Well, Rosalee," Ben said, "what we found was a whole lot of these little fellows . . ." His words trailed as he opened the drawstring and shook out a small mound of gold dust and nuggets onto his palm.

"Oh my goodness, Father!" Rosalee said in a hushed tone. She put her hands to her cheeks, stunned. "Is that what I think it is?"

"Only if you think it's pure, solid, glittering gold!" Ben Finley said, unable to contain himself seeing the sparkle of awe and excitement in his daughter's eyes. "You've just become the richest young woman in Nolan's Gap!"

Inside the crevice, Jack Bell stopped and stood looking down at Delbert Hanks. Delbert sat holding a wet bandanna to the gash on his forehead with his tied hands, the wound on his leg caked with dried blood. "What are you looking at," Delbert growled under his breath. Two feet away, the dog stood with its head lowered, its hackles half-raised, staring at the wounded ne'er-do-well. Before Bell could reply, a squeal of delight came from Rosalee outside the rock crevice.

Delbert shot a sarcastic scowl toward the sound of Rosalee's voice and said, "What's she got to be so happy about?"

"That's none of your business, Delbert," said Bell. "The last time I laid eyes on you, I told you not to ever cross my path again. Now here you are . . . too brash and stupid to heed good advice." Now that Bell had arrived, the dog backed away and laid down near the fire as if a changing of guards had occurred.

"Believe it or not, mister," said Delbert, "I came here to warn you. Figured I owed you that much for pulling me out of the snow slide." He raised his tied hands. "You've got no right to hold me prisoner here. Get this rope off me."

"Save your breath, Delbert. The rope stays on. You're not going anywhere. And I *don't* believe anything you've got to say. I have no idea what I did to get you stuck to me . . . but I get the feeling nothing will shake you loose until one of us kills the other."

Delbert gave a sly grin. "You already showed me you can't kill nobody, Bell. If you could, I'd never have been able to ride away after you pulled me and Rance Hardaway from the snow. You're weak, Bell. You showed it that day, helping us. That was a bad mistake." He shook his head back and forth slowly.

"Speaking of your partner, Hardaway, where is he?" Bell asked.

"Partner!" Delbert spit as if to get rid of a bad taste. "That sumbitch was no partner of mine. He had a yellow streak up his back a yard wide. He never made it back to Nolan's Gap. He died of lead poisoning."

"That figures," said Bell. "I suppose you shot him while his back was turned."

"What's the difference if his back was turned or not?" Delbert shrugged. "Dead's dead in my book, any way you read it." Again he spread the sly grin. "Want to hear something funny? All the mining detectives think you kilt him." He chuckled aloud. "Don't know where they got such a notion. But that's what I came to warn you about. There was a detective killed out there too. Somehow they all think that's also your doings. They sure have it in for you." He grinned.

"You told the detectives I killed two men?" Bell felt his fists ball at his sides in rage. "You rotten punk! I've never harmed you or anyone near you in word or deed. Now, just when things are going good for me, you put me in the jackpot this way."

"I agree it's a damn shame. Don't you just hate people like me?" Delbert snickered.

"I ought to walk you off a steep cliff and watch you fall," said Bell.

"Yeah, you probably ought to," said Delbert. "But you won't. Like I said, I know *weak* when I see it."

Bell let out a breath in exasperation. "I would ask why you're doing this to me, Delbert," he said, "but the shame of it is, you don't really know why yourself."

"Sure I do," said Delbert. "It's because Early Philpot sent me to take care of you, and you fouled up the deal for me — made me look bad. I can't have that, not if I'm ever going to make it in this gunman business."

"We're leaving first thing in the morning, Delbert. I'm taking you all the way back to Elk Horn, and I'm making you tell the sheriff there what really happened."

"Like hell I'll tell him," said Delbert. "I'll deny everything. Nobody's heard me say it but you. It's your word against mine, and you're nothing but a drifter. Nobody will take your word; nobody will vouch for you."

"Maybe somebody will, Delbert. I've got enough faith to think that something as rotten as you can only get so far. You can't keep doing people this way forever."

"We'll see about that," said Delbert. "If you're thinking of the barkeeper in Nolan's Gap vouching for you, you're in for a big disappointment. Last I saw, his saloon was burning to the ground. Odds are, these detectives who're on your trail left him and his woman lying dead on the floor."

"Why, you lousy — !" Bell stepped forward, his hands trembling in rage, ready to reach out around Delbert's throat. But he felt Ben and Rosalee grab him from behind and hold him back.

"Jack! No!" said Rosalee. "Don't let him get to you. He's nothing but a devil in the skin! Can't you see he's only trying to get you upset?"

"I know," said Bell, "and he's doing a good job of it. This lying fool has told every detective in Elk Horn that I killed two men. Now they're out gunning for me."

"But why?" Ben asked, a look of bewilderment on his face. "Why on earth would anybody —"

"Save yourself the trouble of asking, Ben," said Bell, cutting him off. "Delbert here is just a bitter, twisted punk. He doesn't need a reason to hurt people. It's just something he enjoys doing."

Ben looked at the smirk on Delbert's face. Then he looked back at Bell. "What are we going to do, Jack? I just told Rosalee what we found up there. Things is just now looking up for her and me."

"What did you find up there, old man?" Delbert asked. "I hope it's something worth dying for."

"Keep your mouth shut, Delbert," said Bell. "I've never cracked a man's head while his hands are tied . . . but stop pushing." He turned back to Ben Finley. "We're going on back to Nolan's Gap, Ben, just like we meant to before this man showed up. All you do when a foul wind like this blows in is to go on with your life until it passes."

Ben glared at Delbert. "For two cents I'd put a bullet between his eyes."

"Don't stoop to his level," said Bell. "Rosalee pegged him right. He's a devil in skin. We have to manage to live with him awhile. I'm taking him to Nolan's Gap, or even to Elk Horn if I have to. There's a sheriff in Elk Horn. I'll make sure everybody learns the truth. Then they can do with Delbert as they please."

"The truth? Ha!" Delbert jeered. "The truth is whatever they all wanted to believe to begin with. I've already given them that. They had no trouble at all believing you killed those two men. The best thing you can do now is get on your horse and make a run for it . . . hope they all give out before you do."

"No, I'm seeing to it you go back to Elk Horn and face justice, Delbert," said Bell. "Somebody has to expose you for what you are."

Delbert turned his face from Bell and chuckled. "You can *try* bringing this devil to justice if that's what suits you, Bell. But it's going to cost every one of you, I swear to that." He turned his attention to Ben Finley. "What did you find up there, old man? Some gold? Enough to grubstake you and little Rosalee for a while? Well, ain't that real nice?"

"It's more than any grubstake find, mister!" said Ben before thinking. "We've found enough gold to —"

"That's enough, Ben," said Bell, taking Ben by the arm and pulling him away. "Let's talk outside." Bell raised his pistol from its holster and handed it to Rosalee. She took it and held it firmly toward Delbert's face. As Bell and Ben Finley walked outside the crevice, leaving Rosalee with Delbert, the dog stood up from the fire, walked around and stood facing Delbert with a distrustful look in its eyes, a low growl boiling in its throat.

"Before this is over you're going to wish you never heard my name, pretty little *Rosalee*," said Delbert in a mock tone, careful not to speak too loud and anger the dog.

"I already wish it," Rosalee said flatly, the pistol not wavering an inch.

Walking through the snow back to where they'd pitched the saddlebags, Ben Finley said to Jack Bell, "I feel like I've brought all this on somehow."

Bell just looked at him.

"I know you think that sounds foolish, Jack," said Ben. "But no matter how I try to look at it, this gold ain't clean. It's got blood on it. I never came by it the right way. I wonder if this ain't all punishment for my wrongdoings. Maybe I better turn it in like I was thinking while we were up there." His eyes went to the high ridgeline above them.

"That's up to you, Ben," said Bell. "But if you do, make sure it's not because of Delbert showing up here. You had nothing to do with this. Delbert came along before I ever met you and Rosalee. This has nothing to do with either of you. It's trouble of mine."

"I know, but still," said Ben, "I feel like I brought this on some way or other."

"Listen to me, Ben," Jack Bell said firmly, stopping in the snow and turning to face the old man. "There are people who feel they have nothing good coming to them in this life. Delbert's one of them whether he knows it or not. Because he feels that way, he knows nothing else to do except destroy others. There's other people who feel they don't *deserve* anything good in life. Or they think that anything good that comes to them has to have a catch to it, something bad that comes along with it."

Ben shrugged. "You have to admit, it looks awfully peculiar, him showing up right after we found this gold. It's almost like if

Rosalee and me are going to keep this gold, we're going to have to expect some bad things to happen."

Bell gave him a patient look. "Ben, if you're going to think that way, you might just as well toss the gold over a cliff and be done with it — it's going to bring you nothing but heartache. But it will be heartache of your own choosing. The gold doesn't come with any catch to it. It's just a little windfall of good luck after what sounds to me like a long dry spell. Whatever bad thing was going to happen in life was going to happen anyway. Enjoy this as something good while you can."

"Then you're saying keep it?" Ben asked.

"I'm not saying one way or the other, Ben. I'm just saying that either way, life is going on . . . both the good and the bad. Don't turn a blessing into a curse, is all I'm saying. We've got enough trouble dealing with a *real* curse, like Delbert back there. Don't make up punishment for yourself for some wrong you never done."

Ben's voice lowered. "But I did kill that old man. I owe for that. I owe dearly."

"Then be the best man you can be, Ben, and let God collect whatever he thinks you owe. In the end, that's what it'll come down to anyway." He turned and walked on to the rock where the saddlebags lay.

Ben hurried along beside him. "Part of this gold is yours, Jack. I want you to take an even share."

"No thanks, Ben," said Bell, gazing straight ahead. "It's your gold. I've got enough money to get me wherever I'm going. If I need more, it'll come to me. It usually does."

"I'd feel lots better if you took some," Ben said. "Call it a reward for helping Rosalee find me."

"I know you'd feel better if I took some," said Bell. "But I'm not going to. If I ever needed a stake, I appreciate knowing that I could turn to you and Rosalee. That's enough reward for me, Ben." He stepped around the rock, helped Ben Finley pick up his saddlebags, then hefted his own onto his shoulder. "But let's not think of anything else now except getting ourselves down to Nolan's Gap. If those detectives see these bags with the mining company's name on them, you can bet we'll have a fight on our hands."

"But the mine's closed," said Ben. "They don't work for the company anymore."

"I realize that," said Bell. "But that fact doesn't comfort me one bit." He walked out from behind the rock with the heavy saddlebags on his shoulder.

In silence the two walked back to the crevice, their stride in the snow looking strange and awkward to the big cat who lay at the edge of a high ridge, looking down from a distance of a hundred yards. He watched the two men disappear into the wall of rock. He waited, eyeing Delbert's horse tied outside the crevice. He licked the healing wounds he'd gotten from his encounter with the dog. As darkness encroached, something higher up the mountainside caught his attention. He peaked his ears, stood up and gave a lingering look down at the horse. Then he leaped upward as quiet as a spirit and vanished as if made of air.

CHAPTER 22

At dawn, Jack Bell and the Finleys broke camp and prepared to move out along the narrow path leading downward to the main trail. Throughout the night, they'd kept a guard posted at the opening to the crevice, the low growl of the dog having given them grave warning of something lurking in the darkness. They had little doubt the cat was still alive and had returned, stalking whatever prey ventured into his world. Delbert's horse spent a nervous night. Had it not been for the possibility of the detectives seeing the light from the distant valley, they could have built a separate fire outside to keep the cat away. But that was out of the question, they'd decided. Creatures of the wild were not their greatest concern.

"Untie me," said Delbert, limping out of the crevice in the early gray light. Behind him walked Ben Finley with Jack Bell's rifle in his hands. Ben helped Delbert up into his saddle. Bell had bandaged Delbert's leg with an extra bandanna he carried in his saddlebags. Once atop his horse, Delbert said to Ben Finley, "You can't expect me to ride like this. Untie my hands!"

"No," said Ben, handing Delbert the horse's reins. "You can rein him with your hands tied."

"Yeah, but why?" said Delbert. "Look around: It ain't like I'm going to make a break and try to get away. In this snow, you'd catch me on foot! Stop being a couple of asses! Untie me, damn it to hell!"

"Shut up, Delbert," said Bell, hearing him complain. "You're only on the horse until we get to the steep path down to the main trail. Then you're going to have to walk down to the trail on foot. It's too dangerous for your horse with a rider on its back."

"Bull," said Delbert, nodding toward Whiskey and the mule, both animals carrying the heavy saddlebags. "You don't seem to mind that both those animals are carrying loads down the mountainside. I reckon this horse can too. I rode all the way up; I can ride all the way down."

"If you rode all the way up, it's only because you didn't care about taking a chance on killing your horse. You're walking your horse down the same as I am. You weigh a lot more than the saddlebags."

"I'm not going nowhere with my hands tied," said Delbert. "Not unless you knock

me out and carry me draped over a saddle."
He grinned. "I know you ain't going to do
that and risk getting the horse hurt, are you
Mr. *Do-good?*"

Bell stopped preparing Whiskey for the
trail long enough to walk over beside
Delbert's horse and look up at him. "You
really think you've got me pegged, don't
you, Delbert? Well, you're right. I won't
knock you out and lay you over a saddle.
The horse doesn't deserve it. But before I'll
untie your hands and risk you harming one
of these people, don't think I won't roll you
off right now and leave you here. We'll see
how you fit into that cougar's dinner plans."

Delbert looked all along the upper
ridgeline, then back down at Bell. "Hell,
that big tomcat's long gone by now. He
didn't stick around once he saw there
weren't nothing in it for him."

"All right then," said Bell, yanking
Delbert's boot from the stirrup. "Just say
the word. I'll put you off right here."

"Hey, come on, *Do-good,* take it easy now.
I'm going along with you, see?" Delbert
made a show of easing his foot away from
Jack Bell's hands and slipping it back into
the stirrup. "I swear, you people are the
touchiest bunch I've ever seen. Can't you
take a little ribbing now and then? It makes

the time go by so much faster, I always found."

Jack Bell turned from Delbert, picked up the reins to Whiskey and handed them to Rosalee. "You lead my horse. Ben and I will take turns with the mule until we get down to some flatter land." He nodded at Delbert and said, "Stay behind him. If he decides to make a run for it, we don't want him running over you."

Hearing Bell, Delbert turned in his saddle and said, "Now why would I want to leave such good company as this? You people have gold!" His eyes widened in exaggerated excitement. "I want to be around when we get the gold to Nolan's Gap. You might decide to make me a partner by then." He laughed aloud, shook his head and grumbled under his breath, "Bunch of damn fools is what you people are if you think you'll ever make it to Nolan's Gap alive. Those detectives will chew all three of you up and spit you away. If you think I was about to harm this little lady, wait till you see what that bunch will —"

"That's enough, Delbert!" Bell shouted, seeing the cold blank stare in Ben Finley's eyes. He saw Ben's hands grip tight around his shotgun. "Pay him no mind, Ben. You see what kind of man he is. We're just going to have to learn to put up with his mouth until we get to town."

"I know," said Ben. "I don't care what he says to me or about me . . . but I won't have him making remarks about my daughter."

"Father," said Rosalee, "I'm a big girl. Nothing he says matters to me. Don't let this fool upset you."

"All right," Ben grumbled. Snatching up the mule's lead rope, he said to Bell, "Ready when you are."

Slowly they set out along the winding path, Delbert in the lead, followed by Bell, carrying his rifle, then Ben and the mule, then Rosalee on Whiskey. At the rear came the dog, his nose busily at work, probing the air and the snowy ground for any sign of the cat's scent. No sooner had the party rounded the turn in the trail than the dog sniffed along the rocky edge, then stepped down out of sight, moving back and forth along a narrow ledge, his nose to the cold earth until he satisfied himself that the cat was nowhere near.

Within an hour, the travelers reached the path that led down to the main trail. There Jack Bell helped Delbert Hanks down from the saddle and supported him with a gloved hand up under Delbert's forearm as they made their way down the rocky, slippery terrain. At the bottom of a steep, winding elk path, they stopped and rested at the main trail before taking it down toward a short stretch of flatlands below.

Midevening had arrived when they reached the edge of the flatlands. Spotting a stand of rock that would serve as a good windbreak, Jack Bell stopped and looked at the Finleys and Delbert Hanks, seeing their steamy breath, their red, cold faces. Then he looked the animals over . . . all except the dog, who had wandered off out of sight on the steep mountainside. "We better make camp here in these rocks for the night. Get warmed up and rested before heading down again in the morning."

Ben Finley nodded in agreement. He pointed at a thicket of snow-covered bracken a few yards away and said, "I'll take the mule and bring us back something to burn." Halfway down the mountainside, he had turned the mule's reins over to Jack Bell. Now he took the reins back and led the mule away through the snow.

"Keep an eye out for that cat," Bell said, watching him walk away.

"Don't worry, I will," said Ben. As he led the mule, he looked all around for the dog but didn't see him. "Where's that dog off to?" he said over his shoulder.

"Maybe he prefers living by himself in the wilds now that he's getting over his wounds," Jack Bell said.

"He'll be back once there's a nice warm fire for him to lay near," said Ben.

While Jack Bell and Ben Finley spoke back and forth, Delbert slumped down beside a rock and eyed the bulging saddlebags on the horse and the mule. "Black Moe and his detectives will be real pleased to get their hands on all that shiny gold, Bell."

"Don't concern yourself, Delbert," said Bell.

"Oh, I'm not concerned in the least." Delbert grinned, giving Rosalee a wink and blowing a kiss at her as she turned and looked his way. Rosalee quickly looked away from him. "I just think it's a damn shame though . . . you poor folks doing all the work to get it, then the detectives taking it all away from you."

"It's not going to happen," said Bell, seeing the worried look come to Rosalee's face.

"Really?" Delbert chuckled. "I'm real anxious to see how you keep it *from* happening. There's a whole gang of them against just the two of you: one a *do-good*, the other nothing but a crazy old coot."

"There's three of us," said Rosalee firmly.

"Honey, I don't mean to hurt your feelings none," said Delbert to Rosalee, "but in case you ain't noticed, you're just a woman — not a very big woman at that."

"I wouldn't say much if I were you, Delbert," said Bell. "She was big enough to put you out of business."

"Ha!" said Delbert. "She put me out of business all right . . . with the help of a dog, a mule and a horse! If you think that'll even the odds against the detectives, you're more stupid than you look, Bell."

Bell moved over beside Rosalee as they watched Ben shake snow from the dried bracken and break off large clumps of it and pile it atop the mule. "Don't pay any attention to Delbert," Bell said quietly to Rosalee. "He's just blowing off steam because he realizes his little game is about to come to an end."

"I know," said Rosalee. "I just hope he's not going to get any of us hurt before he finally runs out of steam."

Behind them, Delbert chuckled to himself, then said, "I hope you're not talking ill about me over there. And don't you worry your pretty little head about me trying to make a break for it, Miss Rosalee. I'm sticking around to see what the detectives do. I wouldn't miss what's about to happen here for anything in the world."

Bell and Rosalee ignored Delbert and began sweeping away snow from the ground with the sides of their boots until they had a good, wide clearing for a small campsite. When Ben returned with a pile of dried brush and wood for a fire, they helped him unload it into the center of the cleared area. In the shelter of the rocks, the four of them were soon huddled near a hot fire. A coffeepot full of snow had melted and was boiling coffee. The tin skillet lay atop glowing coals; the jerked beef in the skillet was beginning to sizzle. The two horses and the mule had been attended to and stood on the outer edge of the rock stand.

"I'm curious about that dog," said Ben Finley, his hands cupped near the flames as he scanned the mountainside behind them. "I figured he'd be back here by now."

Delbert piped in, "If you ask me about that dog, I'd say that cougar you folks are so afraid of has et him and gone on by now."

"Nobody asked you, Delbert," Bell said quietly, seeing the look of concern on Ben Finley's face. "Ben, that might be the last we see of the dog, sure enough. I meant what I said a while ago. Now that he's mending up, he might want to go back to the wilds."

"I kinda hoped he'd go on back to town with us," said Ben. He sighed. "But if that's not what he wants, I reckon I have to go along with it."

"Yep," said Bell, "maybe this dog's just one of those acquaintances who only pops into our lives long enough to help us do a particular thing. Once that thing is over, he's gone on to somewhere else." Bell looked first into Ben's eyes, then into Rosalee's. "We've all known those kind of people, the kind who are just here awhile, then they're gone."

"Yeah, I know what you're talking about." Ben nodded. "I've met folks like that over the years." He passed a glance to Rosalee, checking her reaction to what he took as Jack Bell's way of telling them both that he would be moving on once they got back to Nolan's Gap. Ben couldn't tell if his daughter had gotten the same message he had, but he saw a look in Rosalee's eyes that he'd never seen before as she looked past him at Bell's face. Ben smiled to himself.

"Maybe this dog is like that," said Bell.

"Maybe," said Ben, "but I hope not. There's few enough good years on this old earth for any of us. The more time we can spend with folks who care about us, the better, I always figured. What does a man ever acquire for himself if he never stays in one spot and enjoys his loved ones and his friendships and the good times he's made for himself? What else does a man get?"

A second of silence passed, during which Delbert grumbled to himself, "You stupid peckerwoods make me sick." The conversation may just as well have been in a foreign language for all he understood it.

"I don't know what else a man gets," Bell finally said. "I've never been in one spot long enough to find out." He gave a slight smile, standing up as he spoke and looking upward on the mountainside where long slices of black evening shadow darkened out the snow-filled crevices and ridgelines. "But I was only talking about the dog . . . wondering myself if we've seen the last of him."

Rosalee felt a slight sting of embarrassment, realizing what her father had been leading up to. She gave Ben a look of exasperation. "Well, whatever the dog decides, we'll all have to be gracious enough to accept. Not all things can come indoors and settle down after a life in the wilds."

"Oh, right you are, Daughter," said Ben. "I wouldn't dare suggest otherwise." His tired smile widened as he looked down, his lowered hat brim hiding his face. "No sir, I wouldn't," he whispered under his breath. "I just saw how much he enjoys the warmth of a fire." He pressed his palms outward to the rising heat and closed his eyes, savoring it.

Two miles behind the campsite, above them on a dark ledge of jagged rock, the dog lay in silence, shivering in the cold. A familiar scent of coffee, warm meat and wood smoke wafted faintly up to him, enough to make him turn his cold muzzle in the direction of the campsite and whine silently as if in longing for those things he'd become briefly accustomed to.

But then, higher up, came a soft sound like the whisper of a breath across a rocky ledge, followed by a spill of broken ice as the big cat moved as quietly and as surely as swift death through the fallen darkness. The dog perked his ears and, as if resolved to some harsh decision he'd forced himself to make, turned his attention to the sound along the high path and resisted the cold and the isolation of the coming night.

Food, warmth, comfort, the gentle touch of a human's hand. Those things meant nothing to him now. He'd come back here for the cat, knowing through no other source or sense save that of premonition that the cat would come. The cat was a hunter not unlike himself. Yet thousands of years of contact and kinship with humankind had forged the dog's instincts toward the protection of man. There were laws unwritten between the two species that could not be broken. A need ingrained deep in the dog's nature demanded he put himself between humankind and the predator looming in their wake. He would do so without questioning, with no regard for his own life.

When the next sound came, the dog rose up into a crouch, his eyes following what would have appeared to be a wisp of yellow smoke as it curled downward, visible through snow-streaked underbrush, past rock and low branches. And as the cat topped a cliff overhang and stood looking back and forth from fifteen yards above, the dog growled loud enough to make his presence known. The cat riveted his eyes into the dog's and responded in kind. With a low, guttural snarl, its long fangs gleaming in its open jaws, the cat slung its head back and forth. Then, with a flick of its tail, it plunged out and down, claws spread, into the dark, rocky field of battle.

Seeing the cat hurling down upon it, the dog leaped quickly aside, the suddenness of the cat's attack still almost catching the dog by surprise. The cat hit the rocky, sloping ground, trying to check itself down against the onthrust of its own weight. But momentum wouldn't allow it to stop. It tumbled forward in a high spray of snow. The dog saw an advantage and took it without hesitation. Plunging into the rolling ball of fur and snow with its fangs bared, the dog rolled along, burying its teeth into the cat's neck and locking its paws around the cat from the side.

The tumbling ball of fur, snow and slashing fangs and claws continued downward until it hit a flat, hard ledge of solid rock. Both animals sprawled for a second, coming apart, the wind knocked out of their lungs. Blood spewed from the cat's neck, the skin ripped and steaming in the cold. Blood and steam flew from the fresh claw marks on the dog's side, where the cat had slashed through the tender wounds and stitchwork of their last encounter.

The dog whined long and low. For a second, the whole fight seemed to have ended, both combatants too dazed and maimed to continue. The cat slid backward up onto its paws, stopped and shook itself off. The dog lay watching, tensed, poised for the cat's next move but appearing ready to call a truce and back away. But then the cat half-turned toward the path leading down toward the flatlands, and before he could even take a step in that direction, the dog lunged with renewed energy.

The cat turned and rocked back on its haunches in time to catch the dog and withstand its weight. For a moment the two swayed in place, tensed and snarling, like two enraged lovers locked in a death waltz. But the embrace ended with the cat's paws spinning on its shoulders, slashing, as the dog clamped its teeth into the cat's face and shook its head violently. The dog's deep-ripping fangs were more than the cat could withstand. Its slashing paws ceased to fight, and it chose instead to pull away and run. But even as it did so, the bleeding dog held tight, ripping skin and deep muscle from the cat's cheek.

The cat sank from the weight of the dog and rolled over onto its back, the dog showing no mercy, burrowing its fangs yet deeper, its head lashing back and forth, its growl muffled by fur, blood and torn muscle. On its back, the cat's hind paws came into play, spinning upward, the claws slashing at the dog's belly like ripsaws. Blood flew. Together the two thrashed back and forth, neither giving an inch. Then, suddenly, they rolled beyond the edge of the cliff and plunged down, writhing and

368

turning in the cold air.

Through the darkness they fell, plummeting over thirty feet before their fangs and claws turned loose of one another. In an explosion of snow and ice, the two careened off the steep slope and tumbled another ten yards before sliding to a halt. The dog gave out a deep, tortured yelp and lay as still as stone. The cat wheezed and gasped until its lungs began working again. Still it lay bucking and jerking for a moment as if in its death throes. When the jerking stopped, the cat let go a spew of dark blood from its throat, rolled up onto its paws and turned staggering toward the dog, ready to resume their fight.

When the dog didn't move, the cat ventured forward a step, blood running freely from its ripped cheek, its torn nose, the wide-open wound steaming in its side. It raised a bloody paw and extended it slightly as if to see if the dog was alive. A low hissing sound came from the cat's mouth. Then it turned and limped down through the deep snow, leaving a thick blood trail behind itself. The dog lay half-buried in the snow, its eyes open and glazed, staring up into the dark sky.

CHAPTER 23

Late in the night, while the others slept, Jack Bell sat with his rifle across his lap. For the past half hour now, the horses and the mule had turned nervous. The change in the animals had been subtle and gradual. If he hadn't already been aware of a cougar prowling the mountainside, the animals' behavior might have gone unnoticed awhile longer. But now that he saw Whiskey stomp and hoof and lower his ears toward the dark flatlands, Bell stood up, walked around the fire and tapped his boot lightly against Ben's leg. Ben sat up and rubbed his face with both hands. "What is it, Jack?" he whispered.

Instead of answering, Bell gave a gesture with his head in the flickering firelight, letting Ben know to follow him away from Delbert, who lay sleeping nearby. Once Ben had stood up around the fire away from Delbert, Bell said in a whisper, "The way they're acting, I believe the cat's circled around us." He nodded at the nervous animals, then continued. "He's out on the flatlands."

"The flatlands?" said Ben, his eyes already searching the darkness beyond the firelight's glow. "Cats don't act this way, Bell . . . at least, none I ever saw. They like staying high up, out of sight."

"Not this one, Ben," said Bell, his eyes also searching the darkness as they spoke. "If it's not the cat, there sure is something out there. Either way, I'm going scouting for it." He passed a glance at Delbert lying rolled up in a blanket, his hat lying over the side of his face. "I want you to keep an eye on him while I'm gone."

"I don't like you going out there, Jack," said Ben.

"Neither do I," said Bell. "But if it's the cat, I want him off our backs before we head the rest of the way down the mountain in the morning."

"I understand," Ben whispered. "Are you going to carry a torch to see by?"

"No," said Bell. "There's enough moonlight for me to find his tracks. A torch might send him away. I want him to come to me. Once I find his tracks, I can get downwind from him."

"All right," said Ben. He looked at Delbert, then at Rosalee, asleep on the opposite side of the fire. "You know I can't go with you, Jack. Not if it means leaving that buzzard alone with Rosalee."

"I know that," said Bell. "That's why I want you to stand watch while I go. We've got no idea what Delbert's apt to do, regardless of what he's said. You keep a close watch on him, Ben. Just remember that whatever I'm looking at out there, it's not nearly as deadly or as deceptive as that blanketful of rattlesnake lying right here among us."

Ben nodded. "I'll remember that, Jack. Don't you worry about me and Rosalee. I've got things covered here." He reached down, picked up his shotgun and cradled it in his arm.

Delbert lay listening, barely making out their words, his slight smile hidden by his hat. He lay dead still, catching a narrow view of Bell walking away from camp toward the short stretch of flatlands. He listened and counted the minutes until he was certain Jack Bell was well out into the darkness. Taking a few deep breaths, he arose slowly from his blanket as if waking from a deep sleep.

"Damn it," Delbert grumbled aloud to himself, rubbing his face with his tied hands. Leaning slightly to one side, he looked around the fire at Ben and said, "Hey, Bell, I hate to bother you, but you or that old man one is going to have to walk me away from camp for a minute. I've got to go real bad."

For a minute, Ben Finley didn't answer. Then, just as Delbert was about to say something more, Ben said, "Jack's not here right now. He stepped away from camp himself. He'll be right back any second though."

"That's fine. I reckon I can wait," said Delbert. A silence passed. Then he added, "Not too long though. That coffee we had was good, but it's going right through me."

Another moment passed, and Delbert stood up and stepped around the fire toward Ben Finley. "What's taking Bell so long?" he asked, looking away from the firelight into the darkness. "I can't wait much longer on him."

Ben raised the shotgun barrel toward him, half coming up from his seat atop a small rock. "Get yourself back away from me," Ben warned him.

"Whoa now — hold on!" said Delbert, acting surprised. But instead of stepping back like he'd been told, he stopped, then slowly took a step forward, saying, "All I want is to attend to nature. I'm not lying; I've got to go bad!"

"I told you to stay back!" Ben stood the

rest of the way up, cocking the shotgun with his thumb.

Delbert froze, raising his tied hands chest high. "All right, take it easy! See? I've stopped!"

"I didn't say just stop!" Ben said, raising his voice. "I told you to get back away from me! Now get!"

"Father! What's going on?" Rosalee scurried up onto her knees, her blanket held tight at her chin. She looked back and forth quickly, then asked, "Where's Jack?"

"He'll be right back," said Ben, keeping his eyes and the shotgun barrel trained on Delbert Hanks.

As Ben had turned a glance to Rosalee, Delbert had advanced another step. Now that he stood only four feet away from Ben Finley, he relaxed, even feigned stepping back, leaning away as if frightened by the shotgun. "I'm glad you woke up when you did, Miss Rosalee! Your daddy was about to put a bullet in me for no reason."

"Shut up, Delbert, and get back! I'm warning you for the last time!" Ben's finger lay tight against the trigger. Still, instead of stepping back, Delbert only appeared to lean back more.

"How much farther back can I go?" Delbert said, sounding frightened for his life. "Miss Rosalee! Please tell him not to shoot me! I've just got to go take a —"

"I said shut up!" Ben said.

"Father, don't shoot him!" said Rosalee, standing up quickly. She started to step forward.

"No, Rosalee! Stay back!" Ben said, turning his gaze to her for just a second.

But a second was all Delbert needed. He lunged into the old man, knocking him backward, farther away from the firelight. The cocked shotgun flew from Ben's hands before he had time to pull the trigger. Delbert scrambled across the ground, his tied hands searching for the shotgun in the dim outer edges of flickering light. When he found the gun, he snatched it up and stood up quickly and pointed it awkwardly at them.

"That was almost too easy!" Delbert shouted, seeing Rosalee and Ben Finley huddle together near the fire. He stepped around wide of the fire, farther into the darkness, wanting to see that neither of them had a pistol before venturing into the light. "Now, both of you raise your hands and get around here and untie my —"

His words cut short as a snarling streak of fur shot out of the darkness and wrapped itself around his chest. The shotgun flew from Delbert's hands as he let out a scream beneath the bleeding face of the wounded cougar. "Help me! God! Please! Help me!" he screamed. Across the fire, the horses and the mule went crazy, nickering loudly in terror.

Ben Finley made a dive into the darkness and grabbed the shotgun as he rolled to his feet. Rosalee ran to her father's side, shouting, "Hurry, Father! Shoot it!"

Ben Finley braced himself against the recoil of the shotgun and pulled the trigger. Delbert caught a glimpse of Ben's action out the corner of his eye as he screamed into the cougar's bloody fur. His scream turned higher when he saw that the shotgun's hammer clicked without firing. Claws ripped flesh from Delbert's chest. Fangs sank into his shoulder. Ben Finley cocked the shotgun and again pulled the trigger. Again the shotgun only clicked.

"God *no!*" Delbert screamed, hearing the sound of flesh being torn away from his shoulder.

"Father, shoot it!" Rosalee shrieked, horrified at the sight of Delbert being ripped to pieces right before her eyes.

"Well, dang it all!" Ben Finley cursed, shaking the shotgun as once again it failed to fire.

Rosalee ran to her blanket and grabbed

the LeMat pistol lying beneath the folded-up coat that she'd used for a pillow. Running back toward Delbert's screams, she checked the pistol quickly. Then she cocked it, raised it with both hands and fired. The cat rolled off Delbert and slunk down on all fours when the bullet grazed the fur on its back. Rosalee only had time to catch a glimpse of Delbert. But a glimpse was all it took to show her that the cat had just ripped most of his throat away. Delbert lay dead in a gathering pool of blood. "Hurry, shoot it again!" shouted Ben Finley, ten feet away, still trying to fire the shotgun.

The cat dropped a mouthful of red gore and centered its attention on Rosalee as she cocked the heavy pistol for another shot. Ben came running, seeing the cat take a low, coiled step toward his daughter, ready to hurl himself between her and the cat. But there was not going to be time, he thought, rushing forward as the pistol exploded in Rosalee's hands, the recoil making her stagger back a step. The shot missed the cat. Now the cat made its spring toward her face. "Rosalee!" Ben screamed, diving but knowing he'd never make it in time.

Rosalee knew it too. There was no time for her father to help her; there was no time to recock the LeMat for another shot. There was not even time to brace herself for what she saw coming at her through the air. She screamed and closed her eyes, swinging the LeMat as if it were a club, not going down without a fight. But at the end of the swing, she hit nothing. The force of the swing sent her falling to the ground. She lay sprawled in the snow, the pistol flying from her hands, the snarl of the cat resounding loudly. Ben Finley landed beside her, grabbing her and clutching her to his chest.

On the ground ten feet away, the dog and cat lay locked upon one another in a raging ball of fur, flying snow and blood. "He came back!" Ben shouted, his breath shallow, spent and weak. "The dog came back!"

"Father, quick! Get the pistol!" Rosalee shouted, coming back from the dead now, ready to continue in her struggle to stay alive.

They both crawled hurriedly around, feeling in the snow until Ben came up with the LeMat. Shaking snow from the big pistol and cocking it as he rose to his feet, he aimed it at the fighting animals. But then he hesitated, unable to make the shot. "I can't shoot!" he exclaimed.

"You have to, Father!" Rosalee shrieked.

"I'm afraid I'll hit the dog!" Ben shouted. Behind the fire, the horses reared as high as their tied reins would allow. The mule brayed and snorted and kicked its heels high.

In the snow outside of the firelight, the dog and cat spun and slashed at one another, nose-to-nose. "You'll have to risk it, Father, for our sake!" said Rosalee.

"I know," said Ben, aiming again, a look of determination on his face. In the billowing cloud of snow, the dog jumped back and forth atop the wounded cat, sinking his fangs in the cat's throat much the same way the cat had sunk its fangs into Delbert's. The dog held on as the cat slung him back and forth, ripping hair, skin and meat from the dog's sides. The cat managed to get its hind paws beneath the dog's belly again, this time kicking and slashing until it tossed the dog in the air.

"Shoot, Father, quickly!" Rosalee shouted.

The dog hit the snow with a yelp. The cat rose up with a long snarl onto its hind legs, ready to pounce again. But now the pistol bucked in Ben's hand. At the same time, a shot rang out from Jack Bell's rifle. Both bullets hit the cat, silencing it. Jack Bell stalked forward as Rosalee and her father turned their eyes to him. At the sound of the shots, the horses began to settle but still bounded back and forth on their front hooves. The braying of the mule had stopped when the snarl of the cat fell silent.

A pitiful whine came from the mortally wounded dog as he dragged himself forward into the firelight, closer to the warmth of the lazily dancing flames. "Oh no — you poor thing," said Ben, hurrying to the dog and helping it make its way the last few feet. He crouched down beside it and felt it try to drag itself closer to the fire.

"Here, boy, I've got you," Ben said, pulling the dog along until he could tell it was satisfied by the way it turned its eyes and watched the flames lick upward into the night. "You take it easy now, ole buddy," Ben said, slipping his hand beneath the dog's bloody chin and laying its wounded muzzle over onto his lap. The dog relaxed and stopped its whining, gasping for breath but settling now as it lay facing the fire as if lying by a warm fireside was all it had ever sought in life.

"Oh God, Jack," Rosalee whispered with tears in her eyes as Bell placed an arm around her shoulders, comforting her. "Isn't there anything we can do? That poor dog gave his life to save us."

"No, Rosalee," said Jack. "Saving him now wouldn't be doing him any favors.

380

Look at him . . . the shape he's in." Jack Bell felt a tightness in his chest, seeing the dog stare into the flames.

"This ole boy just got stuck here by himself, all alone, nobody to look after him." Ben sobbed quietly as he stroked the dog's bloody shoulder. "I swear, I wish none of this ever happened. If I could change it, I would, ole fellow," he whispered to the dog. The dog raised its bloody head enough to lick Ben's hand. Then it relaxed its head and looked longingly into the flames as its breath expelled and stopped.

"Come on, Ben, turn him loose," Jack Bell said in a soft voice, laying a hand on his shoulder. "He's gone."

Ben Finley stood up sobbing and looked down at the dog, shaking his head. "I'm never going to be right after this, Jack. Knowing why that dog got left on his own . . . seeing what my coming up here caused . . . I'm just never going to be right over it."

Rosalee stepped in and held her father's hand while he wept. In a moment, when he'd assured her he was all right, she turned loose of his hand and watched him go to his blanket near the fire and pick up a canteen. "Jack," she asked in a guarded tone, "what does he mean, *knowing why the dog was left on its own?* He sounds as if he thinks he's responsible for something."

"He's just tired, Rosalee . . . worn-out tired and not knowing what he's saying right now."

"Oh . . ." Rosalee stood watching her father take a long drink from the canteen. "Surely he doesn't blame himself for any of this, does he?"

"Of course not. Come on, Rosalee," Jack Bell coaxed. "He just needs to be alone for a few minutes. He'll be all right."

On the far side of the flatlands, camped below a cliff overhang, Black Moe Bainbridge had bolted straight up from his blanket at the sound of distant gunfire. All around him the rest of the men did the same. "If I was to make a guess, I'd bet that was the sound of ole Delbert ambushing Jack Bell and whoever is with him."

"Maybe," said Dewey Sadlo, "but what if it's the other way around? Suppose it's Jack Bell ambushing Delbert?" He stared at Black Moe with his brow cocked. "Think we can afford to let Bell get ahead of us? Once he runs into Delbert, he'll know we're on his trail. If he takes Delbert alive, you can bet ole Delbert will tell him anything he wants to know."

"Hell's blue blazes!" said Black Moe after

considering it for a second. "You're right, Dewey." He looked around the fire at the sleepy faces staring back at him and said, "All right, everybody up! Let's go see what ole Delbert has gotten himself into up there. There's a bonus coming to any man who kills Jack Bell and drags his carcass to me."

While the rest of the men gathered their gear, saddles and horses, Dewey Sadlo came up to Black Moe Bainbridge as Black Moe stood checking his big Colt pistol. "What about the woman?" Dewey asked.

"What about her?" Black Moe responded, spinning his pistol on his thick finger.

"If we kill this Bell fellow, and the old man with him . . . what's going to happen to the woman? I can't see just leaving a poor woman up there to die in the cold, can you?"

"I'd hate to do it to her," said Black Moe, "but if we have to, we will." He stopped spinning the pistol and looked closely at Dewey Sadlo. "Why? What's your notion on the matter?"

"I say we keep her," said Sadlo, his eyes widening in anticipation. "At least for the rest of the winter! Keep her and take her with us!"

"That's real smart," said Black Moe.

"And what do you think will happen the minute we let her go? What do you think the law would do to us for taking a woman against her will?"

Dewey shrugged. "Then to hell with it. We won't let her go. We'll just hang onto her!"

Black Moe Bainbridge shoved his pistol down into his holster and shoved Dewey aside. "You're crazy as a bed tick, Sadlo! Do what you want to with the woman, far as I care. Just get the hell out of my way. I hate leaving early like this — the weather so cold and all. I hope it's not going to ruin my whole day."

CHAPTER 24

Jack Bell, Ben Finley and Rosalee spent the rest of the night preparing for the trip down the mountain. At first gray light, Bell helped Ben carry the dog to a spot between two rocks rising four feet from the ground. They scraped away snow, laid the dog on the ground, then shoved the snow back over him. Ben knew there was no digging a grave in the frozen ground; nor were there enough rocks to pile over the dog. "This is the best we can do for you," Ben said to the mound of snow, patting a gloved hand on it. Bell and Rosalee stood for a moment before leaving Ben alone beside the dog's cold, white grave. On the other side of the camp, Bell took the cougar by the hind legs and dragged it a few yards farther away from the campfire. When he came trudging back through the snow, he found Rosalee saddling the horses.

"That has to be the biggest mountain cat I've ever seen in my life," Bell said. "We all owe a lot to that big cur; there's no two ways about it."

There was a look of consternation on Rosalee's face as she drew the cinch on

Delbert's horse. "Do you suppose the detectives heard the shooting in the night?"

"If they're anywhere out there, they heard it," said Bell.

"Do you think Delbert might have been lying about them?" she said.

"No," said Bell. "I figure if there's one time in Delbert's life when he told the truth, that was it. I figure the detectives are coming. He took too much delight in telling us about it."

"What will we do, Jack? We can't fight them. But we can't let them take you . . . especially if they're as ruthless as Delbert said they are."

"The first thing I want to do is get the two of you around them," said Bell. "If you can swing wide off the main trail, you'll be able to find a pathway down the mountain without them seeing you. You can get into Nolan's Gap ahead of them."

"We can't leave you out here alone, Jack!" said Rosalee.

"You've got to," said Jack. "I'll try reasoning with the detectives — see if I can at least get them to take me back to town."

"And then what?" asked Rosalee.

Bell considered it for a second. "Then, I hope to God Delbert was wrong about Max Brumfield being dead. Max is a fair man."

"But what if he is dead?" Rosalee asked.

"Then I won't have anyone in Nolan's Gap to side with me," said Bell. "But it doesn't matter. I'm still sending the two of you ahead. That way I'll only have myself to worry about. I'm taking Delbert's body back to town. Maybe I can get somebody to understand this whole thing has been him and Early Philpot's doings."

"No one would blame you if you left him out here," said Rosalee.

"I know. But the way my luck's running on this, I'm afraid if I don't show somebody what really happened to him, I'll get blamed for killing him too," Bell said wryly.

Ben Finley walked up and joined the conversation. "If you ask me, somebody needs to grab Early Philpot by the neck and squeeze the truth out of him. I suppose you've already decided to do that though."

While Rosalee finished with Delbert's horse, Bell had stepped in and checked the cinch on Whiskey's belly. He laid the stirrup down the horse's side as he answered Ben Finley. "I don't know of a thing I can do that would get Early Philpot to admit the truth. I'm not sure he even knows what the truth is. He sent those men after me to begin with . . . but from there, he could have been relying on whatever lies Delbert told him.

Besides, if those detectives think I killed one of their men, they're not going to care much what Early Philpot says."

Ben and Rosalee gave one another a look. Then Ben said, "Jack, what if we meet up with those detectives and offer part of this gold to forget this whole thing ever happened?"

Bell lifted the heavy saddlebags as if to lay them across Whiskey's back, but at the last moment he stepped over and laid them across Delbert's horse. He began strapping them down. "That's a kind offer, Ben, but I can't let you do it. Besides, if you let those men know you've got gold, there's no doubt in my mind they would kill you for it."

Ben Finley said, "But Jack —"

"No more buts," said Bell, cutting him off. "This is how it's going to be done. This is trouble of mine that has nothing to do with you folks. I won't risk getting either of you hurt."

"You risked your life coming up here, helping me look for my father," said Rosalee. "Don't you think it's only fair that we stand beside you?"

"If there was room to stand beside me, yes," said Bell. "But there's not. So if you want to help, please do like I ask. Let's find a side trail down this mountainside and get the two of you on it." He turned to his horse, dismissing the subject.

Ben and Rosalee Finley stared at one another for a moment, then turned to the mule and began loading supplies onto its back. As they finished with the mule, Bell stepped in, picked up the saddlebags from the ground and laid them over the mule's back. Ben Finley watched Bell fasten the saddlebags in place. He shook his head, saying, "I'm sorry, Jack. This whole thing is my fault. I just can't keep —"

"That's enough of that, Ben," Jack Bell said firmly, cutting a glance to where Rosalee had stepped over and started pouring the last of the coffee onto the low flames. "Think about Rosalee. Get her away from these men and let me take care of myself. She's the one I'm worried about."

Ben stared at him, running things through his mind. "All right, Jack. I'll go along with whatever you say."

In moments they'd cleared the campsite and headed out across the short stretch of flatland. Jack Bell walked in front, leading Whiskey. Delbert's body lay wrapped in a blanket and draped over the saddle. Behind Bell, Rosalee sat atop Delbert's horse, riding for a few minutes until they reached the downward trails. Ben Finley led the mule behind his daughter. He'd been quiet ever since they'd broken camp. He wore a grim, resolved expression on his cold face. His eyes stared straight ahead beneath his lowered hat brim.

Halfway across the flatland, they veered off of the main trail and trudged three hundred yards through the deep snow until they reached a narrow path leading downward in a winding series of natural switchbacks carved over thousands of years by the hooves of elk and goat and the claws and padding of other creatures of the wilds. Bell looked at the prints of animals along the snow-covered path. "This should get you back to the main trail before long."

"We'll be all right, Jack," said Ben. "You look out for yourself. Rosalee and I both want to see you in Nolan's Gap inside of the next couple of days."

"That's right; we'll be looking for you," said Rosalee, stepping down from the saddle. She stood close to Jack Bell for an awkward second, blotting her gloved fingers to her eye. "Why does it have to be this way, Jack?" she said at length. Stepping forward against him, she put her arms around his neck.

"Have faith, Rosalee," Bell said, returning her embrace. Ben Finley looked away from them out across the cold sky, steam swirling in his breath. Bell gently took Rosalee's arms from around his neck and stepped back away from her. "Now go, please," he said softly.

Bell watched until the two made their way down the path and went out of sight around a turn in the trail. Turning back to Whiskey, he stepped halfway into the saddle, then rolled Delbert's body forward across the saddle horn and swung up under him, letting the body rest across his lap. "Come on, Delbert. You got me into all this . . . let's see if you can't help get me out." He heeled the horse toward the top of the main trail leading down from the flatlands.

Black Moe Bainbridge dropped to the side along the narrow trail and let Dewey Sadlo take the lead. They had been climbing the trail since before dawn, taking their chances in the dark, keeping their horses nose-to-tail, moving slowly. Going into a long, rounding, upward turn, Sadlo saw sunlight creep out over a rock ledge above them and said over his shoulder, "Damn, boys, it's going to be warming up here in a few minutes."

A low, uninspired murmur stirred among the men. Black Moe slipped his horse back into the slow-moving line, between Nate Reardon and Gannerd Woodsworth. "Cheer up, men," he said, "and try to show some spunk! This thing ain't going to last much longer. Ole Delbert's probably up there right now, waiting for us with a big fire and a hot pot of stew!"

Dewey Sadlo chuckled, joining in. "Hell yes. And a full bottle of whiskey!"

They pushed on, each of them beginning to see the long rays of sunlight as they drew closer to the top of the trail. Dewey Sadlo was the first to step his horse over the snowy edge onto the flatland. As soon as he saw the lone rider facing him with a blanket-wrapped body across his lap, he sidled his horse over, put his hand on his pistol butt and said over his shoulder, "Black Moe, you best get on up here. We got company."

But before Black Moe could get onto the flatlands, Nate Reardon rode up, followed by Ellis Dill. They both saw the lone rider staring at them in silence, a cocked rifle lying across the back of the corpse, the rider's thumb across the cocked hammer.

"Uh, Black Moe," said Dill. "Didn't you hear Dewey? He said we got a visitor up here."

"Yes, I heard him, damn it to hell!" Black Moe barked, lunging his horse forward.

"What am I supposed to do, shove everybody off the trail?" He gigged his horse sharply, forcing it up over the edge. Then he stopped abruptly, seeing the lone rider, the large open bore of the rifle pointing at him. He gave Sadlo, Reardon and Dill a harsh glare, as if to say they should have mentioned that the visitor had a cocked rifle in his hands.

"The hell's going on?" Gannerd Woodsworth asked, still down on the trail, stuck there with Finch and Red Tony Harpe.

"Shut the hell up down there," Black Moe shouted back at Woodsworth.

Woodsworth looked at Finch and Red Tony and shrugged. Red Tony only shook his head in pain, sitting drawn into a knot in his saddle, his eyes looking red-rimmed and hollow. "Boys, I can't sit like this too long. I feel like somebody's hammered a spike into my backbone."

On the edge of the flatland, Black Moe Bainbridge said to the lone rider, "Whatever you've got to say, mister, you best get it said. I hate somebody pointing a gun at me first thing in the morning."

"I've got nothing to say," Bell said in a calm, even voice. "I was just headed down when you men came heading up. I'm just

393

waiting for the trail to clear."

"Oh," said Black Moe, surprised by the man's words. "Well then, excuse us, mister." He sidled his horse over a step, but then stopped and said, "Who are you though, if you don't mind us asking."

Bell just stared at him. Instead of answering, he said, "You're the detectives Delbert here told me about, aren't you?"

Black Moe's eyes went to the blanketed corpse. "Delbert, did you say?"

"Yep, it's Delbert all right," said Bell. He reached his boot toe forward and eased the corner of the blanket back enough to expose Delbert's cold, purple face, Delbert's staring eyes large and terrified, as if on some larger, unseen plane the cat still stood atop him. "He told me about you detectives before he died."

Black Moe looked him up and down. "You didn't kill him?"

"No. Why would I kill Delbert?" said Bell. When the men just stared at him, Bell went on. "He said he was helping you hunt for a man by the name of Jack Bell. I can save you some hunting. Bell's dead too. Him and Delbert killed each other. I could only carry one. Delbert and me were friends."

"Who the hell are you?" Black Moe asked again.

"I'm Hardaway . . . Rance Hardaway. Delbert and I have been riding together, working for Early Philpot."

"Uh huh, I see . . ." Black Moe gave him a curious stare, having a hard time doubting him: the calm tone of voice, the sincere look in his eyes. "But you know something?" Black Moe raised a finger for emphasis, his right hand inching its way closer to his pistol butt. "Ole Delbert there told me you got yourself killed by this Jack Bell fellow. What do you think of that?"

Bell offered a slight, thin smile. "I'm not surprised. Delbert was apt to tell anybody anything. Don't know if you ever noticed or not, but he was the most awful liar in the world. If you believed anything he said, you'd have to be about as crazy as he was."

"You don't say," said Bainbridge, studying Bell closely.

Jack Bell held his ground, not giving up a thing in either his eyes or his expression. He could tell that he actually had these men wondering. But could he pull it off? He looked from face to face and decided that yes, he could. "If you men want to go on up, you'll find Bell just up off this stretch of land. He's about a half mile up in a —"

"Jack, I'm coming!" shouted Ben Finley

before Bell could finish his words. With a quick snap of a glance, Bell saw the old man running toward them from twenty yards away. Farther beyond Ben came the sound of Rosalee's voice, shouting for her father to come back.

"Well, I'll be damned," said Black Moe Bainbridge, grinning broadly. "You halfway had us believing you!" His hand had already started to fall back for his pistol, Sadlo, Reardon and Dill following suit.

"I know," said Bell. "I saw it." The rifle exploded, his left hand pulling the trigger as his right hand jerked the Colt from his holster and fired on the upswing. Black Moe flew backward from his saddle, the impact of the rifle shot turning him in a back flip and sending him sailing down the trail onto Gannerd Woodsworth. Woodsworth's horse reared and fell backward with the sudden weight thrust upon it.

Bell's first pistol shot punched Dewey Sadlo high in his shoulder but only twisted him sideways in his saddle for a second. Bell had no more time for Sadlo right then. Ellis Dill's pistol was out, cocking on the upswing, coming up to fire. Bell's second pistol shot nailed him in the forehead, lifting his hat high on a spray of blood and bone matter and sending his body flying brokenly from his saddle.

"Jack! I'm coming!" Ben Finley shouted, cocking and clicking the broken shotgun, still trying to get it to fire as he ran.

Dewey Sadlo had righted himself quickly in the saddle and swung his pistol toward Jack Bell. But seeing the shotgun coming at him, ten yards away and growing closer, Sadlo jerked the gun around and shot Ben Finley twice in the chest.

"No!" Bell shouted. He fired and saw Sadlo fly from his saddle. But out the corner of his eye, he caught a glimpse of Ben falling in the snow. A shot from over the edge of the trail whistled past Bell's head. He flung himself from the saddle, pulling Delbert's body down with him. Gannerd Woodsworth and Floyd Finch came over the edge on foot, firing repeatedly.

Even through the gunfire, Bell heard Rosalee scream, "Father! No! God no!" But Bell had no time to look around. He jerked Delbert's blanketed body up as a shield. Three bullets thumped into the corpse as Bell reached around it and fired. Two bullets hit Gannerd Woodsworth: one in the knee, the other in the top of his bald head as he bowed forward to grab his leg wound, his hat falling off just before the bullet struck. He rocked back onto his behind for a second as if sitting down in a chair. But then he collapsed onto his back in the bloody snow.

"Don't shoot!" Finch shouted, throwing his pistol away and throwing his hands out to show they were empty. "Don't shoot! I give up! I give up! See?" But instead of staying in one spot, he ran backward in the snow, falling but coming back up, screaming like a madman, waving his empty hands until he fell over the edge of a cliff not far from the trail. He let out a long scream as he fell. Then a silence set in, broken only by the sound of Rosalee crying softly over her father.

Bell only had time to give her a glance as he stepped forward, slipping his empty pistol into his holster and snatching up his rifle he'd dropped in the snow. He levered a round into the rifle chamber as he stepped over onto the trail. Seeing Red Tony Harpe sitting bowed over in his saddle, Bell pointed the rifle at him and said, "Drop it!"

Balled up, his chest nearly touching his knees, Red Tony looked at him through his red-rimmed eyes and said, "Drop what? I'm not holding nothing. I couldn't lift a pistol if I tried."

"Then sit up so I can see your hands," Bell demanded. Red Tony struggled and managed to raise both hands slightly. "That's the best I can do, mister. God knows I'd give anything to be able to sit up straight. But I can't . . . not if my life depends on it. I can barely straighten up long enough to relieve myself!"

"Keep quiet," said Bell. He listened closely as he looked back and forth. "Are you the last of them?"

"Me? The last of them?" Red Tony looked frightened. "I hope to hell not!" He groaned in pain as his horse shifted its legs beneath him. "You don't mean the rest of them are . . . ?" His words trailed. "You didn't . . . ?"

"They are. I did," Bell said flatly, his mind and body still racing from the fight. He walked over closer, reached out with his rifle barrel and spread Red Tony's hands enough to make sure there were no guns hidden on his lap. He lifted Tony's chin an inch. Tony grunted and dropped it as soon as Bell removed the rifle barrel. "What's wrong with you anyway?" Bell asked.

"Aw hell, it was stupid of me," Red Tony said. "But I tried raising the bar off the floor at the Western Palace."

"The Western Palace." Bell gritted his teeth, reached up and snatched Red Tony from his saddle. Red Tony screamed loud and long. He collapsed onto the ground but couldn't lie flat. Instead, he hunkered down into a painful ball, his hands raised slightly over his head. Bell reached out with his boot toe and flipped a pistol from Red Tony's holster. It fell into the snow.

"Jack!" Rosalee shouted. "What are you doing to him?" She came running down to Bell, tears still wet on her face. She bowed over Red Tony as if shielding him and looked up at Jack Bell. "Don't kill him — not like this. Not in cold blood! Please, Jack! You're better than they are!"

"Easy, Rosalee. I'm *not* going to kill him like this. He screamed because his back's hurt."

Red Tony looked a bit relieved but not much. "I had nothing to do with killing the bar owner or the woman, if that's what you're thinking. That was all Dewey Sadlo and Black Moe's doings. Nobody else is to blame for that, I swear it."

"Then Max Brumfield really *is* dead . . ." Bell closed his eyes for a second and took a deep breath. When he opened his eyes, he turned to Rosalee. "What about Ben? Is he alive?"

"No, Jack," Rosalee said softly, managing to keep her voice from cracking and coming apart. "Father . . . didn't make it."

"Rosalee, I'm so sorry," Bell whispered, holding his rifle to the side far enough to take her in his arm. "Why on earth did he come back?"

"He said he could never live with himself if he left you to pay for his wrongs, Jack," Rosalee said, weeping against Bell's shoulder. She looked at Bell. "What was he talking about, Jack? I didn't understand what he meant. What wrongs could he mean?"

"No wrongs, Rosalee," said Bell. "At least none that you or I should ever judge him by." With his arm around her, he gestured his rifle barrel toward Red Tony's horse. "Get back on your horse and ride out of here."

Red Tony gave him a strange, pained look. "Well, God almighty, man, why'd you pull me down here then?"

"He told you to go," said Rosalee. "You better listen to him."

"Well, that's fine, ma'am," said Red Tony, struggling up to his feet, still bent over in his back. "I appreciate it. But damned if I can get into a saddle by myself! I can barely straighten up enough to put a clean shirt on when I need one!"

Rosalee stepped forward, collecting herself, wiping her eyes with her coat sleeve.

"All right. Come on. I'll give you a hand. Up you go," she said, hearing him moan pitifully as she held his hand and gave him a shove up into his saddle.

"I won't forget you helping me, ma'am," Red Tony said in a strained voice. "You neither," he added, looking at Bell through pained eyes. Jack Bell only nodded.

When Red Tony had ridden slowly down the trail and out of sight, Rosalee and Bell both took a few deep breaths of cold, clean air. Then they went to work, preparing for the trip to Nolan's Gap. They unrolled Delbert's body off the edge of a cliff and wrapped Ben Finley in the blanket. They gathered the mule and the spare horses. Before heading out down the trail, leading the animals, Rosalee passed a nod toward the saddlebags of gold.

"I don't think I'll ever feel right about that gold," she said.

"Then that's too bad," said Bell, "after all your dad went through for it. Ben wanted you to have that gold awfully bad, Rosalee."

Rosalee thought about it, then said, "All right. It's just going to take some time to get used to it."

"I'm sure it will . . . but you need to try — for Ben's memory as well as for your own sake."

"What about you, Jack? My father would have wanted you to have a share of it. He said so."

"I have no need for it," said Bell, dismissing the subject.

Rosalee stared at him for a moment. "Are you going to be leaving as soon as we get back to Nolan's Gap?" Bell didn't answer right away, and she took that to mean that he was. "I mean, if you are, I understand. There's nothing to hold you there, now that your friend Max is dead. But I just thought if you were —"

"I don't want to leave, Rosalee," Bell said softly, keeping her from finishing her words. "To be honest, I'd like to stay there. I'd like to be with you . . . if you'll have me, that is." He looked away, as if uncertain what her answer might be. "I've never been a husband or a family man. I'd sure like to try though."

They stood in silence as a cold wind blew in off the higher crest of the mountainside behind them. "Will you be going after Early Philpot?"

"I never want to see him again in my life," said Bell.

"You're not out to avenge Max Brumfield's death? Most men would be."

"Then I must not be like most men," Bell

said. "Whatever comes to Philpot will come from a bigger hand than mine. I've never sought vengeance in my life. I don't understand what vengeance does for anybody. I never have. Life's hard enough day to day. If a person can forgive and forget, I think they're better off." As he spoke, he looked around at the bodies lying in the snow. "If anybody here could speak, they'd say the same thing."

"I admire you for feeling that way," said Rosalee, also looking around at the blood and carnage.

Again a cold wind came down from the higher peak. When the wind had passed, Bell said, "So, does that mean you'll have me?"

Rosalee smiled. "I'm certain of it, Jack," she said quietly.

Just after daylight, as the Sporting Life Saloon opened for business, Early Philpot came out of his office at the bartender's beckoning and walked to the stranger at the end of the bar. Looking across the corner of the bar, all Philpot saw was the top of a dusty Stetson as the man stood with his head bowed low over a shot glass full of rye. "You wanted to see me, sir?" Philpot asked.

"Yeah," said a voice full of gravel. "I hear

you've lost some men and need to replace them."

Philpot looked the man up and down, noting the tight black leather gloves as the stranger tapped his fingers on the edge of the bar. A curl of gray cigar smoke drifted up from beneath the hat brim. A gunfighter, Philpot decided. Some tough devil straight up out of hell, he thought. He could have sworn he'd just caught a scent of brimstone rising from the man's shoulders. He grinned. "So, you're looking for a job here?" Philpot asked, hooking his thumbs into his green silk brocade vest, a thick cigar pinned between his fingers. "That's why you wanted to see me?"

"Yeah, to see about a job," the voice said. The glass of rye came up in the tight black glove and disappeared beneath the hat brim without revealing the face. Philpot stooped a bit but still caught no glimpse of the face.

Suddenly Philpot got a bad feeling about the man. Acting on that feeling, he said, "I've lost some good men the past few weeks, that's true. But you can't just waltz in here and go to work. It takes some powerful recommendations to work for me. Who'll vouch for you? Who have you been working for?"

"Vouch for me?" The voice chuckled, low and menacing. The hat brim shook back and forth slowly. The fingers quit tapping on the edge of the bar. "Who have I been working for?" The voice chuckled louder. Then it stopped abruptly. A hand shot out and snatched Philpot by his shirt collar and pulled him forward. "Come here, you!"

Philpot stood powerless, staring wide-eyed as the other hand came up cocking a pistol and jamming it under his chin. "The man I used to work for is dead . . . but if he was here, he'd tell you I'm a man of my word!"

"Mister, please!" Philpot gasped.

"Before he died, I told him I'd kill you," said the gravelly voice as the hat brim turned upward, revealing a tight, scarred mask of death. "And today I keep my word!"

The shot resounded loudly in the Sporting Life Saloon. A fountain of blood erupted from the top of Early Philpot's head. From the back room, a bartender came running out, dropping a case of whiskey as he saw Philpot on the floor, a long shower of blood and brain matter hanging down from the ceiling. Hearing the running footsteps, the stranger turned at the front doors. With the pistol pointed and cocked, he said to the bartender without raising his face, "Your next step won't be worth it!"

The bartender froze, his eyes going back to the gore running from the ceiling. He shrank back a step and watched the stranger walk out the doors and along the boardwalk out front, a translucent figure passing the dusty window in a glittering ray of sunlight. "Good God," the bartender whispered.

At the edge of the boardwalk, the translucent figure stepped down, turned into the alley and stepped up into his saddle. "How did all of this thing go then, you tell me?" said another coarse voice, this one belonging to a large man who sat atop his horse holding both horses' reins.

"He's dead. That's all I wanted," said the gravelly voice.

"Yah . . . he is dead, and so now all the world is better," said the other rider, a large man, his arms and face covered with gauze, the back of his neck scarred and hairless.

"Maybe not all the world," said the gravelly voice as the two turned their horses down the dark narrow alley toward the backside of town. "Maybe just ours."

ABOUT THE AUTHOR

Ralph Cotton has been an ironworker, a second mate on a commercial barge, a teamster, a horse trainer, and a lay minister with the Lutheran church. Visit his Web site at www.RalphCotton.com.